"Why are you here, Malcolm?"

He brushed past Cass to the living room, the length of her yoga mat, then stopped. There was nothing else to do here…but he couldn't seem to make himself leave.

"What you told me…about my sister, Lauren," he said. "That's something only a few people would know about."

"Freaked you out, huh?" she asked.

He nodded.

She stepped closer, her eyes glued to his. They were bright green like a fairy's, he noted.

"You're wrong, you know," she said suddenly. "I didn't kill your sister. Or the woman in the stairwell." She paused and her eyes became unfocused. "Lauren wants you to know that you're being stubborn. She says your stubbornness is always your undoing."

Something inside his head snapped and he leaped forward, reaching for her. She had to stop talking. But he also needed to know.

"Tell me how you're doing this. Tell me…"

Dear Reader,

If you've ever seen John Edward's show *Crossing Over,* then you know he can be frighteningly accurate. He's a medium who claims to communicate with the dead, and passes their messages along to loved ones.

When he was tested by scientists they found his "hit" rate—the number of times he accurately stated something about a person he'd never met before—so high they concluded he had to be telepathic. Because, of course, being a medium was beyond the realm of science.

I loved the idea of scientists having to accept something outside the norm to explain something even further outside the norm. And so my heroine for this story, Cass, was born. Thinking about what it would mean to hear voices from the dead made me wonder…what if some of those voices weren't so friendly? The next thing I knew I had the idea for her story. Cass may be small, she may be a loner, but her bravery comes from a very big heart.

Hope you enjoy this story. I adore hearing from readers. You can e-mail me via my Web site at www.stephaniedoyle.net.

Stephanie Doyle

POSSESSED

Stephanie Doyle

Published by Silhouette Books

America's Publisher of Contemporary Romance

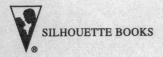 SILHOUETTE BOOKS

ISBN-13: 978-0-373-51430-4
ISBN-10:   0-373-51430-1

POSSESSED

www.SilhouetteBombshell.com

Printed in U.S.A.

STEPHANIE DOYLE

has been writing for ten years and very much enjoys contributing to the Silhouette Bombshell line, where she can explore the depth of a heroine's skill and strength. And while she doesn't have psychic ability herself, she's pretty sure her two cats do, because they always know when she's in the mood for ice cream and will circle the refrigerator until she gives in to her craving. You can visit Stephanie's Web site at www.stephaniedoyle.net.

For my editor, Wanda,
because you get it, even when I don't write it.
Thanks.

Chapter 1

The hiss of steam hitting milk inside a pitcher echoed. The smell of strong coffee permeated the air. Beyond the bar where Cassandra Allen worked creating espresso concoctions, she surveyed the coffeehouse. Overstuffed chairs. Coffee tables littered with books and magazines. A few straggler customers taking in that last bit of caffeine, hoping that it wouldn't keep them up all night or maybe hoping that it would.

A tingle on the back of her neck told her it was coming. But from who? One of the customers? She turned to her colleague, who was wiping down the pastry counter in preparation for closing. The sensation grew stronger.

In her mind another familiar sight took shape. A square, white room. Empty except for her. She stood in the center, looking at a lone closed door.

The door opened and a rush of energy blew at her, causing her body to jolt. Cass smothered a gasp. A woman stood on the other side of the threshold. Her features were blurred by the hazy fog that enveloped her, but Cass could sense she was older, plump, and her hair was the color of faded brick. The woman's voice was faint when she spoke, but her words were clear.

She has to talk to him. He's so upset. She's so angry. I can't go until I know they're okay.

The door closed suddenly, and, just as quickly as it had formed, the image of the white room was gone.

Her mind clear, Cass cursed as the hot froth foamed over the top of the pitcher and down her hand. Shutting off the steam, she set the heated milk aside and rinsed her hand under a stream of cold water in the sink. It helped to take the sting out of the burn, but the remnant pain of contact still lingered.

The song of a cell phone muffled by a large purse broke through the sound of running water.

Cass sighed, shut off the tap and did what she had to do. "That's going to be your dad."

Her fellow barista, Susie, continued to wipe down the counter and ignored the chirping phone under the counter. Her hair was a bright red, probably enhanced by chemicals, but the resemblance was there.

Cass shrugged at the nonresponse. She took the settled milk and poured it over two shots of black espresso into a massive mug, making sure to keep it light on the foam per the customer's request, then called out, "Large latte, light foam."

She placed the mug on the counter for the customer, who was on his second drink, to come and collect it. With a silent nod he took his order and returned to his table with his book.

"You're going to have to talk to him eventually," Cass said after the ringing stopped.

Susie stared at the purse under the cash register and scrunched her face in denial as she continued to wipe the now perfectly clean counter in front of her. "You don't know who that was."

"Call it a hunch," Cass said.

Susie paused in her task and looked at Cass with a mix of skepticism, suspicion and maybe a hint of fear.

"You are so freakin' weird," she accused.

Cass shrugged. It wasn't like Susie was wrong.

The girl let out a huff. "It doesn't matter if it was him. I don't want to talk to him."

"It's not about what you want. It's about what your mother wants," Cass said calmly.

Although the contact had been brief, the message had been plain. Cass was able to fill in the rest from what Susie had told her.

There had been an accident. Four months ago. Her dad was driving. Her mom didn't make it, but he did. It was no one's fault. Just a slick road and fate. Susie was having a hard time coping with the loss. What girl who had lost her mother wouldn't? But Susie's mom knew that the only thing that would help both her husband and her daughter was for Susie to find a way to forgive her father.

"Whatever." A typical response from an eighteen-year-old.

Cass decided she couldn't, wouldn't, push it. After all, it really wasn't her business. It never was.

Rubbing a hand over her face, she suddenly realized how tired she was. It was almost ten—closing time. They still had a couple milling over cappuccinos in one corner, and the man with his recently poured latte and a thick book in another. Cass hated to shoo people out of the establishment. Shooing, in her opinion, was not good for business. But the manager of the coffeehouse had strict rules about keeping the place open beyond operating hours and, besides that, she needed to get home. At this hour, her neighborhood in Philadelphia became slightly more threatening as the denizens of the night came out to do business.

Then the cell phone started singing again.

Okay, so maybe it wasn't any of Cass's business, but the high-pitched digital song was starting to give her a headache. "Really, Susie, he's not going to stop until you pick up the phone."

"Stop saying that. You don't even know if it's him," she snapped.

"Yes, I do," Cass said simply.

As if she were hoping to prove Cass wrong, Susie reached into her bag and extracted the phone. Her face gave away everything when she spotted the incoming number. With a muttered "Hello," she waited for the other person to speak.

"No, I'm not coming home tonight, Dad…I'm staying with Peter."

Trying to give the girl some privacy, Cass turned her back on the conversation. She knew Susie's father didn't like her choice of boyfriend. Susie had said as much. Staying with him certainly wasn't going to help the situation between her and her father.

Again, none of her business. It was just an unfortunate side effect of her unique gift that made her privy to people's secrets.

Struggling against the physical weariness that seemed to flood her system, Cass rubbed her jaw, twisting it gently from side to side. Her back ached, and her feet, despite being encased in very practical black sneakers, started to communicate to her how long she'd been on them.

The jingle of the bell over the front door chimed and captured her attention. Glancing down at her watch, she saw that there were only ten minutes to closing. Yeah, she was going to have to make sure this coffee was to go. Good business habits or not, she was ready to call it a night.

"You! Are you her?"

Cass lifted her head at the sudden barking. The first thing that registered was the man's wild, red-rimmed eyes. The second was the gun in his hand.

"Oh, my God! He's got a gun!" This from one of the lovebirds in the corner.

"Shut up! Shut up, all of you. I just want her."

Cass had no doubt who he was referring to. She heard Susie drop the phone on the floor. She saw the man in the chair who had been reading his book preparing to stand, and she immediately held up her hands to prevent anyone from doing anything rash.

"I'm right here."

"I have to talk to you," he said, the gun shaking in his unsteady hand. He wore a pair of jeans topped with a white, long-sleeved shirt and nothing else, but she doubted he felt the late October freeze that had recently descended upon the city.

"Okay," Cass said calmly. "We can talk."

Susie burst into tears, but everyone else in the coffeeshop was deathly silent.

"You have to tell her how much I miss her. I know you can do that. I heard from someone…about you. About what you do. I need you to talk to her."

Surreptitiously, Cass reached under the coffee bar for her oversize handbag even as she answered him. "Yes, I can tell her."

"Prove it!" He moved closer to her, the gun in line with her face.

"I'm just going to come out from around the bar."

Adjusting her apron carefully over her black trousers and black sweater, Cass emerged from behind the bar, ducking under the opening rather than lifting the partition. She moved slowly so as not to alarm him until she was standing directly in front of him.

"How do you want me to prove it?"

"Tell me her name."

"I don't know her name."

"You're supposed to. You're supposed to know her name or the first letter or something. Like they do on TV."

Cass shook her head. "Maybe if you put the gun down. You're scaring these people."

"I don't care," he whispered. He ran his free hand over his scruffy face, then rubbed one of his eyes with his fist. "I need to talk to her, and he told me that you could make that happen, but I want proof."

Cass closed her eyes and tried to concentrate. The white room started to take shape in her mind, and as soon as it did, the door flew open, slamming back against the white wall. A stinging sensation lanced her brain as the rush of energy hit her. When she opened her eyes, a woman stood on the other side of the door. She was younger. Dark and pretty and dressed in a silk purple teddy. She cried as she spoke.

Cass focused her attention on the desperate man in front of her as she listened to the voice in her head.

"She bought a purple teddy," Cass relayed. "Your birthday was last month, wasn't it? The tenth?"

His hand clenched more tightly around the gun and he wet his lips. He nodded. "Yes. It was a Monday."

"She wanted to surprise you. Shock you a little, I think. But every time she put it on, she always took it off right after. She thought it made her hips look fat. She was very self-conscious."

His lips wobbled into a distracted smile. "She hated her hips."

"I know," Cass said gently. "She wants you to put the gun down, Jess."

"How do you know my name?"

"She told me."

"She can't," he whimpered. "She can't talk anymore."

"Yes, she can," Cass countered softly as she moved a step closer toward him. The gun practically touched her nose. "And she wants you to give me the gun. She says it's for the best."

"Don't..." Jess muttered.

The man in the chair started to move again, and his actions startled Jess. Predictably, Jess panicked at the sudden movement and in retaliation pushed the end of the revolver against the center of Cass's forehead.

"Don't move, man—I'll kill her. You don't know. I'll do it. I have nothing to live for. Nothing."

Cass shuddered at the feel of the cold steel pressed between her eyes. Trembling slightly, she still managed to lift her hand to signal to Large Latte Light Foam to stay back.

"It's okay. Sit down." She turned her head and felt the tip of the gun graze her brow as she made eye contact with the wannabe hero. He was shaking, and she could see that he wanted to act. Not that it would have been an easy task considering he still held a book in one hand and a coffee mug in the other.

Mentally, she commended him for the effort. However, if he moved, she had no doubt she would be dead before he overtook Jess. Cass wasn't overly concerned about the prospect, but she knew it didn't have to end this way.

"You're not going to kill me, Jess," she told him, turning back slowly so that she once again made eye contact. "You're going to give me the gun. She wants me to remind you about what you said on your wedding day. You said you would never hurt her. You said you wouldn't hurt a bug if that's what she wanted. That's how much you loved her. She doesn't want you to hurt me."

With that, he dropped his head and wept deep, gut-wrenching sobs. His arms fell to his side, and the .38 revolver hung loosely in his hand. She reached out and took it. He didn't seem to notice.

"I need to talk to her," he gasped. "I have to let her know I'm sorry."

"She knows."

"I thought the purple teddy was for…"

"It wasn't, Jess. It was for you."

"I know that now," he snapped. "I read it in her diary."

Once again she met his wide, wild eyes, and her body tightened in reaction. She placed the gun on the counter behind her, then slowly reached inside the useful pocket in the front of her apron where she typically kept squeeze bottles filled with caramel.

Before she could get her hand free of the pocket, he grabbed her. His fingers wrapped around her upper arms, squeezing them painfully. "You have to tell her something for me. You have to tell her I didn't mean it."

"You can tell her yourself," she replied calmly, tugging gently to extract her hand from the apron. "You've always had the ability. Now, I have to make some calls. I'm very sorry. This isn't going to hurt. Much."

His body jerked abruptly and for a second the grip on her arms tightened even more, causing her to wince. Then he fell lifelessly to the ground.

Large Latte Light Foam moved to stand over the prostrate man. "What did you do to him?"

Cass held up a strange-looking weapon. "It's a stun gun. It gave him a jolt, that's all. Susie, call 911."

"You're hurt," the man said, raising his hand with the book in it, probably for the first time realizing he still held it, and pointing at her nose.

Cass reached for her face, and when she pulled her hand back she saw the blood on her fingers. Inwardly, she cursed. A result of the connection. Jess's wife had been more intense than Susie's mom. She dug out a tissue from her apron pocket and held it against her nostrils to stem the flow.

"It's just a bloody nose. I get them."

Susie was still staring at the body. "Oh, my God, that was so scary and weird and…"

"911, now!" Cass barked. She didn't have time for hysterics. There was no way of knowing how long the man would stay down.

"And tell the dispatcher he'll need to call Homicide," she instructed. "There's been a murder."

The couple from the back had joined the group. The girl clung to her boyfriend as they both stared down at Jess, whose right leg twitched uncontrollably.

"I don't get it," the boyfriend said. "What was that all about? What did he want? Who *are* you?

"I work here," Cass said.

Large Latte Light Foam snorted. "Why did you want her to tell the cops that we needed a homicide detective if he's not dead?"

"Because he killed his wife."

"You can't know that," the girlfriend said, muffled

against her boyfriend's chest. "Right? She's freaking me out, Ted."

"Sorry," Cass apologized to the girl. But it wasn't as if she could help it, and she wasn't one to hold back the truth, no matter how bizarre it was.

"How?" Large Latte Light Foam wanted to know, his tone clipped, his face a picture of suspicion. It was an expression Cass was used to. "How do you know he did it? He didn't say he did it."

"No, he didn't," Cass agreed calmly. "But she did."

Chapter 2

"Cass!"

Cass glanced up at the sound of her name and scowled.

"Dougie, you better have a really good reason for this," she warned.

She'd been summoned down to police headquarters, located in Center City, Philadelphia, about a half hour ago. It was past one in the morning, and after the night she'd already had she was beyond exhausted.

And the lobby's hardwood bench was killing her ass.

But Dougie never called unless it was important. When she'd walked into her apartment, the phone in the kitchen had been ringing. Despite the strangeness of the hour, and the likelihood that the call was important, she'd let the machine pick it up. When she'd heard Dougie's plaintive voice calling to her from the machine, she'd groaned, knowing she wouldn't be able to resist him.

Once, she'd thought it was his big brown eyes that were irresistible, but now she knew it was his voice. Half man's, half boy's, his voice compelled every woman within earshot to want to either save him or cook for him.

Since she'd been pumped up from the adrenaline rush of almost being shot, and since the possibility of falling asleep had seemed remote, Cass had buckled and returned his call.

Now her butt was numb, the adrenaline high was completely over, and all she could think about was how she would have absolutely no problem getting to sleep. Instead, she was at police headquarters, a place, she had learned from experience, where nothing good ever happened.

Detective Doug Brody stopped and checked over his shoulder for any other cops who might be lingering in the area, then shook his finger at her, accompanied by a stern look. "How many times have I told you not to call me Dougie?"

"I can't help it. It's your name."

"*Doug. Doug* is my name. *Dougie* is what my mother calls me."

Cass smiled, knowing he truly didn't mind because *Dougie* was also what his wife used to call him. Then she turned her smile into a grimace.

"Don't mess with me tonight, Detective. I'm crabby and tired. Did you hear about what happened at the coffeehouse?"

"Yep."

"Then you know we were all stuck there for almost two hours giving our statements."

"Yep."

"I had just gotten home when the phone rang," she elaborated. Dougie should understand the nuances of a guilt trip when it was being given. His mother was a professional at it.

"I know that, too," he said.

"What are you? Psychic?"

"Cute." He smirked. "Real cute. No, I heard about the husband and what happened, which was what made me think of you for this in the first place. I called one of the officers, hoping he would bring you here directly, but you had already left."

"Did he make a statement?" Cass wanted to know. "Jess. Did he tell you where he…put her?"

"Yeah. I wasn't in the room, but I got it from Steve. He broke down and confessed to the whole thing before Steve even started questioning him. They sent a team out to the house. Turns out he buried her in the basement."

Cass wrapped her hands around either arm. How sad for both of them. Maggie—that had been her name— had loved her husband. But he'd been too wrapped up in jealousy, pride and ego. He claimed he'd come to Cass for help, but she believed he wanted to be caught. Maggie's message had been very clear about stopping him, and the dead didn't lie in her room.

The room itself was nothing more than a mental image she constructed and projected to help her deal with her gift.

As a child Cass had been assaulted by images and voices that accompanied a strange burst of pain that she couldn't predict. The inability at first to understand what was happening to her, then to control it, had nearly driven her mad.

Over time, with the help of others who understood her mental anguish, she learned to recognize the precursors of contact: the tingling sensation on the back of her neck, sometimes a subtle change in the feel of the air around her. Once Cass was able to determine when contact was about to happen, she could set the imaginary room as a stage for the dead, with them on one side of the door and her on the other as a way to keep herself separate. When the door opened, she knew to brace herself for the searing burst of energy that always followed.

Crossing the barrier between the living and the dead was never a gentle moment.

For her the gift wasn't like what was described in movies or on TV talk shows. It wasn't letters of the alphabet, dates and different-colored flowers and serene images of a heavenly place. It was real images and actual voices. It didn't mean those TV people were frauds: only that for her the gift was different.

Cass likened it to talent. Some people had musical talent or athletic talent or artistic talent. And even within a type of talent there were different strengths. Some artists used watercolors, others oil, still others used metal.

A gift, like a talent, was unique to the individual.

Hers just happened to hurt, which is why she did everything she could to prepare herself for the impact. Conjuring the door to ready her body and mind for what was coming was one way of dealing with it, and using yoga and Pilates to strengthen her body physically so that she was better able to handle the impact was another.

"Are you okay?" He had covered her hands with his and was rubbing strongly to warm her up as well as offer support. "You look a little pale."

She glanced up into his narrow face and brown eyes. He was smiling gently, caringly. She might have wondered how he managed to stay untouched by the ugliness and despair that surrounded murder and in turn surrounded him. The answer was obvious.

Because he was a good man. Just not her man.

Deliberately, Cass backed away from his touch. "I'm good now."

He sighed but took a step back as well. Then he crossed his arms over his chest and looked away. "Apparently, he was saying a lot of stuff in the conference room." *Conference room* being a euphemism for *interrogation room.*

"You said it was Steve interrogating him?"

He nodded. "We both switched to the late shift."

"Steve thinks I'm a wacko," Cass said. "I can't do anything about that."

"Fortunately, with the confession, you shouldn't need to get involved. Once the uniforms dig up the body, it will be a slam dunk."

Cass turned to reach for her purse, which she'd set on the evil wooden bench. "You know, it wouldn't kill you guys to spruce up the waiting area a little. Some cushions. Maybe a chair pillow or two."

"Police stations aren't designed for making people comfortable," he returned. "I know it's been a long night for you, and I wouldn't have called you down here after all that, but I need your help with something."

"What is it?"

"A case. A girl, about twenty, stabbed yesterday, not too far from where you live. I've got her brother, a man named Malcolm McDonough, in for questioning. The name ring a bell?"

"Should it?"

Dougie shrugged. "I guess not."

"You think he did it?"

"I don't know. This guy is a city bigwig. Construction, money, politics and all that shit. He's got the mayor in his back pocket, and if I push too hard and he's innocent, it's going to be my neck on the line. I've been pressing him for hours, but I can't get a read on him. He's ice. Some people, that's how they react when someone close to them dies. But it's also how someone acts if he's a sociopath. I need a feel one way or the other."

She knew exactly what he meant. It wasn't the first time she'd worked with the police. After she and Dougie had met, he'd come to respect her in ways that few people ever had. He saw her talent as something that could be helpful, not hurtful, and periodically, usually over the grumbles and jests of his colleagues and superiors, he was given the authority to hire her as a consultant. While she didn't possess the more common psychic gifts used by other law enforcement agencies, in certain circumstances she could be useful.

Like in determining a suspect's innocence or guilt.

"We can't hold him much longer. He's been in since this afternoon. He hasn't lawyered up yet, but he's getting impatient. It's just a matter of time."

"Your captain knows I'm here?"

"He knows that a friend of mine might be stopping by this evening."

"A friend?"

"Whose consulting services will be well compensated for."

Cass smiled. Unlike Steve, the captain didn't believe she was a wacko. However, he also couldn't reconcile the fact that she was what she was. His skepticism had been obvious the second they'd met. But a wise man didn't look a gift horse in the mouth, and the captain was a pretty smart guy. The fact that in all the time she'd been doing this she'd never once been wrong didn't hurt, either. And the extra cash always came in handy.

"Ten minutes," Dougie said, urging her along. "Talk to him. Do your thing and then I'll take you home."

"I have my bike."

"You mean your scooter?"

"Scooter, motorcycle, whatever."

"Calling a scooter a motorcycle is like calling a go-cart a car," he pointed out. "I'm not letting you go home on your own at two in the morning. The damn thing will fit in the back of my Cherokee."

She was about to point out that she managed to make her way home every other night on her own, but she knew it was useless to resist. Still, pride had her making an effort. "You're being ridiculous."

"Please. Let me be chivalrous."

She smiled indulgently. Chivalrous was the only way he knew how to be. Plus, he was looking at her with his warm, puppy dog eyes. Between them and the voice, she knew she wouldn't be able to deny him anything.

"Have you ever not gotten what you wanted?"

Suddenly, the intentional puppy dog expression was gone, replaced by something much more sorrowful. "Yeah."

"I'm sorry, Dougie. I didn't mean to bring up Claire…"

"I know. Forget it. Just come and talk to this guy, okay?"

"Okay."

She tried to brush her short, dark hair into place over what she was sure was an unnaturally wide forehead. The rest of it she just made sure was flat. It was so short it didn't really have anywhere to go, but if she was consulting on a case, she imagined she should look somewhat respectable.

Although that probably wasn't going to happen tonight, neat hair or not. She'd removed the work apron, but she was still dressed in her all-black uniform. An old but serviceable green trench coat covered the simple ensemble and kept her warm on the trip over. Added to that she'd tossed a purple wool scarf around her neck for more warmth and at least a pretense of fashion. Her practical sneakers squeaked against the linoleum as she and Doug made their way through a series of hallways.

She didn't need a mirror to know she didn't look like a cop or a lawyer. Which left either victim or criminal as a reasonable guess. Pride had her wishing it were the latter, but a hunch told her it was the former, and once more she tried to straighten her hair. Then she removed the green coat and slung it over her arm, hoping that the bulk of it would cover the milk stains on her clothes.

A few right turns past some doors into different hallways and she found herself in the homicide wing. Precincts with detectives assigned to them were scattered about the city, but all the homicide cops worked out of central. Dougie had started as a beat cop, earned his shield and worked the south division for a while, before moving to Homicide.

The move hadn't been a promotion, though, so much as it was a calling. Death had touched him, and because it had, he needed to touch it back. Cass had been one of his few friends at the time to actually support the switch. Despite the ugliness of it, contrasting with his inherently good nature, he was a great champion for the dead and for the living who suffered as a result of death.

"Over there."

The room was open and broken up into two sides with several desks making up each row. There was a smattering of detectives sitting around, some on the phone, others standing together talking about the Eagles' shot at the Super Bowl this year. The mood was casual, as the graveyard shift sometimes could be, depending on what the night brought.

Cass was convinced it took a certain kind of person to work the hours from midnight to eight when everything was dark and quiet and most people slept. Sure, the night could be peaceful. But it could also be a time when even the most innocuous things turned sinister. When a bush outside a window transforms itself into a monster in front of a scared child's eyes.

Or when a man who loves his wife suddenly becomes her murderer.

The night shift, like Homicide, didn't really fit Dougie's personality. He was an optimist. Nights at a police station rarely fostered optimism. But she imagined there was some reason he had made the switch.

A tingle at the back of her neck intercepted her thoughts. The room in her mind formed quickly, and the face beyond the door was familiar to her.

"Ow," she blurted as she reached for her ribs.

"You okay?" Dougie asked, his hand at her back guiding her forward.

"Yes, just a hitch in my side," she told him. She turned to study him and noticed the dark circles under his eyes that hadn't registered before the visitor in her head pointed them out. "You're looking tired, Dougie. Are you getting any sleep?"

"I sleep," he replied enigmatically.

"Enough?"

"I sleep," he snapped. "Jeez, you sound like my mother."

"I've met your mother. She's a smart woman and she

worries about her son." He stopped walking, so she did, too. "I take it that's him?"

There was only one man in the room who appeared to be a civilian. Dressed in a dark gray suit that screamed quality from a hundred feet away, he sat stiffly in a hard-backed chair. His eyes stared out the window to his right as if he were in a trance, but Cass could see even from this distance that his jaw was tightly clenched.

"Mr. McDonough," Dougie called to him as they approached the desk.

The man turned, and his steel-blue gaze landed first on Dougie, then switched to her and he came to his feet. Once more, she reached up to brush her bangs down over her forehead.

"This is Cass Allen," Dougie introduced her. "She works for us from time to time on a consulting basis. I wondered if you wouldn't mind taking a few minutes to speak with her."

"I do mind." His words were clipped. Although his tone was seemingly neutral, Cass could feel the heat of anger in the air. "Am I under suspicion? I came here after hearing about…after seeing what he did to her…to answer any questions that might help you in your investigation. That was over ten hours ago. I wanted to avoid calling my lawyer, but if this is going to go on…"

"I told you we just wanted to talk to you," Dougie assured him. "There is no reason to call your lawyer. Unless of course you think you need counsel, then by all means…"

The muscles around his jaw flexed. "I don't."

"A few more minutes," Dougie said.

"A few more minutes," he repeated softly. "That's a few more minutes that you're not out there looking for my sister's murderer."

"Looking for someone, until we know everything there is to know about Lauren, her habits, her friends, her routine, would be a waste of time. Let us do our job. Talk to Cass. She's going to ask you some questions."

Cass's eyebrow shot up, but she resisted the urge to shoot Dougie an uncertain glance. She didn't have any questions. She just needed to spend time with McDonough to see if anything happened. Dougie was counting on the fact that something would, but nothing was ever certain. There was never any way of controlling it. Some people she connected with and others she didn't. She used to question it, but it became pointless when she learned she was never going to find an answer.

As the tingle started she acknowledged this was one she connected with, and she focused on forming the room in her mind. The familiar door opened slowly, almost cautiously, and Cass waited for impact.

A powerful blow shot to her midsection, causing a whoosh of air to escape. She could sense both men looking at her, but she straightened slowly and ignored their curiosity. Instead she smiled and concentrated on breathing.

A serene face greeted her on the other side of the door. Beautiful. Blond.

Lauren.

"So, you're Malcolm McDonough? And your sister was Lauren," Cass stated.

He merely stared at her, his eyes moving up and down, taking in first her sneakers, then the rest of her apparel, with a slight sneer.

"You don't look like a consultant."

"I got her out of bed," Dougie told him. "Can't really expect her to be at her best at this hour."

"I suppose."

"I think I need some coffee," she said.

Dougie hesitated for a moment, but then nodded. He walked off, his agile gait eating up the distance between the desk and the coffee machine.

Carefully, the man in front of her took his seat again. *You have to help him. He won't know what to do. How to handle this.*

Cass felt the words inside her head and tried to make sense of them even as she focused on the seated man. It was sort of like trying to have a conversation with someone while listening to someone else speak into her ear. Like people tried to do with their hands-free cell phone units and usually failed. However, for Cass, keeping the two conversations distinct while acting normally had become an art form. While dramatic pauses made for great television for TV psychics, in real life they tended to make people uncomfortable.

The space between the desks was tight, and she found herself having to step over McDonough's feet in order to get to the chair that was across from Dougie's desk. Turning the chair a little, so she could face him, Cass struggled with what to ask him.

"Long day?"

His face hardened noticeably. "Yes."

He's so hurt. I can't leave until I know he's going to be all right. Make him talk to you.

"What's the matter with your eye?"

"I'm sorry?" Cass looked up and met his gaze.

"It's bruised. Did someone hit you?"

"Uh…no…uh, I'm clumsy and I bent down and you know…bang."

He said nothing.

"I know that Lauren lived on Addison. I live on Addison. It's a nice neighborhood, but it's going downhill a little. I just moved a couple of blocks down the street to avoid the danger zone."

He continued to say nothing.

"Did she have any friends that lived nearby?"

"Of course she had friends. She was a very sweet girl."

"Anyone you know?" When he remained silent, she pushed. "Were you two close?"

"No."

"Oh." She waited for him to say something else, but she was getting the impression that he wasn't the type to volunteer information, so she had to ask the obvious. "Why not?"

His jaw clenched. "There were several reasons. She is…was…my half sister. There were many years between us. And we were very different."

We were close. As close as he would let anyone. He loved me. He wouldn't hurt me. Remind him…about the nurse.

"I think you loved her. I think you're putting on a

pretty good facade right now, but inside you're hurting." Cass gulped when his face remained impassive. "You strike me as someone who needs to be in control. I hear you're somewhat of a big shot. You have your own business. Something like this happens, and all of a sudden nothing is in your power. Nothing that you can change. I imagine it's extremely difficult to accept that. But you have to know that Dougie, Doug, will find whoever did this."

"Who are you?"

Cass avoided the question and instead turned her head, searching for Dougie. He was still on the other side of the room with two cups of coffee in his hands, waylaid by one of the other detectives.

"I'm...a consultant," she answered pathetically.

"I see. What kind?"

"I'm not sure that matters."

"Oh it absolutely matters," he told her, his voice colder than it had been when speaking to Dougie. "You suggested that this was difficult for me? This afternoon at my office two police officers came to inform me that my sister was dead. That she was slain in her apartment, murdered in cold blood, stabbed several times and, for the final injustice, had her tongue removed with a knife. The blood that poured out of her mouth seeped into the floor so that eventually it could be seen by the people who lived in the apartment below her. That's how they discovered she was dead. I demanded to be taken to her apartment to see what had happened, and now that image will forever be burned into my memory.

"Since then I've been made to sit here for hours while I've been asked and have answered the same questions over and over again, including those about my whereabouts during the time in which she was murdered. All this while my sister's killer continues to walk free. And then the detective gives me you. You with a coat that I wouldn't give to the Salvation Army. You, who, if I had to guess, is barely over the legal age limit. You, who has absolutely no idea what you're doing. So I'll ask again. Who are you?"

Tell him about the nurse.

The door to her room closed, and Cass now focused all her attention on Lauren's brother. Who was innocent of his sister's murder.

"My name is Cassandra Allen, and Dougie wanted me to talk to you."

"Detective Brody wanted you to *talk* to me?"

"Yes."

"Why?"

Cass shrugged. There was no point in lying to the man. She'd stopped hiding who and what she was years ago. But somehow she suspected that what she had to tell him was not going to go over all that well.

"He's hoping I'll be able to determine if you killed your sister."

He breathed audibly. "And how exactly will you be able to determine that?"

"Actually, he was hoping Lauren would tell me."

"Is this some kind of joke?"

"No, sir. You see, sometimes…the dead…they speak to me."

His jaw dropped slightly, then his eyes narrowed. "You're a psychic."

Although the way he said the word, it sounded more like "fake."

"I have a gift."

"You see things?"

"No. I'm not clairvoyant."

"Feel things then. Isn't that how it's done?"

"That's clairsentience. And I don't have that gift either. I can't read your mind or see the future. I'm a medium, Mr. McDonough. I make contact with those who have passed through their loved ones. That's all."

"That's all," he repeated, his voice calm and moderated but as sharp as glass. "You disgust me. People like you who prey on the innocent and trusting. The grieving. A gift? More like a sham. You are the worst sort of con artist. How do you live with yourself?"

"I'm sorry you don't believe me."

"Don't apologize. Detective!" He stood then and raised his voice enough so that Dougie turned and came rushing back to the desk. "Are you part of this ridiculous scam?"

Dougie looked at Cass, and she merely shrugged in defense. "Mr. McDonough, Miss Allen has been a consultant for the PPD now for some time and…"

"I don't give a damn what label you stick on her. I am done with this pretense of an investigation. Psychics! That's who you bring in to help. No wonder you haven't found Lauren's killer. Is the mayor aware of your current police procedures?" He shook his head. "I'm leaving. If you insist I stay, you'll be insisting to my lawyer."

"It's okay, Dougie." Cass squeezed through the two men, who were facing off and looked pretty close to coming to blows. At the slightest brush of her shoulder against his chest, she felt Malcolm shrink away from the contact, his revulsion evident.

The physical slight didn't stop her from revealing the truth. "You can let him go. He's innocent."

McDonough quickly turned his angry gaze on her, pinning her in place with his fury.

"You sure, Cass?" Dougie asked, not giving an inch of ground. "The guy sort of looks to me like he has a bad temper."

Instantly, Malcolm pulled his eyes away from Cass to meet Dougie's hardened cop face.

"I'm sure. You see, Mr. McDonough hates blood. Can't stand the stuff. He gets physically queasy any time he sees it. Something he's worked his whole life to hide, especially when he's on a construction site. When Lauren was young, she had to have her tonsils out. A nurse came into her hospital room to draw some blood while he was there. Malcolm saw the needle, went after the nurse, pushed her off his sister and then stuck the needle in the nurse's…well, in her bottom."

"How could you…" McDonough cut off his words, his incredulity proof enough that the story was true.

"What's that got do with what happened to Lauren?" Dougie wanted to know.

Cass shook her head. "Don't you get it? He didn't stab his sister. He certainly didn't watch her bleed to death or cut out her tongue. He couldn't have. He wasn't her killer, Dougie. He was her hero."

Chapter 3

"I'm really sorry. I had no idea he was going to go off on you like that," Dougie said.

He had won the battle and was driving Cass home, her motor scooter tucked safely in the back of the Cherokee. After everything that had happened that night, she hadn't put up much of a fight. It was late. At midnight, the neighborhood was sketchy, so she couldn't imagine things improving at 3:00 a.m. It made sense. It just didn't sit well with her to have to rely on anyone, even Dougie.

"He was definitely pissed," Cass agreed. Although the word *pissed* barely scratched the surface of the man's outrage.

"I didn't think you would actually tell him about…you know."

She shrugged. "I wasn't planning to, but he kept pushing. And you know I don't lie about that stuff anymore. Anyway, he never really even yelled. Just spoke to me in that kind of tone that makes you feel like you're ten years old. I had this irrational urge to show him my ID and prove I was almost thirty."

Dougie glanced over at her quickly, then focused again on the road in front of him as he navigated the narrow city streets around Logan Square. "He wouldn't have believed it. When you're fifty you're not going to look thirty."

She pointed to the thin, elfin nose that tipped up ever so slightly at the end. "It's the nose."

He laughed and made a right turn then slowed to a stop in front of her apartment building.

"You should move closer to Old City."

"Ugh. I just moved to this place because you were on my case. It's fine. I'm not saying I'm going out jogging on my own after midnight, but I haven't had any problems," she said.

He double-parked in front of her building. She hopped out and made her way to the trunk to get her scooter, but Dougie had beat her to it and was already lifting it to the ground.

"I can take it from here."

He merely scowled at her and rolled the thing toward the building. It was only three stories tall, each apartment having its own entrance off of a series of cement steps. Hers was the basement apartment. Walking in front of him, she made her way down the steps and used her key to let herself in.

"Seriously, Dougie. I could have carried it," she said as she stood back and let him set the scooter inside what she called the foyer but what was really part of the kitchen. "I do it every day. I'm not as weak as I look."

"You look like you're barely five foot and a hundred pounds wet."

"Ah, ha! See how wrong you are. I'm five foot two and a hundred and four pounds wet."

He chuckled and set the scooter aside, using the kickstand to stabilize it. He proceeded to check the place out, looking for bogeymen in the closets, she imagined.

"Where are the creatures?" His affectionate term for her cats.

"They're probably on my bed sleeping."

"Good," he muttered.

"You really need to get over this paranoia."

"They don't like me."

"Maybe that's because you look at them and wonder why they're not dogs."

"All pets should be dogs," he insisted.

"Spoken like a dog lover. What I don't get is, if you love them so much, why you don't just get one?"

He opened his mouth and then snapped it shut. "My schedule is too…whatever. Hey, check that out. Is that furniture?"

He was pointing to the futon she'd recently purchased that sat in the corner of her sparse apartment. The foyer off the door opened up to a small kitchen that was no more than a space with a stove/oven, a counter with a sink that held most of her dishes and a refrigerator. Beyond that was the living room, although *living room* seemed too fancy a name for the compact square area beyond the kitchen.

Dougie's joke about the futon wasn't completely off base. Cass liked to call herself a minimalist because it sounded as if there was a reason for the lack of furniture. Mostly, she just didn't like clutter. She was a lousy housekeeper and the less she had, the less she needed to keep clean. Plus there were fewer places to leave dirty clothes.

She had a low Japanese-style table where she knelt to take her meals, a small TV to catch the evening news, a yoga mat that spread almost the length of the living room and some Pilates bands that she was incorporating into her workout. And now the futon. The cushion covering the oak frame was bright red and amazingly comfortable for napping.

Down a narrow hallway there was a bathroom on one side and a large closet that she liked to call her bedroom on the other. As a home, it wasn't much, but the economic apartment and everything in it suited her needs. Which, in her mind, was all space and furniture were supposed to do.

She shrugged off her coat, hung it on a hook on the foyer wall and turned to putting the events, *all* of the events, of the night behind her. She didn't kid herself that it would be easy. McDonough's harsh words stuck with her.

How do you live with yourself?

Not easily, she thought, but not for the reasons he assumed.

Cass tried to be understanding. After all, his sister was dead and he was devastated. Sometimes people didn't mean to hurt others, but they did anyway. No one knew that better than she did.

Or she could forget about trying to be sympathetic and just write him off as a jackass. Maybe not as noble that way, but it was a hell of a lot more satisfying.

"Is there going to be any fallout? From tonight, I mean. Can McDonough make trouble for you?"

"Like I said, he's got connections with the mayor. If the mayor talks to the chief about you... The chief knows about what you do, but you know he's never liked the idea. If the mayor brings heat...I don't know." Dougie walked over and sat on the futon. His expression indicated that he was as surprised as she had been at how comfortable it was.

"What is the connection with the mayor?"

"Business. McDonough is one of the up-and-coming contractors in the city. A real rags-to-riches sort. His dad was an ironworker who married a socialite, Lauren's mother. Malcolm went to college but eventually got into construction. He made money by establishing a reputation for bringing in jobs for less. Then he started speculating and he was never wrong. He had all the right money contacts because of his stepmother. And the union loves him because they think he's one of them."

"But he isn't?"

"What do you think?"

Hard to tell. There was something about the way he carried himself. The way his suit fit. It all screamed class, money and sophistication, making it hard to picture him in a pair of jeans with a hammer in his hand and a tool belt around his waist. Plus, with his short, dark blond hair, blue eyes and chiseled face, he would have to be described as classically handsome rather than ruggedly handsome. He wasn't as tall as Dougie, maybe only six foot. Still, to her five-foot-two frame, he'd seemed rather large. Especially when he was standing over her, berating her and calling her disgusting.

Putting aside his appearance, however, there was definitely a hardness about him that acted in contrast to the sophistication. So, while she couldn't readily see him with a hammer, something told her he knew how to use one.

"You sure he didn't do it? I mean really sure?"

"Nothing's for sure, I suppose. The messages are never that clear. But I got the feeling she was worried about him. Worried how he would handle her death. Like she knew it was too much of a shock for him to take in. If he was shocked by it, he couldn't have done it. That and the story about the nurse and the blood…she told me that for a reason."

"Maybe. Maybe he lost it, and the shock was about what he had done. There were bruises on the body. She was engaged in a fight with her killer for some time before he eventually stabbed her."

"But the tongue thing…that was done after?"

Dougie winced. "Yeah."

"That smacks of a process. Intent. Not something a man might do after he'd realized that he'd just killed his sister in a rage."

He stood then and moved toward her, close enough to knock a finger under her chin. "Listen to you, Miss Detective."

"Comes from spending too much time with you."

"Ah, you can never spend too much time with me." He smiled charmingly, then his gaze sharpened on her face. "Hey, McDonough didn't get rough with you, did he? You've got a…"

"Bruise. I know. I bent over at work and *bang*. It's nothing." She pulled away a little, not wanting to encourage further inspection. Dougie didn't know what it cost her to make contact, and she wanted to keep it that way.

He nodded. "I've got an idea. I know this bar that stays open until six in the morning for the restaurant people. We'll go. We'll have a few drinks, unwind and forget about McDonough and his sister."

"I don't think so. I'm really beat."

He shoved his hands into his pants pockets. "You find an excuse every time I ask you out."

"I do not. We've gone to lunch plenty of times."

"Lunch, yes. But never dinner. Never drinks."

"Dougie…" She sighed.

They'd covered this ground before, earlier in their relationship. She wasn't sure why he was bringing it up again, but she knew that she didn't want to have to rationalize why they couldn't date. He didn't know what had made their one night together such a disaster but she would never forget it. What had happened would always be reason enough for her to keep her distance romantically. There were times she thought it might be easier if she simply told him, but not tonight. Three contacts in the span of a few hours. It was a lot even for her. She was exhausted.

"All right. I'll let it go. For now. But someday I'm going to convince you."

No, he wouldn't. He was trying to move on with his life. She granted him that. But he had no idea how much further he still needed to go before he'd be over his wife's death. If he would ever be.

"Lock up behind me," he said as he made his way through the kitchen to her front door. "And thanks for the help. My gut was telling me he was clean despite the ice man routine, but confirmation doesn't hurt. You're right about the tongue. There was something about it that smacked of…psycho-city."

"Psycho-city." She smirked. "There's a technical term. I take it to mean you think this person is deranged."

"I…I should shut my mouth. Who knows what this is. I don't want to give you bad dreams."

"Thanks for seeing me home."

"Sure." He paused for a second, but she was a good two feet away from him. Too far away to even attempt a move if that's what he was thinking.

"She wants you to get some sleep," Cass told him, understanding more than he did why he didn't leave right away. "I connected with her briefly back at the station. She doesn't think the insomnia will go away just because you've switched to nights. You're not sleeping during the day, either."

"I wasn't going to ask."

"Oh." It would be a first if it were true. Dougie loved his wife. More than most, she supposed. Her death had almost killed him with grief. Cass often worried whether or not their friendship stemmed from the fact that she was his only link to sanity. His only link to Claire. She liked him enough that she didn't dwell on it. He was her only real friend. If she had to give him a message from Claire from time to time to make him happy, she was willing to do it. But it forever prevented their relationship from going any further. "Well, she does. It's why I mentioned it."

He nodded, then turned, and she shut the door behind him.

Maybe it was some new phase of his recovery, she decided. Maybe he was truly ready to move on. If that was the case, she would be thrilled for him. He was a good man who deserved someone special in his life.

That person just couldn't be her.

Turning the dead bolt and linking the chain, Cass thought about maybe asking him to lunch so they could talk about it. There was no way she was going to risk their friendship over one night's weakness that for whatever reason he couldn't seem to put in its proper place.

The locks secured, Cass turned around and smiled when she spotted her feline friends. Two shorthair Americans, one black, one gray, both with mint-green eyes. They practically materialized out of nowhere to welcome her home.

"Oh, I see. He's gone so it's okay to come out."

They didn't answer. They didn't need to. They simply walked toward her, then through and around her legs, purring affectionately.

"Come on, girls. Let's go to bed."

She was about to bend down to pick them both up when she saw that the red light on her combo phone/answering machine hanging on the wall was still blinking. She had erased the message from Dougie earlier, which meant this had to be new. She didn't know that many people, and it was too late for work to be calling.

Unless maybe it was Susie wanting to talk about what had happened or Kevin, the coffeehouse's manager, checking in to see what exactly had gone on that night. Susie had called him right after she'd called the police.

Cass hit the button, heard the soft dulcet voice inform her that she had one new message, listened to the beep, and waited.

"Cassandra, it's Dr. Farver. I would like to talk to you. I've been trying for some time. I'm surprised you didn't let me know your number had changed. But...that's not the point. I'm calling because there's someone I want you to meet..."

She hit the erase button before he could finish. She didn't have to listen to the rest of the message to know what he was going to say. She'd heard the same song often enough before, which had been her reason for not giving him her new number. Not that it had worked...obviously.

And the fact that he had called after 1:00 a.m. was no surprise. Once Leonard Farver struck upon a new idea or found a new candidate to research, he could be relentless. She knew that from experience.

Someone he wanted her to meet. More like someone he wanted her to read so he could test, monitor and poke at her. Not anymore. Cass had promised herself a long time ago that she was done being his lab rat despite what he'd done for her.

She waited for the guilt that usually surfaced anytime she blew him off, but this time she felt nothing. Exhaustion trumped guilt every time.

She made her way down the short hallway and let herself fall face forward into the double bed that took up most of the room. She could have gone with a twin bed and added a vanity or dresser, but the cats slept with her and they needed their space, too.

Bone-weary, Cass considered crashing in what she was wearing, but knew the discomfort of her bra would only wake her up later. Sitting up, she shucked off the shirt, toed off her sneakers and kicked out of her pants. Then sighed blissfully when she unhooked and discarded her bra. In nothing more than a pair of white panties, she scooted under the covers.

"Spook. Nosey." She felt one then the other leap onto the bed. One settled by her feet, the other against her side. Their soft purring served as the best kind of lullaby. After what could have been only seconds, she felt her body and her mind drift off to sleep.

Cass dreamed she was at a ball. There were women in gowns and men in tuxedos. A champagne fountain emitted tiny bubbles in the center of the ballroom, and tables laden with all sorts of exotic foods surrounded a large dance floor. And she was on that dance floor, moving, spinning and twirling like a little girl playing Cinderella to the beat of an orchestra that played a waltz.

When Cass glanced down at her feet in amazement, knowing that she had never danced like this before, she saw that she was wearing sneakers instead of glass slippers. Black work sneakers coated with the dust of coffee beans and dry milk. She wore her apron and her green Salvation Army coat.

The ballroom now silent, she stopped, aware that everyone was watching her.

Looking to the side, she saw her grandfather on the edge of the dance floor, shaking his head. She couldn't decipher his expression; she'd never seen it before.

Talk to me, Cassie. Please.

But she didn't want to talk to him. Her grandfather was synonymous with betrayal. And worse—guilt. She didn't want to ever have to talk to him again. She turned to leave, but a gasp from the crowd as Malcolm McDonough walked out onto the dance floor stayed her. It was his party.

She wanted to hide, she wanted to run, but her feet were stuck to the floor.

"Who are you? Why are you here?"

Cass opened her mouth to tell him that his sister had invited her, but before she could get the words out, the ballroom was gone and she found herself alone in an empty white room.

This place she knew. Here, she was comfortable. This is where they came to talk to her. Where she welcomed the dead who wanted to speak.

Cass stared at the door and wondered how she could be here, now, in her sleep. Was it possible that she was preparing to make contact? Part of her mind rejected the idea. The definition of a medium was being in the middle. A conduit between two people, one living and one dead. If the dead were trying to come through, then who did they want to talk to?

Her? In the dream, she'd seen her grandfather. But she'd always been able to block his connection. It had been so long since he tried that she thought he might have given up, if such a thing was possible of the dead.

The door to her room slammed open. Cass struggled to brace herself for the energy to hit her, but the image that was forming beyond the door had her gasping for breath. It wasn't a man or woman.

It was a monster.

With a piglike snout and horns that burst out through its head, it reared back and shouted with a horrible reverberating baritone voice. It was the size of a man, had a powerful chest and stood on two legs. But hooves replaced hands, and fangs replaced teeth. It shouted again and the sound was as crippling as the pain of impact. In the room, Cass dropped to her knees.

When she looked up, she saw it was moving toward the door. The certainty that if that thing reached the entrance it would do what no one else had done and cross into her room filled her with a strange panic.

Struggling against a lethargy that pulled at her, Cass pushed to her feet and forced herself to move across the empty space. She reached for the door and watched as the thing on the other side stepped closer and closer, the whole time shouting indecipherable words at her.

Instinctively, she did the only thing that seemed logical. She shut the door in its face.

As she let out a heavy sigh of relief, the white room faded away.

Cass woke up with a start, clutching the covers to her chest.

Someone had brought a monster from the beyond. Who? How?

The questions assaulted her, as did the essence of danger, which meant she needed to stop for a second and regain her mental balance. Using techniques she'd learned through yoga, she took a cleansing breath in and then let it out slowly.

Cautiously, she sat up in bed, wondering what the physical effects of the strange encounter would be. Although the pain was in her head, her body always manifested physical evidence of the contact. A bruise here or there, a bloody nose. This time the energy that had overwhelmed her had been intense. Her mouth hurt. With her tongue, she stroked her bottom lip. It was swollen as if she'd been hit.

Checking for her cats, who routinely slept at her side, Cass noted their absence. It was morning, early morning based on the hazy quality of light outside her single bedroom window, and earlier than she normally would have awoken. Typically, the girls never left the bed until she did. This morning they were gone. She wondered if she'd thrashed about during the strange dream.

"Spook? Nosey?"

No morning meow to signal they had gone in search

of the dry stash that she left out in the kitchen. No gal-loping feet to suggest they had been caught napping on the new futon during what was supposed to be their nightly vigil. The silence was disconcerting. The memory of what she'd dreamed…experienced…made it that much more unsettling.

Cass rolled out of bed. Dismissing her discomfort, she found a robe in her closet and made her way from the bedroom down the short hallway to the living room.

She found her girls in the foyer, sitting silently, mo-tionlessly, in front of the locked door. As she came to stand behind them, their two heads turned, one clock-wise, the other counterclockwise, in her direction.

There was a message conveyed in their feline eyes. Cass thought maybe she was being dramatic, but, after what had happened, she didn't think so. The lingering sense of evil still shook her, and she knew without a doubt that death waited for her on the other side of the door.

Chapter 4

Cass stood unmoving as she and her cats stared at the door. She was certain there was something wrong outside. She didn't need any kind of psychic ability to know that. This was pure gut instinct.

Someone had brought that monster into contact with her. It was the only way her gift worked. The monster was on the other side so there had to be someone on this side. Someone living. Someone close.

Was that person still out there? Was he waiting for her? More important, could someone who had been touched by something as horrific as that monster in life not be a possible threat to her physically? Because whoever had brought that thing to her room last night had known evil. Had lived with or had been connected to evil.

It stood to reason that a person like that had a pretty good chance of being evil, too.

Backing away from the door, she considered hiding in her bedroom for a time, waiting until she was sure the person was gone. However, as soon as she found herself hesitating, Cass pushed herself into action. Because there was another possibility.

What if the person the monster was trying to contact needed her help?

With hands that were less than steady, she undid the series of locks and opened the door. Her bare feet made contact with cold concrete and she winced, reminded that she was still dressed in a robe, panties and nothing else. Bolting back to her bedroom, she threw on a pair of sweats, a tank top and some flip-flops that were the first pair of shoes she saw.

It was early and the narrow city street was still thick with parked cars on both sides. A cyclist sped past, and an old woman bundled in a coat and a blue wool hat walked her dog. Cass could hear the sound of the pooch's claws tapping the pavement, as well as the occasional yap, but nothing else.

No one cried out for help. No one leaped out from among the cars to attack her.

She stopped halfway down the road and shook her head. Maybe it had been a dream. Maybe the monster hadn't been real. After almost twenty years, she thought she had a grasp on her gift, but she'd never experienced anything remotely close to that beast. Yes, there had been impatient messages, sad messages, even angry ones. Mean *spirits*.

Cass was never sure what name to apply to those who made contact. Ghost, spirit, soul. To her they were people. They just happened to be dead. Wasting time on semantics or philosophizing on the religious implications of what her gift was about didn't interest her. Getting the messages and giving them to the right people so that the dead would stop hassling her and the living would know some resolution—so she could go on with her life—that interested her.

But this *thing* last night had been different. Angry, yes, but anger swirled around it, mixing and blending with other emotions. If she closed her eyes, she could remember the fear she'd felt because she knew that on the other side of her door was everything that was wrong with the human element. Hatred, rage, greed, power and pain. Pain that it liked to inflict on others.

And it had almost come inside. A trickle of unease had sweat pooling under her arms and dampening her palms despite the coolness of the crisp fall morning. Part of the purpose of her mental room with the single door had been to keep the dead at a certain distance. Cass lived with the very real fear that one day contact wouldn't be enough for them, that only possession would suffice as a way to express their message.

What if the monster was some kind of foreshadowing? What if the images from last night, the sense that it was getting closer, were a way of letting her know that the dead were coming for her?

She wouldn't allow it. Mentally, she was too strong to let herself be used. Wasn't she? A lingering memory of a night about a year ago flashed behind her eyes. She and Dougie on a bed. Entwined. Connected. And Claire, his dead wife, in the shadows of her mind just beyond the door…watching. Instantly, Cass quashed the remembrance. She didn't want to go there. It was too disturbing and opened up too many questions she didn't want to have to answer.

The small dog that was being walked by the old woman broke loose from its leash and took off down the quiet street, yapping frantically. The shrill sound snapped Cass out of her thoughts, reminding her what she was doing outside in the first place.

There was something wrong out here.

Following the dog's direction, Cass jogged down the street after the woman, who was desperately calling her pet. The older woman was moving as fast as she could but was losing ground to the animal, which had an impossibly speedy gait considering how short its legs were. The dog rounded the corner and descended steps that led to a brick apartment building similar to Cass's. The old woman came to an abrupt stop on the sidewalk in front of it.

The woman's stillness was unnerving—and it wasn't because she was simply out of breath. Cass came up behind her and circled her so she could meet her head-on. The old lady's mitten-encased hands covered her mouth and her eyes were wide. She was so pale Cass feared she might faint.

"Are you all right?"

The woman merely pointed to the steps that dipped below the level of the sidewalk. Two slim, bare feet stuck out from around the bend of the cement steps.

They didn't move. The dog, out of sight around the corner along with the rest of the body, continued to bark.

"Call 911."

The older woman shook her head. "I…don't…I don't…have a cellular phone. My daughter wanted to get me one, but I said I didn't want one. I don't like cell phones very much and…"

Cass put a hand on the woman's shoulder in an attempt to calm her before she carried on about the evils of cell phones in general.

"Down the street a little farther, there's a convenience store," Cass pointed out. "It's early, but they sell coffee in the morning so they should be open."

"I buy my Powerball tickets there," she muttered.

"They'll have a phone. Tell them to call the police. Tell them they need to get in touch with Doug Brody. Can you remember that name? Detective Doug Brody."

"Doug Brody," she repeated mindlessly.

"Good. Go on now."

"Is that girl dead? Is that why Muffy won't stop barking? I've never heard him bark that way."

"I'll watch Muffy. You go."

The woman hesitated but seemed ultimately to understand that she didn't want to have any part of walking down those stairs. Swinging her arms as if to speed up, she took off down the sidewalk for the convenience store.

Cass took the stairs slowly, watching to see where she stepped, knowing from what she'd seen on TV shows more than anything else that even a flip-flop can mess with evidence. By the time she got to the bottom, she could see around the bend of the brick portico that framed the apartment door.

Muffy, a brown cocker spaniel, barking unceasingly, stood steadfastly at the head of the victim, who unfortunately could no longer hear him. The woman wore only a sheer nightgown. It wasn't ripped or torn to suggest the attack had been sexual, but there was no doubt that it had been deadly.

The stranger's eyes were open in a death gaze that, for all her experience with the dead, Cass had never seen. The worst, however, was the blood. It was smeared all around her mouth and face and underneath her body. Cass could see that the welcome mat was saturated with it. She thought about what McDonough had told her earlier about his sister and shuddered. So much blood.

And why?

Not wanting to disturb the scene any further, Cass moved around the body to the dog and plucked him up and into her arms. She stroked him until he calmed down, limiting his barks to about one every other second.

Backing out and up the stairwell, Cass and Muffy waited for the old woman, the police and, most important, Doug. He would understand what this meant. She could only hope he would know what to do about it.

A light from a street-level window above the stairwell caught her eye.

Palm Reader—Fortune Teller.

It was a red neon sign with the outline of a crystal ball in its center. Cass could see that it belonged to the same apartment whose doorway the woman lay in. Guessing from the nightgown, Cass had little doubt that it was the dead woman's apartment, which meant that she was likely the palm reader. Not that Cass could ask her.

Cass turned back and stared down at the still motionless feet.

"I'll bet you didn't see *this* coming," she mumbled, more to break the morbid silence than anything else.

There was no reply to the bad quip. Not that Cass expected one. She never communicated directly with the dead. Except in one case, which was completely different altogether.

Of course, there was the monster to contend with, but the resolution of what that thing was, was still too far off to consider. Was it connected to the woman at the bottom of the steps? Was it too much of a stretch to believe that it wasn't?

Cass wasn't ready to think about it. Better to wait for Dougie and let him decide what had happened before she started leaping to conclusions she couldn't back up with facts. She trembled involuntarily and Muffy squirmed in her arms. She set him down, careful to keep a firm grip on his collar so he couldn't return to the body. Turning to her right, she spotted the older woman scurrying down the sidewalk as fast as her aging body would carry her.

"The police are coming. They're coming," she huffed as she came within hearing distance of Cass.

Cass nodded in thanks, then handed her back her dog. The woman reattached Muffy's leash and together they all stood in front of the stairwell like sentinels standing guard over the body.

Minutes later, sirens broke through the early-morning quiet. Two cars screeched to a stop as uniformed officers popped out and started barking orders to one another.

"Do we need an ambulance?"

Cass shook her head at the stocky officer who approached her first. "No. Maybe to take her to the morgue…"

The cop's face didn't change with her answer. "Right. We're going to ask you to wait over there. We'll need to ask you some questions in a little bit." He was pointing to a stoop a couple of feet away and numbly Cass nodded. Sitting suddenly seemed very necessary. She tugged on the arm of the woman, who was trying desperately not to look down the steps as the uniformed officers secured the area.

"Come on. We should get out of their way."

From the third step of the stoop, Cass watched as two standard-issue city cars pulled up. She wondered how it was that detectives were always so shocked when they were made so easily by the criminal element. The car reeked of cop.

Dougie's long form emerged from the vehicle and instantly he spotted her. Ignoring her for the moment, he checked on the scene. The uniforms had taped off the stairwell, and soon the techies would be by to snap photographs and collect evidence from the apartment and from the victim. Evidently satisfied with the progress they were making, Dougie made his way to where she sat with the old lady at her side.

"How…"

"I don't know. I think she was stabbed."

"No, I meant how are you here?"

Cass knew what he meant, but there wasn't an easy answer. She certainly didn't want to elaborate with the woman, Ethel, she'd come to learn was her name, and her dog sitting next to her.

"My Muffy found her. My Muffy was very brave," the woman interjected.

"Yes, ma'am," Dougie replied politely. "Very brave. The PPD thanks you very much for calling this in and for waiting so that we can question you. If you would head over to the officer with the blond hair, he's got some questions for you." Dougie pointed to one of the uniformed cops, who looked to be just out of school. Surely someone so young wasn't able to handle the responsibility of standing between evil and the rest of society? Someone with a job like that should at least be shaving, Cass decided. Then again, given her youthful appearance and the fact that Ethel called her honey as if she were soothing a child, she guessed she couldn't throw stones.

"Just tell him everything you saw and heard. And don't leave anything out," Dougie said.

Ethel nodded slowly as if to suggest that she took her civic duty very seriously. "Of course I will."

Cass stood and reached for the woman's elbow, helping her to her feet even as Dougie reached for the woman's other arm. On legs that probably weren't as steady as they had been when she'd set out that morning, Ethel managed the few cement steps until she was back on the sidewalk. "You'll catch the person who did this? That's your job."

"Yes, ma'am."

Satisfied, Ethel led Muffy to the blond kid in the blue uniform.

Once she was out of earshot, Cass asked, "Does the PPD thank me, too?"

"No," he growled softly. "The PPD wants to know what the hell you're doing here."

How could she tell him? What would she tell him? *There was a monster in my mind.*

To her it sounded a lot like having one under your bed or one in your closet. Like the kind of nightmare a child might have. Only she wasn't a child and it, whatever *it* was, hadn't been a nightmare. She was pretty sure of that now.

She was afraid that Dougie, despite all his good intentions to be open-minded where she was concerned, wouldn't get it. He might believe she spoke with the dead, but this was asking too much of anyone.

"I think you must be grumpy because they got you out of bed."

"Absolutely I'm grumpy but not because of a lack of sleep. It's the lack of answers that's annoying me right now. Talk to me, Cass."

She took a breath and tried to explain. "I had a thing. A weird thing. I felt…"

Fear. A deep and gut-wrenching fear of the dead, something she'd never felt before. And a darkness. She'd felt that, too. Beyond the beast, there had been inky blackness rather than the hazy fog she'd become used to.

As if the horns hadn't been sinister enough.

No, there was no point in telling Dougie this. Not when she couldn't explain what it meant.

"I heard a dog barking," she said. "I came out here, followed the sound and there she was."

"That's not even remotely convincing."

Cass shrugged. "It's the best I can do for now. Let's just say…I had a gut feeling."

"Right." He snorted somewhat disgustedly. "Look, I'll let it go for now until I can pull all the facts together. But we're eventually going to have to talk about this. Whatever happened to this girl…"

"She had her tongue cut out, Dougie."

He didn't bother to issue the standard police line that nothing was certain and that until evidence was gathered and analyzed nothing would be accomplished by leaping to conclusions about the relationship between two seemingly unconnected victims. She knew better.

"I don't have to tell you to keep this quiet."

That made her laugh. "Who am I going to tell?" Her world consisted of about three people, one of whom was standing in front of her.

"I'm just saying we don't need the press…"

"Dougie? It's me. I'm not going to talk to the press. Ethel you might have to talk to."

"Yeah." He sighed. "Two women, a few blocks apart, both missing their tongues and no signs of sexual assault. This doesn't smell right."

"At least one thing is for sure," she reminded him. "You know now that Malcolm McDonough didn't kill his sister."

"Great," Dougie muttered unenthusiastically. "Mr. Connections goes free, but there's a wacko loose in the city."

"A psycho-city wacko," Cass repeated, recalling his description from last night.

Dougie looked back to the stairwell where they were finally bringing the body up. That they had tried to be careful with her was obvious, but the body bag was still covered in the woman's blood.

"Definitely."

Chapter 5

Cass walked through her front door and instantly started shivering. She hadn't realized how cold she'd been, almost numb from it, until the warmth had started to creep back into her skin. She didn't know what she'd been thinking, running out of the house barely dressed late in October.

Actually, that was the point. She hadn't been thinking. She'd been reacting and she found the idea unsettling.

To combat the cold, she found a sweater in her bedroom and then went back to the kitchen to make some soothing lemon tea. Five minutes, that's all she wanted. Five minutes to not have to think about anything.

But that wasn't going to happen. The image of the woman's body being carted off haunted her. Then, as people came outside ready to start their day, a crowd had gathered around the scene, as tends to happen when there is trouble. Neighbors spoke about the woman, talked about suspicious characters that she called customers. Apparently there was no boyfriend in the picture, no obvious enemy. Nobody that anyone could instantly finger as a murderer, anyway.

After an hour of Cass sticking to her story about simply hearing the dog, Dougie had relented and let her go. It wasn't as if telling him about the monster was going to get him any closer to the person who did this. Trace evidence, detective work, finding out whatever link there was between Lauren and the palm reader—that would be helpful to him.

Ghostly monsters in her head…not so much.

Cass dipped her tea bag and sighed. She was lying to herself and she wasn't very good at it. The real reason she hadn't told Dougie about it was because she didn't want there to be a connection. She didn't want to believe that she was ever going to have to see that *thing* again. Shame descended on her as she considered what she'd done. If the monster was related to the murder and she was ignoring it because of that god-awful fear that she'd experienced during contact, then she was nothing better than a coward.

What had the palm reader suffered? What had Lauren? Certainly more than mere fear.

Thinking about Lauren brought Cass back to the night when Lauren had been killed. There hadn't been any monster then. No unusual dreams at all that she could recall. Did that mean that the monster and the murders weren't related? Or did it mean that maybe Lauren's murder and the palm reader's death weren't related?

No, that didn't make sense. They had to be. Dougie had said so. Two women, blocks apart, both stabbed and both with missing tongues. Philadelphia could be a dangerous city, but such gruesome deaths weren't exactly standard fare.

Who the hell cuts out a tongue?

"A sick bastard," she told the empty room. *Who the hell else cuts out a tongue?*

Cass thought about the serene young woman who had made contact through her to reach out to her brother. Lauren was beautiful. And there was an aura around her spirit that suggested sweetness and gentleness. Two qualities that her half brother obviously didn't share. To have her life end that way—so abruptly, so brutally—was wrong. Unjust.

Of all people, Cass knew better than to expect fairness in life. She hadn't been born cynical. Growing up with television and movies, where the good guy always won, the bad guy always got caught and the right thing, whatever that was, always happened in the end, had given her a rose-colored view of life and the people in it. Being raised by old-fashioned grandparents who believed in things like trustworthiness and honor only reinforced those lessons.

But that all ended the night the nurse locked her into her room at the asylum.

A phone ringing startled Cass out of her memories. There was no point in going back there, not when it only brought sadness. She put down her cup of tea and reached for the phone, but stopped when she recalled that Dr. Farver now had her new number. She waited for the three rings to pass and for the answering machine to pick up.

Only it wasn't Dr. Farver—it was Kevin, the manager from the coffeehouse.

"Uh, hey, Cass, I heard about what happened last night from Susie. Look, I hate to do this, especially over the phone, but...you don't need to come back to work. It's just...nobody will work a shift with you. You've wigged them all out and if it's a question of you or everybody else...well, I've got to let you go. If you could mail back your apron and keys that would be cool. I'll mail you your final check. You don't have to worry about stopping by. Uh, well, see ya."

Fabulous.

She didn't have to worry about stopping by. Translated: please don't show your face around here anymore. Fired. By a kid who she knew carried a fake ID.

Cass took her tea, flopped down on her futon and waited for her cats to come and comfort her, which they did in short order. There was no point in getting upset over it. It wasn't as if this was the first time she'd lost a job because of her gift; it was just that jobs in general weren't the easiest things to come by for her. She didn't have a college degree; for obvious reasons, she never had good references to offer a prospective employer; and if anyone looked too closely into her past, there was that whole "committed to a mental asylum" strike she had against her.

Fortunately, her lifestyle didn't require much money. The minimalist style she'd adopted helped to keep costs down while giving her flexibility if she needed to leave in a hurry, as she did when she'd decided to leave Dr. Farver and the institute in D.C. Not to mention, she wasn't the type of person who needed things. Cass imagined that came from a very intimate understanding few people had: possessions didn't follow you to the other side.

Luckily, this time she would have a check for her consulting work, which would be enough to tide her over until she found something else. Maybe another coffeehouse or an ice-cream parlor. Something where she could connect with people because she believed it was important for her to do that, but not so many people at once that the connections overwhelmed her. Like at the waitressing job she'd taken last year at a popular roadhouse. She'd been so bombarded by energies knocking at her door that she'd ended up dropping more plates than she'd served.

Better to wait and find something that fit. If she had to, she could always go back to doing readings for money.

Cass cringed. The thought of using her gift to make a living had always made her uneasy. Oh, she knew others who had done it, had in fact grown rich as a result of their talent. She didn't resent them, but to her it too closely resembled selling herself. Not unlike a hooker.

"Get over it," she mumbled to herself. "You'll do what you need to, to survive. You always have."

A knock on her door had the cats bolting off the futon in opposite directions.

"Let's see," Cass said as she stood and made her way to the door. "This day started with a monster, then a murder, then being fired. What do we think is behind door number two, Stan?"

More than likely it was Dougie coming to bug her again for answers she wasn't ready to give. Cass checked the peephole and gasped in surprise at the ominous presence of Malcolm McDonough.

This just wasn't her day.

Cautiously, she opened the door. "What do you want?" Instantly, she found herself on the defensive. Considering his prior verbal assault, she decided it was the smart place to be.

"To talk."

"We talked last night. I heard every word you said."

As she moved to shut the door, he put his hand against the frame. Part of her felt no qualms about slamming the heavy door against his fingers. A few broken append-ages might teach him a lesson, but it wasn't her style.

"Let me rephrase. I *need* to talk to you."

And that's when it occurred to her why he had come. He knew about the second victim.

"Someone told you."

"I have…"

"Connections," she finished.

"Yes. Can I come in?"

Against every reasonable instinct she had, she backed away from the door and let him inside. "For a few minutes. That's all."

Malcolm came in but stopped short as he took in her apartment. "You don't believe in furniture, or you can't afford it?"

"Don't need it," she answered quickly, remembering his comment about her coat. She took note of the Rolex watch on his wrist. Even his blue jeans sported a brand name that probably wasn't often found on construction sites. This was a man who believed in having things. She almost felt sorry for him. Almost. "Don't worry. I'm not a destitute waif." Just jobless and short.

"I'm not," he said quickly. "Worried that is. What happened to your lip?"

"Bit it. You wanted to talk."

Malcolm hesitated. Staring down at her in her pajama bottoms and oversize sweater, he was immediately seized with the realization that the idea that had brought him rushing to her door could very well be absurd.

Suddenly agitated, he moved inside the spartan room.

It's just that when he received the call about the second attack, his contact at the police station had told him that the body was found by the same woman who had questioned him at the station the night before.

It couldn't be a coincidence. Instantly Malcolm had phoned Brody to let him know that he wanted her brought in for questioning regarding the murders, but he'd been practically laughed off the phone and assured that he was wrong.

He should have suspected as much. Detective Brody had seemed quite friendly with her. The two of them must have some sort of relationship. He concluded that they were sleeping with each other. Maybe she had seduced the detective to protect herself from suspicion. Or possibly to get close to the case. To know every move the police made. It didn't matter.

What did matter was that she was involved in his sister's death. There was no question about that in Malcolm's mind. He knew it because she had obviously known Lauren. She'd spoken with her, learned about her life and her history with him. Heard the story about the nurse from her.

It was the only explanation. If she knew Lauren, had gotten close enough to her to extract such insignificant details like that story, then why hadn't she said as much to the detective?

The only reasonable answer was that she'd had something to do with her death. If the police weren't going to arrest her or even question her about it, then he was.

However, standing here now in front of her, he didn't see how it was possible.

Lauren was at least several inches taller. Probably twenty pounds heavier, too, yet she'd been overtaken, beaten, stabbed…by a waif?

"I'm sorry, I don't know what to call you," he began, unsure of how to address her.

"Cass is fine."

"Short for Cassandra?"

She nodded once.

"Cassandra is lovely name," he said, stalling for time. This was insane. He should go, but the story kept banging around inside his head. Only Lauren, him, the nurse and his parents had known about what happened in that hospital room. Yet she knew. How?

Exhausted after being up for more than thirty hours, he tried to force his brain to make some sense of the facts. The waif knew Lauren. Lauren was dead. The waif was lying. To protect someone?

What if the murderer was here? Or, if not, maybe he left something behind. He should search the apartment. Search it and find…what? The bloody knife lying in the sink under a stack of dirty plates? It didn't seem likely.

"It's Greek legend stuff," Cass said, filling in the silence. "Cassandra could predict the future. Apollo came down from the mountain one day to woo her, but of course she would have none of it. Apollo sounds like an ass, doesn't he? Always forcing himself on the mortals."

"I wouldn't know. I'm not up on Greek mythology."

Malcolm moved beyond the kitchen into the living room and saw the cats. He also saw the yoga mat and next to it some rubber bands that he knew from his experience in gyms were Pilates equipment. He turned and studied her again, this time concentrating on her body under the oversize sweater. Thin, yes. But that didn't necessarily mean weak.

"Ahh." She winced and gripped her stomach with her hand.

"What's the matter?"

"Nothing," she said. "Cramps. Anyway, when Cassandra spurned Apollo, he cursed her. No one would ever believe her prophecies again. A hell of a thing to know you speak the truth, but to have no one believe you. I give my mother credit. She picked the absolute right name for me before she split."

He looked up from his continuing assessment of her

body when she stopped talking. He knew she'd caught him looking at her, staring really, but he didn't care. Maybe she would chalk it up as typical male perusal. With her elegant face, jet-black hair and green eyes, he had to imagine she was used to the attention.

In fact it occurred to him that she was stunning. He hadn't noticed that last night when he'd called her disgusting.

The knife, he caught himself. He was supposed to be looking for a knife.

"Do you mind if I use your bathroom?" he asked. "I want to splash some water on my face. It's been a long night."

She hesitated. He could see it. But eventually she shrugged. "Sure. First door on the right."

He made his way down the short hallway and took the time to check the door on the other side of the hall. An unmade bed dominated the tiny space. Turning away from the room he stepped into the bathroom and shut the door.

A small shower with a solid blue shower curtain. A toilet and sink. There was a faded bath mat on the floor, an oversize towel that hung from a rack and a toilet seat cover. All in soft blue. Simple and small. A far cry from his hundred-square-foot master bath.

In fact, it reminded him very much of his first home. The same type of run-down apartment he and his father had lived in before his father had married Malcolm's very wealthy stepmother. In hindsight, he knew that Lauren's mother, Becca, hadn't been as fabulously wealthy as she'd looked through the eyes of a twelve-year-old. But she'd had enough money to make everything easier. It had definitely been a step up for him and his father.

A step that had led to him getting into the right prep school. The right college. Meeting the right people, making the right friends, so that when he was ready to graduate, it seemed the world was open to him, where for so long it had been closed. He and his dad were going to own their own business, make good money together.

But that wasn't to be.

In a blink one day, his father was gone. A heart attack at a young sixty and it had been over in an instant. Becca died a year later of what Malcolm believed was a broken heart. It had been just him and Lauren, but it seemed like enough. Like family.

He worked hard. For his father's memory. For Becca's memory, too. To make her proud of him and to assure her that the opportunities she had given him hadn't been in vain. But mostly he worked for Lauren. He needed to know that he could give her everything that his father and Becca would have given her if they had lived. That she could have anything she wanted. Not that she ever asked for anything other than his time and attention.

Now Lauren was gone and none of it mattered. And he was standing in a stranger's bathroom looking for traces of blood in the sink.

He saw only chipped porcelain.

Turning the faucet on, Malcolm took a moment to splash some water on his face. It didn't help wash away the images in his mind. Not knowing what else to do, he opened the cabinet above the sink and studied the contents. Sample lotions of varying sizes, a tube of toothpaste and an eyelash curler.

Nothing extraordinary. No prescriptions for depression or mental conditions that he'd been hoping for. Nothing that told him she'd done it.

Everything about her seemed to be simple. Except for herself.

"You get lost in there?" she called to him.

"Sorry."

He opened the door and brushed past her to the living room. He considered sitting but decided he needed to stay mobile, so he paced the length of the yoga mat and then stopped and turned. There was nowhere else to look, nothing else to do here, but he couldn't seem to make himself leave.

"What did you come here for, Malcolm?"

So he hadn't been subtle. That wasn't a shock. "I told you. I wanted to talk."

"But so far you haven't said a thing."

"What you told me…about the nurse…that's something only a few people in this world would know about."

"Freaked you out, huh?"

He nodded. It was either that or verbally accuse her once more of being a liar.

She took a few steps closer and paused, her eyes glued to his. They weren't just green, they were bright green like a fairy's, he noted. Perfect for a woman who had the face of an elf.

Elfin face, waiflike body, mythological name. Was she even real?

"You're wrong, you know."

"I don't know what you...wrong about what?"

"I didn't kill your sister. Or the woman in the stairwell." She paused and he saw her eyes lose focus for a second. "She wants you to know that you're being stubborn. She says your stubbornness is always your undoing."

His whole being rebelled against her words. "Stop it," he hissed. "Stop talking as if you can actually...stop it."

"And...there's something else. Something in her apartment. Something there she wants me to find..."

"I imagine there is," he said, feeling the rage build. His suspicions weren't unfounded. He knew that now. She needed to get back inside Lauren's apartment. To get whatever it was she'd left there that would incriminate her. That must have been her game all along when she'd convinced the detective to let her talk to him. But how could she have known he would come here today? She couldn't have.

Cass's eyes stayed on his. "I know why you came. You think I'm involved with her death. You thought you might find something here, but you're wrong."

"Am I? Why do you want to get into her apartment? What did you leave there?" he demanded to know.

"Nothing," she stated calmly. "I was never in her apartment. I didn't know Lauren."

"Liar. You knew about the nurse."

"She told me about the nurse last night. She told me about your suspicions today."

"That's not possible."

"It is if you believe that I can communicate with her."

"I don't."

She nodded slowly, as if she was coming to some kind of decision. "When you were thirteen you knocked a small hole in your closet wall so you had a place to hide the lone *Playboy* magazine you managed to score from your friend…Charlie."

"Son of a…" he breathed even as he shook his head in denial.

"Lauren never told you, but she found the hole. She strongly believes that Miss April's breasts were fake."

It was too much. Something inside his head snapped, and he leaped forward, reaching out and circling her delicate neck with his hand. She had to stop talking. He needed to make her stop talking. But he also needed to know. "Tell me how you're doing this. Tell me!"

"You're hurting me," she gasped, but she didn't try to pull his hand away.

The sound of her breath catching fizzled his burgeoning rage in an instant. And something else. An overwhelming feeling of peace and gentleness filled his body. It was as if Lauren herself had reached out somehow to make him back off. Like she was here, with him, instead of gone.

Stunned, he saw his fingers digging into Cass's soft neck and immediately released her. He watched as she stumbled back and then he looked down at his own hands in disbelief of what he'd done. In his life he'd never raised a hand to a woman. Had never hurt anyone who was weaker than he was.

"I…I don't… I'm sorry." He moved toward her, but of course she backed away. "I swear I didn't mean…I would never…"

She ran a hand over her neck as if checking to see if he'd left permanent dents. Then, as if physically shaking off the pain, she refocused her attention on him. "I still need to see Lauren's apartment."

In shock, knowing he'd been a second away from true madness, he dropped down on the brightly colored futon and felt the cushion collapse under his weight.

"Now," she insisted. "We should go now."

He needed to think. He needed to find an explanation to what was happening—who this woman was and how she could possibly know the things she did. "The police have it secured as a crime scene."

"You said you have connections. Use them."

He raised his head and saw her still standing there looking at him. He expected disgust, anger, but there was none.

"Why aren't you calling the police on me? Or at least telling me to get out. I hurt you."

She shrugged. "Not badly."

"Does that matter?" he asked incredulously. Maybe having a man put his hands on her in violence wasn't an unusual occurrence. He thought about the bruise under her eye last night. And now her lip was swollen. His gut twisted with revulsion, but this time it wasn't aimed at her. Who could hurt such a fragile thing?

Him, apparently. He shut his eyes in disgrace.

Cass stepped toward him and knelt down in front of him. She started to reach out to touch him, but stopped herself and instead folded her arms over her stomach. He opened his eyes finally and met her gaze.

"Look, you're exhausted. And you're the type of man who sees everything in black and white. I just threw a big gray ball in your face. Several, as a matter of fact. You flipped, but you're over it now. Right?"

"Who are you?"

"You keep asking me that, but you don't want to listen to the answer. That's fine. Just trust that there's something in your sister's apartment and I need to find it. I think it could help."

"I couldn't protect her." He dropped his face into his hands. "She was so damn innocent, and I couldn't even come close to stopping this from happening."

"I know. I know it's eating you up inside. But you have to believe it's hurting her more. She feels your pain and it's just as hard for her to bear it as it is for you. You've got to let the guilt go."

He rubbed a hand over his face and stared at her hard. "I can't believe you."

"Okay."

She made it sound so easy. But it wasn't. None of this made sense and because none of it did, the only answer seemed to be to keep moving forward. To the next step, the next course of action. "You want to see her apartment?"

"Yes."

He nodded. "All right."

She stood and walked to the kitchen to grab the cordless phone. She tossed it to him. "Call whoever you need to call. I'm going to get dressed."

Malcolm stared down at the phone, everything she'd told him still running through his head. Then he smiled softly.

"You're right, Lauren. Miss April did have fake breasts."

Chapter 6

He won't hurt you.

Now that was irony for you. Cass had heard those words in her head at the same moment Malcolm's hand had wrapped around her throat.

Not that what he'd done had hurt exactly. It was odd. It had been so long since she'd had any kind of physical contact, anything beyond the occasional comforting gesture by Dougie—and even those she didn't let linger—that it had startled her more than anything else.

Then she saw in his eyes the rage and sheer despair that he was forcibly holding in check, and fear had crept in. Lauren told her it was going to be okay, and Cass chose to believe her.

As soon as Lauren spoke to her, he seemed to snap out of it. As if…as if he had heard his sister, too. Or felt something.

Cass leaned her head back against the soft leather headrest of the luxury car and wondered what his reaction would be if she asked him if he had also heard Lauren or maybe felt her presence in the room with them.

Probably best not to do that while he was driving.

Carefully, so as not to attract his attention, she shifted her eyes to her left and studied his stern countenance. He'd offered to drive the short distance and she'd accepted because the idea of walking even one block seemed too onerous a task. Looking back on that decision, she realized it hadn't exactly been a smart one. Moments before, he'd attacked her. Hours earlier, he'd been suspected, albeit briefly, of causing a violent death.

His dead sister vouching for him—what did that really mean? Cass never had siblings so it was hard to know how far loyalty would take them. Would the dead lie to protect someone who was still living? It was a sobering thought, but she quickly dismissed it.

The dead had always been honest with her. It was the living she couldn't trust.

Reaching up to massage a pressure point at her temple, Cass closed her eyes and hoped to ease away her tension headache. The stress of everything that had happened in the past twenty-four hours had finally borne down on her until it was hard to distinguish the pain of contact with the dead from the real thing.

Since this pain wasn't going away as quickly as the

former usually did, she had to assume it was the real thing.

"You okay?"

"Hmm," she answered. It was the sort of noncommittal answer that hopefully didn't elicit more conversation.

"Seriously… If I hurt you…"

"You didn't." She opened her eyes and looked at him directly, partly because she didn't want him to think he'd actually scared her. Even though he had. And partly because she knew he was still freaked out by what he was capable of. There was absolutely no reason for her to put his mind at ease after what he'd done, but she knew he wouldn't stop until he'd apologized a hundred more times.

He wasn't an abusive man. She knew it even without Lauren's assurances. And that was why she'd agreed to get in the car with him in the first place.

"It's just a headache."

"Do you get them?"

She eyed him suspiciously. "Sometimes. Like most people. It's not like it's related to…the thing." An excellent way to describe her unique and awesome gift to a man who clearly did not believe.

"Oh."

His cell phone rang and he reached for it in the console between them with the ease of someone who was used to navigating traffic and speaking on the phone at the same time. "McDonough," he answered.

He said nothing other than a brief thanks after a moment and snapped the tiny silver phone shut.

"We have clearance to get inside her apartment."

"Wow. When you say you have connections, you mean it."

"I know people. It's not like I bribed anyone," he said quickly.

Cass nodded. "Right. Black and white. White being lawfulness and black being crime. You definitely strike me as the law-and-order sort."

He turned to take in her expression. "And you're not?"

"I've been known to stray to the dark side from time to time. But only to survive."

"That's interesting," he commented.

"Trust me, it sounds sexier than it is."

"It doesn't sound sexy at all. A person shouldn't have to 'stray to the dark side' to survive. That's what family is for. To help."

"Maybe that would have worked, if I'd had a family." That wasn't really fair, Cass thought. She'd had a family. Her grandparents had cared. But ultimately they'd let her down, and that, she had a hard time getting over.

There was a moment of silence. "I'm sorry," Malcolm offered.

"Please stop apologizing. You're going to wear yourself out. Besides, it's really not necessary."

"I do seem to be doing a lot of that around you."

"That's because you're a gentleman. It's in your nature to apologize for things you can't fix because it's the only thing left to do. Admit it."

"I'll admit that I hate not being able to fix things," he replied.

"Close enough."

She watched his jaw tighten, but he didn't comment

further and she was grateful. They were almost there, and she needed to think about what Lauren had wanted her to find.

Cass had received instructions from the dead before. Tell him I love him. Tell her the money is in the suitcase. Tell her not to forget to brush the dog's teeth. Innocent instructions that meant nothing to her but invariably made whomever she was speaking to weep.

This message, the way it sounded in her head, the way the image of Lauren shifted in her mind, it wasn't something prosaic. It was important.

They missed it. It's in the apartment. You need to go there. Now.

Assuming the "they" were the police, and the "it" was some kind of clue, Cass figured Lauren wasn't wrong in her urgency.

Two nights. Two women. Two murders.

Shaking her head against the sudden rush of dread she felt, Cass figured she'd had enough of the silence. "What did you tell them, your connections, by the way? To get inside her apartment?" she clarified.

"That I need to choose an outfit for the…for the funeral."

"Oh."

Funerals were so final. It was one of the most painful obstacles the living had to hurdle during their grief. Although it was better than the alternative. Not attending a funeral could leave a person without the necessary closure. Missing her grandfather's funeral had been the biggest mistake of Cass's life. It was easy to see that now. A year ago, it had been impossible.

"They're going to release her body from the morgue either this afternoon or tomorrow. I'll need to make arrangements."

She could tell he was speaking more to himself than he was to her. "What about her mother?"

Malcolm shook his head. "She died a few years ago. Not too long after my father. Other than a great-aunt on her mom's side, I'm basically the only family she has. Had. God," he breathed, rubbing a hand over his face roughly as though he could wipe away the pain as if it were dirt.

He couldn't. And there wasn't anything she could say to make it better. She shouldn't even want to try, given both his treatment of her and his suspicion that she was somehow involved. Not to mention nearly strangling her.

Cass reached up to touch her neck. She thought about the pressure of his hand on her skin. The way it had felt. Skin to skin. There had been something different about it. She didn't want to dwell on it, but her mind kept wandering back. It was like a rush of energy that she had felt flow from his body into hers. Cass hated to overdramatize the sensations and feelings that went along with her gift, but she knew it was important to document each new experience. If nothing else, Dr. Farver had taught her that.

Control came only through understanding.

And it had been a new experience, hadn't it? Cass thought about the last time she'd touched or had been touched in any meaningful kind of way. The fact that she knew that it was a year ago bothered her. It was a sign of how far she had distanced herself from others.

An image of Claire surfaced, but she pushed it aside. Claire wasn't connected to Lauren.

"You're touching your neck. I know you don't want me to apologize again, but I will."

Cass turned and saw that he was looking at where her hand rested over what she guessed were some faint bruises. "I don't. Seriously. Don't worry about it. It wasn't a big deal, okay?"

"It was to me," he said gruffly. "I've never been so out of control before. Right now I feel like I'm standing on some sort of precipice. I'm not sure which way I'm going to fall."

"That must be a hell of a thing when you're used to always being on steady ground."

"Yes," he said quietly.

Cass nodded. Despite his hostility she could at least offer him her experience with this. Death was something she knew a lot about.

"That's what it's like with Lauren's kind of death. It's different from an illness, even different from a sudden accident. Murder tends to shake the living to the core, not because you can't prepare for it—no one can ever prepare themselves for losing someone. It's the violence of the act. It's not just that she's gone; it's the fact that she was *taken* from you, forcibly, against her will and yours. It's going to make you a little crazy. Probably for some time to come."

She couldn't tell if her words penetrated as his eyes stayed focused on the red light hanging above them.

"It doesn't give me the right to take my pain out on anyone else," he finally said.

"No, it doesn't," she agreed.

"Especially you."

That had her raising her eyebrows. "What does that mean?"

"I just meant that, well, you're very…small," he finished awkwardly.

Cass smirked. "*Small* doesn't always mean 'weak.'"

He turned his head and studied her for a moment. She couldn't imagine what he was thinking. After a second, his scrutiny became almost uncomfortable. Fortunately, the light turned green.

"We should go," she prompted.

It was no more than eight or nine blocks from Cass's apartment to Lauren's. Parallel parking with ruthless efficiency, Malcolm settled his SAAB into a tight spot. Cass had reached for the handle when he put a hand on her arm and stopped her.

"Wait."

He exited, circled the car and opened her door— the habit of someone who had been taught manners and used them.

"Gentleman," he said. "Remember?"

He offered his hand, and Cass looked at it as if it were a snake. She didn't want to touch him. It was too soon, and she still hadn't processed all that had happened when he'd touched her the last time. Misinterpreting her reticence, he scowled slightly but moved away from the car door to let her out.

Lauren's apartment was the top floor of what was essentially a row home. The block was lined with narrow, three-story buildings that were kept in only moderately good condition. Cass had surmised from what Dougie had said that Lauren didn't live far down on Addison Street from where Cass's current apartment was, and her old apartment was just a few blocks further up. She knew the neighborhood well enough to know that there was nothing high-class about any of the buildings in this particular section of the city.

She considered all the money Malcolm had at his disposal, not to mention what she knew about how Lauren had grown up, and figured that Lauren must have rejected that lifestyle. It could have been a pride thing. She wanted to make it on her own, or it could have been a family split. She wondered if Malcolm would comment, but he said nothing.

"It's this one," he indicated, pointing to the third house on the right. There were front steps that led to a door that, once unlocked, led to another door that served as the entrance to the downstairs apartment. Another set of stairs, still blocked by yellow tape, would take them to where Lauren had lived.

Together they climbed to the top, where they stood on a handwoven mat that covered the small landing, while Malcolm unlocked the door.

Cass glanced down at her feet.

Blessed Be.

Malcolm pushed open the door, then took a few steps down to allow Cass to proceed ahead of him. It was well past midmorning at this point, and the light from the sun was more than enough to illuminate the tiny space.

The first thing that caught her eye was the stain of

blood that could be seen so clearly on the floor. Large and ghastly, it resembled a small lake covering the cream linoleum of the kitchen floor. It got even darker as it spread out to the cheap, pale beige carpet.

"You don't have to come up here," she said, looking over her shoulder to where he stood still two steps down.

"I've already seen it," he muttered.

"That doesn't mean you have to see it again."

He pinned her with a gaze that suggested he didn't need to be coddled, and she guessed he was right. It wasn't her place to tell him what he could or could not bear.

He was on his own.

Ignoring him, she stepped into the apartment and focused her senses. There was something here that Lauren thought was important. Something obscure enough that the police had missed it.

It stood to reason that if they had missed something, it wasn't going to be easy to find.

Cass waited for the tingling sensation to hit her, but, for a long moment, there was only silence. "I'm going to need a little help here," she mumbled.

"Help with what, exactly?" Malcolm asked as he stepped inside, closing the door behind him.

"Uh…I was sort of talking to her," Cass admitted.

She watched his jaw tighten, but this time he managed to maintain his cool.

The space wasn't as she'd expected, but then she'd probably been associating Lauren too much with her brother. There was nothing austere or elegant or high-class about it. Instead, it was a chaotic mess of knickknacks, wall hangings and two shelves that were filled with books and tiny porcelain figurines. At the center of all of it was a plump, bright-yellow couch and an end table covered with more books and magazines and…well, stuff.

There was also a hint of vanilla, she determined, in the air. Cass couldn't understand how that was possible, given the blood that had been lost, but it was there.

Heading for the end table, the first thing she spotted was an oblong, carved wooden bowl that held two slim sticks inside of it. She lifted a stick, sniffed the top of it and knew where the vanilla had come from. Next to the incense holder was a box with a pentagram carved into it. As she scanned the book titles and magazines on the table, a picture began to form. *Magickal Digest, Spells and Cants for Beginners, The Wicca Almanac.*

A set of pentagram chimes blended with a dream catcher that hung from the ceiling near the window that overlooked the street below, and, moving to one of the bookshelves, Cass could see rows of tiny figurine fairies that sat almost as if protecting the reading material behind them. Gently pushing past them, she pulled out *Advanced Spells*. It looked unread.

The reading material, the pentacle box, the doormat out front.

"She was a witch," Cass said, lifting one of the porcelain pieces. It wasn't particularly well crafted, but it was whimsical and said a great deal about the person who would buy it in the first place.

Behind her, she felt Malcolm's approach, and before she could close her hand on it, he was snatching the fairy out of her grasp and placing it back on the shelf. Hard.

"She was into a lot of things," he explained.

And maybe that was true, but one of the things she was very much into was the practice of Wicca. Although based on what Lauren had been reading versus what had been left untouched, Cass was guessing she'd just recently pursued the religion.

"There's nothing wrong with having alternative spiritual beliefs." As so many of the people she'd been committed with in the asylum had told her.

Malcolm cringed, and Cass had to admit she took a perverse pleasure in it. She could only imagine his reluctance to listen to his sister prattle on about nature, the moon cycles and which herbs were best for love spells. She could see him now trying to reason her beliefs right out of her.

Did he feel guilty? Now that she was gone, was he sad that he had so quickly dismissed her and her beliefs as nonsense?

A bright bolt of pain smacked her, and a voice echoed in her head.

He didn't like it, but he always listened. He never made fun of me.

Lauren's voice startled her, but Cass quickly worked to construct her room so she could hear clearly what Lauren had to say.

Interesting. "You were okay with her being a witch." Cass was astonished.

He straightened the figurine so that it was exactly where it was before she had disturbed it. "Lauren believed what she did. Practiced the religion she chose. She was a grown woman. I might have thought it was

ridiculous, but it was her life and not my call to inter-
fere. Why are you looking at me like that?"

Cass immediately shook her head to try to erase
whatever expression she was currently wearing. "I'm
sorry, it's just so unexpected."

"Unexpected of me? How? You don't even know me."

The reproof hurt. Mostly because he was right. She
didn't know him at all, but she did know how he had
reacted to her and to her gift. For someone who saw
things in black and white, was being a medium very
much different than being a witch?

"You didn't give me a whole lot of leeway when I
told you what I was," she countered.

"You pretended to be talking to my dead sister."

Pretended. *Ouch.*

"Don't," he said, holding up his hand as if to stop
her. "Please don't tell me anything else 'she said' or
what you know about me. I just don't think I could
handle it right now."

Since he appeared to be even more exhausted than
he'd been an hour ago, she let it drop. She wasn't the
type to showboat her talent, but with him, there was this
irrational need to prove something. He was right,
though. This wasn't the time or the place.

"Okay."

"You were looking for something."

Cass closed her eyes for a second to better concentrate on the voice inside her head.

There was a ticket. Find the ticket.

"A ticket," Cass stated. "I'm looking for some kind
of ticket."

"A movie ticket, theater ticket, plane ticket?"

But she could see that the door was closing. Lauren's face disappeared behind it, and Cass stood alone in her room. The mental image faded, and she shrugged to let him know that was all the information she was going to get.

The two of them moved around the room. Thankfully, there wasn't a large area to search. The couch took up most of the space. The shelves lined the walls of the rest of it. She had a framed picture of her family. It was a snapshot taken outside of what looked to be a downtown restaurant. Cass's eyes fell to the strawberry blonde in the shot. Lauren was more beautiful alive. Clearer, more vivid.

Malcolm searched the kitchen, but it was tidy, with only a single orange mug in the sink that still had an herbal tea bag in it. She heard him opening and closing doors, and she moved from the shelves back to the end table. The magazines had been stacked next to the books, no doubt by the cops who had gone through them. Given all the natural clutter, Lauren didn't strike Cass as overly orderly.

She'd bet a million dollars, though, that everything in Malcolm's place was in neat piles.

Shaking the useless thought from her head, she forced her attention back to the magazines. The one on top had a shiny cover that was coated with a fine, black powder that suggested it had been fingerprinted. Probably not the best surface to extract a print, but the thought process behind it hadn't been bad.

Neither the lock on the door downstairs nor the one

to her apartment had been tampered with, and Lauren
had been killed inside her apartment. She'd let whoever
did it inside. One of the reasons why Malcolm had
been an easy suspect. If it had been a friend or someone
she'd known casually, it was conceivable that that
person might have sat on her couch, rifled through a
magazine, maybe…

Cass lifted the first magazine and shook it gently by
the seam, letting the pages flap about freely. She did
the same with the one underneath that. By the fourth
magazine, she was growing discouraged when a short
stub fluttered to the table.

She picked it up and studied it. It was the second half
of a train ticket. Baltimore to Philadelphia.

"You found it." Malcolm could see through the open
kitchen area to where she was standing.

"It was stuck between the pages of one of the magazines," she told him. "Had she been outside Philadelphia recently?" Cass read the date on the ticket. "Within
the last two weeks?"

"No. She just got a job. Some New Age store a
couple of blocks from here. She was excited about it.
I know for a fact that she was working at least six out
of her last seven days."

"Did she have any friends who lived in Baltimore?"

"Not that I know of."

Cass had grown up in Baltimore but kept that information to herself so as not to trigger another round of
suspicion. Not that it was anything more than a coincidence, anyway.

"Last night, you said you weren't close."

Reluctantly, he nodded. "We weren't close in age. I didn't spend much time around her friends, as I'm sure you can imagine. They were all…like her."

"Witches."

He frowned. "Can you not use that word?"

"It's politically acceptable within their practice."

"You know about…witches?"

"I know a lot about people who are on the fringe. The unaccepted. The unusual."

"Because that's where you fit," he logically reasoned.

"It's where I belong."

He didn't respond but instead looked away when he finally answered her first question. "No, we didn't hang out together a lot. But we spoke on the phone at least once a week. She would have told me if she was having company from out of town."

"Even if that company were male?"

"Especially that. Lauren was always very excited about the prospect of meeting her true love. She'd had three of them by the time she was seventeen. If a man was coming to visit, one she cared about, she would have told me and…" He sighed. "She's never going to have that now, is she? There's never going to be the one. Not for her."

"You said she had three."

"That was school stuff. Childish, immature crushes."

"Love is love. And whoever said there had to be only one real thing and it had to come when you were ready? You can't spend your life thinking about what she missed. You have to remember what she had."

"Yeah. Are we done?"

"I found what I came for."

"So what happens next?"

"We find out who from Baltimore came to visit Lauren."

"We?"

"The police," Cass amended. "I know you don't completely trust me. But you can trust them."

Malcolm stuffed his hands in his pockets and looked away from her. "It seemed like too much of a coincidence that you happened to be there this morning. It wasn't the most ridiculous theory."

"No, I suppose it wasn't."

"This time I'm definitely not going to apologize. Not for what I thought."

"I didn't expect you to," Cass told him. "You're the type who can apologize forever when you know you're wrong, but you won't budge if you think you're right."

He turned back to her, his gaze sharper. "You keep assigning me these types. Why do you do that?"

It was a fair question. She imagined because it made him easier to deal with if she believed him to be a black-and-white, close-minded, high society, inflexible man. If he was all those things, then he was to be kept at a distance. If he wasn't…then she wouldn't know how to deal with him.

That idea slightly unsettling, Cass replied by going on the defensive. "Please. You pegged me as a nut the moment we met."

"I didn't peg you. You did that yourself when you

told me what you were." He closed his mouth abruptly. Then he tried to apologize. "I didn't mean to say you were actually crazy. I just…"

"It doesn't matter." But she could hear the bitterness creeping back into her voice. It was her fault for using the term *nut*. It conjured too many bad memories of her grandfather after he stopped being her family and instead became her jailer. Deep down they had all believed she was crazy. A nut. Her grandfather, the doctors at the asylum, all of them.

"We should go," she said quickly, cutting him off before he could say anything. "Do you need to get…you know, the dress?"

He paused for a moment but then nodded and made for the room off the living room that was separated by two folding doors. When Malcolm pushed them aside she could see that the room was almost as small as hers back at the apartment. But Lauren had a dresser. Nice.

Cass watched him sort through the different hangers, stopping occasionally to give one outfit more consideration. Or maybe he was just remembering the last time he'd seen her in it. Again, she felt a twinge, just a twinge, though, of sympathy for a brother who was now alone in this world.

Finally he extracted a hanger.

A small pain behind her eyes signaled contact, but Cass didn't even bother with forming the room. This message was quick and clear.

Not that one.

"Not that one," Cass called to him. He scowled, but she shrugged it off. "Pick again."

Blue.

"Something blue," she added.

He pulled out a soft, periwinkle dress that was light and whimsical. The perfect dress for a practicing witch who regularly purchased fairies.

Perfect.

"Perfect," Cass told him.

"Is that you talking or…" He stopped himself before he could finish the thought.

"Both."

He sighed. "Right. I shouldn't have asked."

Chapter 7

"I don't get it," Dougie began after they sat down in a back booth in a downtown Philadelphia bar near Penn's Landing. "After the way he spoke to you, why would you agree to go anywhere with McDonough?"

Cass had called Dougie as soon as she'd gotten home and told him everything. Malcolm's visit, the message from Lauren, the ticket. Everything but the near strangling attempt. She knew Dougie would go macho on her, and she wasn't in the mood for a lecture on why she should avoid Malcolm McDonough.

Reaching up she brushed her neck with her fingers, sliding them over the sensitive skin. That tingle of sensation she'd felt when he had touched her had stayed with her all afternoon, had even followed her into her

sleep when she had tried to make up for the rest she'd
lost the previous night.

Even now, several hours later, it still bothered her.

Something had happened when he'd touched her.
Some feeling or energy had been transmitted. Cass had
no vocabulary to explain it, only that it had happened
and that it was related to Lauren.

When he'd dropped her off at her place, he'd again
performed the ritual of opening her car door for her and
she'd paused for a moment. The temptation to ask him
if he'd felt anything…odd…when they'd touched had
been palpable, but, in the end, the words wouldn't come
out. Besides, with his reluctance to rehash the incident,
she'd doubted he would have told her the truth anyway.

"Worried he might kill me?"

"Not really. Worried he might make you feel bad
though."

"He didn't. He has enough regrets as it is. He says
they weren't close, but they were in the ways that count.
He loved her and she loved him, or the connection
wouldn't be as strong."

"Is that true? It's stronger when…"

She knew where he was going and nodded. "When
the connection between the two people is strong in life,
that seems to follow after death. At least, it's easier to
hear the person speaking and understand what they're
saying. Lauren was loud and clear and pretty insistent."

"You never told me that."

No, because it invited the inevitable question,
which she now had to answer. "When I hear Claire,
she's very clear."

He frowned. "I didn't ask."

"Okay." Cass reached into her purse and extracted the Ziploc bag containing what could be evidence. She slid it across the table toward him.

Dougie smiled as he held up the Baggie. "Worried about contamination?"

"I wasn't sure."

"It's doubtful we'll get prints off of it, but we'll see. You ever had a voice tell you about a clue before?"

"No, but keep in mind it might not be a clue to her murder."

He scrunched up his face. "Huh? Why point you to something unless it could help solve her murder?"

"Sometimes the dead aren't very interested in the means of their death. When they make contact, it's typically because they want resolution. That ticket could be about anything, really. Her relationship with her brother, with someone else. It's not necessarily tied to her killer."

"So you're telling me even the dead make lousy witnesses."

"To their own murders? Yep. It's not as if they're casual observers."

"Yeah, but you went over there for this. My guess is you think this is related."

It was a gut hunch. Nothing more. Cass nodded. "I think it might be."

Dougie held the bag up and studied the ticket a little more closely. "I can't believe our guys missed it."

"It was stuffed in the pages of a magazine. The magazine was dusted for prints, but I don't think anyone not specifically looking for it would have found it."

"Baltimore," he murmured. "Early a.m. That's a huge commuter train; it's going to be tough to pin down."

They were interrupted by the appearance of their young waitress. "Wings and beer to start?" he asked Cass.

Wings and beer: that was seduction, Philadelphia-style.

"Sure," Cass answered carefully, wondering if this had just turned into a dinner date. Doug had insisted on meeting her for dinner when she'd told him about the ticket. When she'd hesitated, he'd pointed out that either she needed to come to his place to drop it off or he was coming to her to get it, so unless she wanted to cook for him, her only other option was to meet him out.

Cass could only really cook eggs. The choice was obvious.

The waitress took the order and left. Dougie non-chalantly pocketed the Baggie in his coat.

"You're not going to lose it?"

He raised his eyebrows. "I've got two dead women in two days, with their tongues missing, and you think I'm going to lose what might be my biggest break. Hello, do you know me? I'm Doug Brody. I've been a detective for ten years."

"Sorry," she mumbled. "I guess I'm nervous."

"Yeah and I know why. You ready to talk about what brought you outside this morning?"

"What was her name?" Cass interjected in an obvious attempt to move him off the subject. "The dead woman from this morning?"

"Silvia, Silvia Biagi. She lived in the apartment where you found her. Made a meager living with tarot cards, palm readings, tea leaves. Whatever. Also seems she did some late-night telemarketing. The way it looks, our guy came in for a reading and then he attacked her. They fought. There was definitely evidence of a struggle. We found some hair that wasn't hers. Short and dark colored. We also got some skin from under her fingernails, but so far no matches. Then our guy stabbed her and took the tongue. Only this time, he did it while she was still alive. He ran out and left the door open. She was crawling outside to get help. We think she was hoping to get up to the sidewalk where someone would find her, but she bled out before that happened."

Cass wrapped her arms around herself to keep away the sudden chill that descended on her. She'd still been alive. What possessed a person to commit such a brutal act?

A memory of the monster flashed behind her eyes. Maybe there were more of them out there than she knew.

"The coroner is still working on it, but he puts her death at sometime around four in the morning," Dougie finished.

Cass processed the information. A psychic. Was it possible that it wasn't a coincidence? "Did you know Lauren was a witch?"

"Yeah." He sighed. "We saw the 'woowoo' stuff all over her apartment. Our first thought was that it might be some kind of ritual killing."

"'Woowoo stuff,'" she repeated. "People who practice Wicca aren't by definition 'woowoo' or ritual killers. Open your mind, Dougie."

"It's about as open as it can be when it comes to you. All I'm saying is we saw the stuff and know what she's about. Has it escaped our notice that the two victims were both into practices considered outside the norm? No. Has it escaped *my* notice that you're connected to both…no."

But Cass shook her head. "The only reason I'm connected to Lauren is because you brought me in to consult."

"I was talking about the fact that you also live on Addison, relatively close to both victims, you are also a woman, and that you are also…"

"Outside of the norm."

"Yeah."

The waitress served them their wings with extra plates and lots of wet wipes and put two pints down in front of them. Forgetting the case for a moment, they concentrated on the food and beer in front of them, using one to quench the fire of the other. With a final swig, Dougie pushed his empty glass aside.

"I'm officially worried about you, Cass. I want to know what the hell you were doing at the crime scene this morning. Don't put me off. If for no other reason, any other possible connection you might have with these women could be important."

"I don't have a connection with the women." She had it with a monster. A monster that was trying to connect to someone. She reasoned if the killer was close enough—Silvia Biagi lived only a block and a half away—that could have triggered the incident.

She'd never connected over such a distance before, but if the killer had at some point passed by her door…

"Another beer?"

Disrupted from her thoughts, Cass looked at the nearly empty glass in front of her; she ran a finger up and down the smooth, cold surface of the glass. She still needed to get home and, besides that, she wasn't sure she had enough cash to cover her half of what they'd already had. If she let him pay, what should have been basically a working dinner would definitely become a date.

"I'll pass."

"You've got to be kidding me. What's the matter? Afraid you'll have some fun?"

She raised her chin defiantly. "Detective, are you encouraging someone who is at the legal limit to go beyond that and still drive her motorbike home?"

"No," he said irritably. "I saw you doing the math in your head, and I know you're thinking about your half of the bill. I'm picking up the tab and I'm putting your bike in my truck. Then I'm dropping you off at home. Now do you want another beer or not?"

His normally easygoing countenance had shifted. She'd annoyed him, but she didn't care. "Dougie…you can't do this. You can't take care of me."

"What if I want to take care of you?" he returned. He leaned forward across the table with purpose. "What is it, Cass? Why do you keep running away from what happened that night? Was it not good for you? What?"

She pulled away from him, pressing herself against the back of the wooden booth.

"Dougie, don't go there," she pleaded.

It wasn't that the sex hadn't been good; it was that everything else about that night had been wrong. She'd been distraught when he'd come over. Alone like she'd never been before, not even during her days of confinement in the asylum. He'd still been struggling with Claire's death, probably had felt equally alone in the world, and so he had offered her a deal. They could make each other feel good for a time. No strings, just sex and relief.

It had started out easy, but then his touch had triggered a wave of pain, and before Cass could block her out, Claire was beyond the door. She had looked on as her husband had made love to another woman. Cass had felt caught between them, but by the time she tried to pull away it had been too late—Dougie was inside her, and Cass could only ride out the storm.

When it was over, guilt had mingled with shame even though she'd tried to tell herself she'd done nothing wrong. Cass had fled to the shower, and when she'd come out he was gone. Since then, she'd done everything she could to distance herself from him. She hadn't counted on his persistence.

Calls, unexpected visits. He'd bombarded her with platonic companionship and he'd never pressed her again to resume the physical aspect of their relationship. He just insisted he wasn't losing her as a friend.

Which made sense. How else could she pass along messages from Claire occasionally?

Cass hated the skepticism that was so much a part of her makeup now, and for a time she'd been able to shelve it where Dougie was concerned. Mostly because she needed a friend and he was a good one. But there was no way she could ever have any kind of intimate relationship with him. Not knowing Claire was watching.

"I want to go there. I want to know why you won't let me back in."

"You know why not. Your wife."

"My wife is dead," he stated as coldly as he possibly could. "She's not coming back. I'm moving on."

"I think that's good. I would be truly happy for you if you could do that, but the last person in this world you can 'move on' with is me. Ask me. Go ahead. You've wanted to since the second I sat down. Ask me."

"No," he refused, looking away from her. "I'm done with that."

"But you're not. You're certainly not done with her and maybe you never will be, but at least with someone else, you might have a chance to move forward. With me, it would always be about the past. Because of what I do, what I am, she'll always be with us."

"I care about you, Cass. *You.*"

His words were sincere—she didn't doubt them— but the resignation in his voice was telling. Feeling safer, she reached for his hand and when he pulled back, she stretched farther to take it. Holding it tightly, she met his gaze directly. "I know you do. And your friendship means the world to me. You have to know that. You're all I have."

"That's all you want?"

"That's all I can have." Cass's eyes dropped to the

hands that were linked on the table. She saw their fingers intertwined.

Skin to skin. She felt nothing. But she also wasn't connected to Claire. A year ago she had been.

"What? Is she saying something? Are you listening to her now?"

Cass refocused her attention on that night a year ago. She'd been drinking, but wasn't drunk or else Dougie wouldn't have touched her. Her senses definitely had been dulled, though. Then there had been the pure grief over the death of her grandfather and the guilt about what she hadn't done. It had all been raging inside of her ready to spill over.

All she'd wanted was some kind of relief from it, a temporary cessation from the pain, and Dougie had given it to her. Cataloging each moment of the experience hadn't been a priority. But now a vague memory came back. A memory she knew she had intentionally kept at bay.

It was the way he had held her. Not like a man held a woman in comfort, and certainly not like a man engaged in a meaningless one-night stand. Claire had been gone for only a few months. Dougie was still fighting to cope with her death. They were supposed to be two people looking for some comfort in a world full of pain.

But the way he'd held her…almost as if she had been his dead wife come back from the grave.

In the here and now, Cass watched his eyes focus intently on the point of contact between them. Almost like he was willing something to happen. When he glanced up and discovered she was studying him, his face flushed with what could only be guilt. Slowly, she pulled her hands back and crossed them over her body.

"Oh, my God. You can feel her through me. Can't you? Oh, my God."

"What? Cass? Don't be crazy."

"Don't call me crazy," she snapped. "I didn't figure it out before. I don't touch many people, never really have. But you. You touch me all the time. A hug, a pat on the back, a shoulder rub. You do it all to get to her."

"You're being ridiculous. Maybe I don't have a problem with physical intimacy like you do."

She saw his lips thin and it only made her angrier. "Do not attempt to blame me for this. You felt her that night. I was connected to her. I couldn't keep her out. I was horrified afterward. I tried not to let you know, but you did know. Somehow you knew she was there. You weren't fucking me. You were trying to make love to your dead wife."

"Cass, don't do this. Don't go there."

Exactly what she'd asked him not to do, but he did it anyway. "I felt something today. McDonough, when he touched me, there was definitely something. I saw it in his eyes. It was as if someone had slapped him, he reacted so abruptly. I thought about how long it had been since I'd touched someone, and I realized the last time was that night with you. There's a reason why I avoid contact. Subconsciously, I must have sensed that this thing that I have, this *gift*, it's changing. It explains everything. How you were with me, how I felt the next morning."

"And how did you feel?" he asked angrily.

"I felt used," she stated coldly. "But I'd thought that

Claire had been the one using me." She grabbed her purse. "I'm going to be sick. You have your ticket. If you need anything else from me have one of the other officers contact me."

Cass pushed herself out of the booth and scrambled for the front door. Not quick enough. She felt Dougie wrapping his hand around her arm, pulling her back. She tugged but couldn't shake off his hold. It infuriated her. Turning to face him, she gritted her teeth and tried to give the appearance of a woman who was about to pitch a major fit in a public place.

"Just settle down and talk to me, Cass. It's not what you think, okay. Yeah, maybe sometimes I can feel…I don't know…whatever, but that has nothing to do with us."

"How can you say that? Don't you see, you're no better than someone who rents a girl off the streets and makes her tell you her name is Claire."

"That's not true," he said tightly. "It isn't like that. It's not dirty. It's me and Claire together and there was *nothing* ever dirty about that."

"You're wrong. It is dirty. As sullied as it would have been to invite me into your bedroom when she was still alive. Now let go."

"What are you going to do if I don't," he taunted.

Cass practically snarled at him. "I'm so sick to death of being bullied by men today. Get your damn hand off me or I will bring this place down around your ears and you will be explaining to your superiors why you felt the need to accost a woman on your free time."

Her determination must have shown through her eyes because after a second he released her arm.

She shrugged it out of his open grasp and bolted for the door. Outside in the fresh air, she leaned against the brick building and tried to rein herself in. The sudden burst of nausea she'd felt at the realization of what had actually happened that night had dissipated, but in its place were loss and humiliation. Neither of which were going anywhere.

When had the gift changed? It was bad enough hearing the voices; she'd learned to cope with that, even control it to some extent. Now she was some freak ghost conductor. It was maddening.

An image of Whoopi Goldberg in *Ghost*, inflating with the spirit of a dead husband, mocked her. There was nothing funny about this. This wasn't what she wanted.

She'd never wanted any of it. A steady dribble of rain began to pelt the top of her head. Lifting her face to it, she felt the sting of the cold on her cheeks, but it made her feel cleaner.

In front of her, the street was filled with normal people. Lots of normal people—young people it appeared—moving from one bar to the next. Second Street, which was just a block off of South Street, was busy every night of the week but more so on the weekend. Once people were done shopping for the strange and unusual on South Street, they would make their way to a bar to show off the strange and unusual purchases, flirt and pass time with friends. When it got late and they got drunk, they would make their way back to Pat's King of Steaks for a cheese steak wit' Whiz.

Like wings and beer, it was a Philly tradition.

One that she no longer let herself be a part of. There was a time when her younger coworkers at whatever meaningless job she had would invite her out after work. Inevitably, they figured out that she was different. Ultimately, the invitations would stop. Then one day one of those coworkers, who had once told her she should come and hang out with him, would call her up on the phone and fire her.

She shouldn't have been surprised that her talent had mutated without her knowing it, because she was so damn removed from everyone. What the hell was she going to do now? She'd built a life designed to maintain some control over her world: few possessions, few friends and simple jobs that allowed her to use her gift without being overwhelmed by it.

Now she had to add avoiding all physical contact? It was as if she were building her own prison, stone by stone. A prison that would be far worse than anything she'd experienced in the asylum. Knowing there were no answers forthcoming, Cass pushed off the wall at her back and made her way across the cobbled sidewalk to the crosswalk.

Thoughts of Dr. Farver and the Institute of Psychical Studies floated through her consciousness, but she rejected the notion. She wasn't going back there. Yes, he might be able to help her set up a controlled environment to start testing what was happening to her, but in the end he wouldn't believe it was real.

Dr. Farver had other ideas concerning her special talent. None of them had anything to do with the dead.

Spotting her bike, where she'd left it chained to a parking meter, Cass stepped toward it, then stopped. A tingling sensation on the back of her neck was sounding the alarm.

Instantly she scanned the street, trying to see who might be her point of contact. But everyone was still bustling along seemingly without noticing the woman standing near the edge of the street. She concentrated on forming the room.

Across two lanes of traffic on the other side of the street, Cass saw a figure in an oversize hooded sweat-shirt and baggy jeans stop abruptly. The hood was pulled low over the person's head, so Cass couldn't make out any features—for that matter, couldn't even tell if it was a man or woman.

However, she could feel a set of eyes on her, staring. The sensation unnerved her so much that she moved out of the light of the streetlamp, allowing the night to keep her in the dark.

A burst of sharp pain stabbed her between the eyes as the door to her room opened without her consent.

On the other side of it was the monster.

Chapter 8

Cass focused on her breathing and tried not to panic as she saw the monster draw nearer. In her mind she acted as she had before, moving across the room in an attempt to close the door and shut it out. But by the time she got there, the hooves of the beast were already wedged into a space between the door and its frame. It pushed against her, forcing her back into the room.

It was so close this time. Its nose was pushed up against its face like a pig's snout, and two large fangs hung down over its mouth, dripping with spit.

What do you want?

It tilted back its head and shouted. The noise penetrated her whole body, shaking her internal organs. *Sha-a Uh-h-h!*

Cass couldn't decipher the answer to her silent question. She didn't even know why she had tried. She *listened* to voices from the other side. Before now, it had never occurred to her to speak back.

The monstrous thing moved steadily forward into the room, past the defenses she'd constructed. Slinking back, she thought to avoid contact altogether until she could... Do what? Escape? Was that possible from a room she had created?

Before she could formulate an answer, a beefy arm swung at her and missed. Then its other arm came at her, and this time she felt the contact against her ribs. Or at least that was how her mind interpreted it. The power of the impact was like nothing she had ever experienced. It was if she had been hit with a baseball bat. She could barely think beyond the pain.

Only, she needed to think. The monster hadn't just come of its own accord; it had to have been brought. That's the way it had always worked. And at the moment that she'd felt the sensation on the back of her neck, she'd seen someone. Across the street.

Cass tried to turn her attention to what her eyes saw. A crowd on either side of her. A smattering of people in front of her. And there, beyond the sidewalk, on the other side of the road, was the figure in the hooded sweatshirt standing rooted in place. Staring at her.

It was an ominous stare, but before she could think about why, another swing from the monster hit her in the face. Her concentration divided between what she saw in her mind and what she needed to see in front of her, Cass couldn't mount any resistance against the powerful beast. Another blow rocked her to her foundation, and, inside the room, she fell to her knees. Her palms were flat against the smooth, white surface of the room, but inexplicably she felt the scrape of stone under her fingers and small pebbles digging into her palms.

This wasn't right. She was in trouble.

Inside the room, she lifted her head, trying to find the monster's position to determine where the next attack would come from. It was moving toward her again, and she wondered if another blow might kill her. If that was even possible. She'd never come close to experiencing anything like this before.

Her focus shifting again, her eyes widened as two beams of light flashed at her, forcing her back to the world of the living. In less than an instant, Cass determined she was not on the sidewalk but was in the middle of the street instead. She had to move. A car wouldn't see her on her hands and knees. The twin beams of light grew larger.

Mentally, she closed her eyes against the monster, deciding that facing the physical danger was more imperative than facing the spiritual one. She tried crawling forward, but she felt the presence of the monster block her path. Cass couldn't fight off the need to stop. The only way out was to turn around. To run from it.

The sound of the car's engine paired with the bright lights compelled her to move faster. She scrambled backward, trying to get to her feet, using her hands to push herself up and out of the way.

The car was louder, a near roar in her ear. Or was that the monster shouting again, moving closer for the final blow?

Don't look at it, she ordered herself. *Just move.*

Her legs felt sluggish. Her whole body, which she'd honed to be lean and strong, able to withstand the punishment of connecting with the dead, worked against her now as she tried to stand. So she pushed harder. Finally making it to her feet, she managed to stumble back, but it was too late. The car was there, practically on top of her, only a few feet away. A blaring horn announced that it had seen her, but it wasn't going to be able to stop in time. The squeal of brakes indicated as much.

It was going to hit her.

Suddenly, Cass felt something clamp around her arm. She was being pulled. Hard. So hard that she flew backward a couple of feet onto her ass and watched from the cobblestone sidewalk as the car screeched to a halt well past the spot where she would have been standing if she hadn't been yanked out of the way.

"What's the matter, you crazy bitch!" the driver called through his open window. "Are you drunk? I could have killed you."

A cranky older man, who evidently felt that almost dying wasn't enough of a punishment, decided to take the time to roll down the car window and yell at her for almost getting killed. Evidently satisfied that he'd scared her, he put up the window and continued on his way.

"What in the hell were you doing?"

Malcolm McDonough crouched down next to her. It took Cass a few seconds to process that he was the person who had dragged her out of the way. It took a few seconds after that to realize that whatever had sent her to her knees in the middle of the street was gone.

Without answering him, she looked up and searched the other side of the road, looking for the figure in the hooded sweatshirt. He was gone, too. Only a gaggle of gapers stood around staring at her as she lay sprawled on the sidewalk. No doubt wondering, like the driver, if she was drunk. Why else would a person throw herself into the middle of a busy street?

Malcolm reached out to cup her face, his thumb brushing against her cheek. He squinted as if trying to see by the dim light of the streetlamp. "Did you hurt yourself when you fell?"

Her tongue felt thick inside her mouth, almost as if she had had too much to drink. She waited a moment for the adrenaline to leak out of her system so she could catch her breath. The monster was gone. The person under the hood was gone, but at least now she suspected how the monster was getting through. There had been someone on the other side of the street. Watching her. The monster wasn't penetrating the barrier between life and death on its own.

"I said, are you hurt?"

Cass blinked a few times and then turned to him. "No. Help me up, please."

He stood, and she noted he wore the same jeans and dark sweater from this morning. He stretched out a hand and she took it, then felt herself being lifted to her feet with the same strength he'd used to pull her out of the car's path. Her hand made contact with his chest and she felt the soft material of the sweater and a hard wall underneath it.

Immediately, she drew her hand back. She couldn't touch him. She couldn't touch anyone anymore.

Finally, the strangeness of his sudden appearance registered.

"What are you doing here?"

"I think I get to ask the questions," he said. "What happened? You were standing there and then you just doubled over. People called out to you, but it's like you couldn't hear them and then you fell into the middle of the street like someone had pushed you."

Cass didn't need the instant replay. She still hurt from the monster, and alongside the pain was the frustration of feeling like she was onto something. Why had that person in the sweatshirt stopped so abruptly? Could it have simply been someone from the coffeehouse who had recognized her? Or more than that? How was he connected to the monster? Too many questions without answers.

There was no point in mentioning any of this to McDonough. He wouldn't understand and the last thing she wanted to do was create a false connection between what had just happened and his sister's death.

"I need to get home," she finally said, choosing not to deal with why Malcolm had been there in the first place. She had too much to think about. Not the least of which was how the monster had gotten past the door. It seemed, to her horror, that whatever distance she'd been able to keep between the real world and the other world was fast coming to an end.

"Okay." He took her elbow in his hand and guided her down the sidewalk and around the corner to where he'd parked his SAAB. She was only a step away from the car when she heard the sound of his remote disengaging the locks and starting the engine. This wasn't what she meant.

"No. My bike. I have to…"

"It's chained up. It will be safe for a while. I'll drop you off then come back for it."

She didn't question the logistics of how that was all going to work. She didn't even put up a mild protest. Defeated, wounded from battle, all she could handle was the idea of putting one foot in front of the other.

He circled the car, opened the passenger door and poured her into the bucket leather seat. When she didn't move, he was forced to bend over her to secure the seat belt for her. She pressed herself back, but even the threat of touching him wasn't enough to motivate her to fasten the seat belt herself.

Never before had she been so drained from contact. Then again, never before had she seen someone who had been murdered. Never before had she lost her only friend. Tears threatened to surface as she considered the ramifications of losing Dougie. With him in her life she was simply a solitary person. Without him she was alone.

But what he'd done she couldn't forgive. If he'd been honest about it the next day, she could have believed that he had been just as surprised and disgusted by what had happened as she'd been. That the whole thing had simply been an accident brought on by her gift. But he hadn't. Instead, he'd done everything in his power to maintain their friendship while at the same time trying to work his way back into her bed.

No, not her bed. Claire's bed.

The betrayal cut deeply. Before this, Cass would have said that Dougie wasn't capable of such deception. Now she felt as if she'd never really known who he was. He'd taken that away, too.

Refusing to cry, as it served little purpose and tended to give her a headache when it was all over, Cass closed her eyes and concentrated on breathing.

Malcolm situated himself behind the wheel and moved the SAAB out into traffic. Cass tried not to dwell on why she was letting him shuffle her around like a rag doll he'd picked up off the street when she'd been stubborn about letting Dougie pick up her half of the check.

He hadn't answered what he was doing there, and the idea that it could have been a coincidence seemed too far-fetched. But she had no energy left in her to ask. Beyond the pain that was sapping her strength was the cold-blooded fear.

What the hell was happening to her?

The luxury vehicle moved with precision through the narrow, car-lined streets, and, before Cass had a chance to look up, she felt him once again parallel parking the car with a skill she couldn't help but admire.

They'd stopped. Cass figured that was her cue to get out, but she was overcome by a sense of inertia. Her legs felt weighted and her arms were numb.

Next to her, Malcolm said nothing but instead got out of the car and came around to her side.

The heavy sweater she'd worn to meet Dougie downtown was now soaked and plastered against a too-thin chemise, which was also wet and stuck to her body. The cold penetrated to her bones. Involuntarily, she shivered.

"Do I need to carry you?"

She turned her head and saw that he was leaning over her, his face close to hers. His eyes assessing her condition. He didn't force her to answer quickly, nor did he immediately take the decision out of her hands as Dougie might have done. She appreciated that. However, since the choice was hers, she naturally had to make the tough call. For that she cursed him.

"I can do it. Back off."

He moved away to give her some space and watched her carefully while she used the car door and frame to help lift herself out. Her ribs hurt, throbbed, really, and she had trouble taking a deep breath. But she made it up and onto her feet. When she buckled slightly, he was there with an arm for her to lean on.

"Keys."

This time he didn't ask but rather held out his hand, expecting he would get them. She decided the points he earned by not hauling her out of the car instantly were lost. Unfortunately, she wasn't in a place to argue.

Cass fished inside her jeans pocket for the key ring that held only a few keys. None of which were for her bike. It had a starter button on it. Her bike. The thing she would need to get to her new job every day. Once she found one. She'd just left it out there on the street.

"I need to go back and get my bike."

"I told you I would have it taken care of."

She handed him the keys and thought about why she

should believe him, but she didn't really see that she had a choice. She was in no shape to put up another fight tonight. First Dougie, then that thing.

Not that she'd actually put up a fight against either of them. She ran from Dougie, and the monster…well, she'd gotten creamed. In addition to everything else that needed to be considered, she was going to have to add that one to the list. She was a poor excuse for a fighter.

He unlocked the door, pushed it open, then stepped back so she could enter first. Typical of his manners. Cass moved past him and went inside and reached out to hit the switch that would illuminate the kitchen. Before the light went on, she saw the red button blinking on her phone, letting her know she had a message waiting.

Maybe Kevin had called back to say he'd changed his mind. The coffeehouse was pretty shy on staff now that so many had gone back to college. Yeah, right. Like the light was going to be good news, given her recent track record. Cass decided to ignore it. She moved gingerly, shuffling to where her bright red futon waited for her. Cautiously, she settled into the cushion.

It was okay, she thought. She was safe now. The beast was gone. She was home. There was blessed silence in her head.

"You need to get out of that sweater."

Just not blessed silence in her living room. How could she have forgotten he was there? He needed to go. She couldn't handle a visit from Lauren in her current shape, and the longer he stayed, the more likely it would become.

"Look, I appreciate what you did, but I'm sort of wiped so…"

Dismissing her obvious brush-off, he shut the door behind him and leaned against the island that bordered her living room, his arms crossed over his chest, his expression pensive.

"I pulled you out of the way before a car could hit you. Some might call that saving your life."

Apparently he wasn't the type to do that without wanting something for it. Funny. She didn't expect that of him. Then again what the hell did she know about anything? Just one more by-product of the Doug Brody Betrayal.

"What do you want?"

"For now I want you to take off your sweater. It appears to be wool, and it's soaking wet. You'll be freezing in a few minutes if you don't get it off."

"I'm a big girl."

"Not really." He moved closer and before she realized what was happening he was leaning over her and tugging at the bottom of the wet wool sweater.

"Stop it," she hissed.

"Lift your arms," he instructed firmly.

Her aggravation was extreme. She had no power to make him go away and she knew it. Still, she couldn't stop trying. "How dare you give me orders in my home? Leave. Now." She injected into her voice what she hoped was a note of imperiousness that someone of his ilk might respond to.

"No. Lift your arms."

Okay, so her imperious tone needed work.

Finally, like the child she felt like, Cass obeyed and he pulled the sweater off. However, with it came the white chemise she'd worn underneath the garment to protect her from the scratchy fabric, leaving her in nothing but a simple pink cotton bra. Her nipples, she knew, were hard and pronounced.

She heard his reaction rather than saw it because her head was still stuck in the neck of the sweater.

"What the hell…"

Not exactly the same reaction Dougie'd had when he'd seen her nipples for the first time. Cass felt the sudden release of the fabric as he yanked it over her head and then saw that his attention wasn't on her breasts but on the side of her body where the monster had struck.

Of course it hadn't actually hit her. It had been simply a mental projection that had resulted in a physical manifestation. Like the way she would form a bruise after making contact with the dead. This, however, was a pretty big bruise. Cautiously, she brushed the area with her fingertips. No, this was no bruise. This would have to be classified as a welt.

"Who did this to you?"

"You wouldn't understand," she mumbled, crossing her arms over her chest to conceal the pink bra she wore, as well as her extended nipples.

Obviously unaffected by her pert breasts, Malcolm's finger gently traced the red mark that ran along her right rib cage.

"Is it the cop?" he asked, his voice soft but tight. "I saw him with you at the restaurant, but you left separately. Are you dating him? Do you let him do this to you?"

That was so typical. As if she would ever let someone do this to her. "You think Dougie beats me?"

He lifted his hand and brushed back a lock of her bangs, studying the same eye he had squinted at before under the streetlamp. "This, too. The car didn't do this to you. You weren't even hit."

"Why was that?" she asked.

Their eyes locked. His hand fell from her face but rested against her uninjured side. His palm was warm and the penetration of heat through her skin made her shiver in a way that had nothing to do with the cold this time.

He was touching her. Intimately. Only this time there was no ghostly connection. There was, however, a physical one, which was possibly even more threatening. Cass shifted to her side, but his hand moved with her. His eyes were pinned on her and she wondered if his heart was racing nearly as fast as hers.

This was crazy. It wasn't what she wanted. She wanted answers. She shifted again and this time, he pulled his hand away. "You just said you saw Dougie with me. You were watching us. Why?"

He moved and took a seat on the end of the futon. There was a weird sort of intimacy even now that they weren't touching. Him sitting on the edge of the place where she typically rested her head. It seemed more natural than it should have.

Deciding that she needed space more than she needed answers, Cass rolled off the other side of the futon away from him. "Forget it."

Her knees shook, but she managed to tug her clothes out of his hands and make it down the small hallway to her bedroom. She dumped the sweater in the corner of the room and reached inside her closet lined with shelves to find a T-shirt that she could pull on. She'd never considered herself modest, but the idea of Malcolm seeing her, touching her, in nothing more than her underwear was a bit too much to handle.

Her cats sat side by side on the bed, their bodies tucked against each other in a way that always made her smile. Popping their heads up, they watched her move about the room. She opened her mouth to coo at them, but saw them turn with synchronicity toward the door.

"The fact that you're telling me I don't have to answer," he said from the doorway of her bedroom, "leads me to believe you think you already know the answer. Did my sister tell you that, too?"

The cats got up from their nest and slowly walked to the edge of the bed as if standing guard against the new intruder. Nice of them this time, since last time he'd visited they had stuck to the bedroom. Not that it mattered. Cass didn't imagine they could be all that effective against a full-grown man anyway, but she appreciated their effort. Right up until Malcolm stepped closer and held out his hand so that they could shamelessly rub their heads up against him.

"You're a cat person."

"Hardly," he replied with a hint of a smirk, even while his other hand reached out to stroke the long feline bodies. "Haven't you heard? Men aren't supposed to like cats."

Rolling her eyes, she made a noise that indicated what she thought about the concept of manliness in general.

"You didn't answer my question. Was it my sister that... Did you communicate, or whatever it is you do with her, again?"

"No. You can relax." No doubt her earlier encounter with the beast had temporarily drained her of the ability to connect with anyone. Maybe that's why his touch hadn't conjured up any kind of connection. Thank God. For a while she could live just among the living.

"You're not curious?"

"I was. Now I'm too sore to be curious."

She moved around him and out of the bedroom. Having him there was worse than sitting with him on the futon. But when she got back to the living room, she realized there weren't a whole lot of other choices. She stood in the middle of her space with her arms crossed over her chest and waited for him to appear.

"Look, it wasn't because I suspected you or anything," he clarified. "I knew this morning that you weren't involved."

"Well, thanks. I think."

"That doesn't mean I don't think you're...connected."

"*Connected.* There is a nice, safe word. How exactly do you think I'm connected?" she pressed.

"I don't know," he answered tightly. "I don't know, other than you seem to be the only link to two women who I believe were killed by the same person. You're also the only thing I can do."

His choice of words had her raising her eyebrows. "Excuse me?"

"I didn't mean it… I meant that you're my only way of staying involved. I followed you because, yes, I wanted to see if something else happened. If you stumbled on another dead body. But that didn't happen."

"Nope."

"No," he said carefully. "No dead body. But you did stumble into the middle of the street for no apparent reason. I told you why I followed you. Now you tell me what the hell pushed you into the middle of the street."

This time he was the one folding his arms over his chest. They made quite a picture, the two of them standing across from each other, both of them in a you-can't-touch-me pose. She tilted her head slightly, already predicting how he would handle the truth.

"What if I told you it was a monster? A monster from the other side hit me and pushed me into the street."

"Given everything that's happened today…I would tell you it's not the strangest damn thing I've heard."

Chapter 9

It certainly wasn't the reaction Cass was expecting. Not that he would laugh outright in her face. He was too polite.

"A big, beefy, overmuscled monster," she elaborated, purposefully trying to shake his stoicism. "With huge fangs that hang from its mouth and a nose that's pushed up against its face like a pig's. Its eyes are set deep and black and when it opens its mouth…"

A shudder overtook her body just thinking about the darkness that had permeated her being at the sound of its strange call. So much rage.

And she had just stood there, figuratively, and taken it. Earlier, Malcolm had suggested that she had let Dougie beat her, and she'd thought the idea ridiculous. But wasn't that what she had done with that thing?

She hadn't even considered fighting back. She didn't know if she knew how. It wasn't like she'd been forced to face off bullies at school. She'd been a loner from the start and most had obligingly left her alone. In the asylum, she'd been segmented from the violent population, so no one had been a threat physically to her, although she had gotten into a few pushing matches with a patient over a chair in the rec room. Certainly nothing that had prepared her for what she'd faced in her room.

She imagined she could deliver a good slap across the face—a gift most women were born with. But no man had ever prompted such an action. Hell, she hadn't even slapped Dougie.

"Let me do something," he said, breaking the silence that had ensued after she could no longer continue with her description. "I'll make you some tea."

Unable to help herself she smiled. "Tea?"

"I'm told it helps calm people down."

"Oh, I get it. You think I'm hysterical."

"I think you're upset, yes. I know you're in pain. Do you have tea?"

"In the kitchen," she said, pointing beyond his shoulder.

Her cats followed him.

Traitors.

Oddly enough, watching him move about her small kitchen, filling her ceramic cow teapot with water, searching for mugs and the tea bags that she kept in the cabinet over the refrigerator, did have a calming effect. Something about the mundane act made her feel normal again.

"Tell me some more about this monster," he urged.

With two filled mugs in his hands, he stopped in the center of the room. "Why don't you have any furniture?"

"I told you before I like to keep things simple."

He handed her a mug and then pulled over the lone bar stool adjacent to the counter and sat. "Okay. Talk."

"Why?" she wanted to know. She found the futon again and was happy to have the length of the apartment between them.

There was a pause as she figured her question stumped him. "Because you claim that this thing was responsible for what happened to you tonight."

"Yes, but you don't believe me. You don't believe I can communicate with the dead. I'm reasonably certain you think I'm nuts. And you wouldn't be the first. Why should I tell you about something that's only going to confirm your worst suspicions of me?"

He sipped from the mug that she'd pilfered from the coffeehouse. It had a chip at the top and they'd been about to toss it, which was why she'd considered it fair game. Now she looked on it as part of her severance package.

He said nothing in response to her accusations but, instead, seemed content to sip his tea.

"Please. Just go," she asked impatiently. "Thank you. I do mean that. That car might have hit me."

"*Would* have hit you," he corrected.

"Maybe, but it's over now."

"Is it?"

No. Not by a long shot.

Her silence was answer enough for him. "Look, I don't believe people can communicate once they're dead. I don't believe in ghosts. In fact, I'm not entirely convinced that there is anything at all after death. But if there were, I certainly don't think anyone living could hear or see someone after they've passed. It doesn't seem right. But…I also don't think you're a liar."

"That's sort of a logic problem for you, isn't it?"

His mouth twitched. "It is. But let's just go with it, okay? Why are you seeing this monster?"

"I don't know. I can't be sure," she whispered. Leaning forward, she placed the mug on the floor and gripped her head with her hands. "It's never been like this. I hear voices. I see images. When I was a kid…they would just pop into my head with a burst of pain."

"Pain? It hurts you?"

"Yes, but not too badly. Still, the pain tends to manifest itself on my body. A black eye, a bloody nose."

"A fat lip," he finished. "You had one this morning. And a black eye last night."

"It's the price of doing business."

He shook his head. "I don't understand. I've seen other mediums do readings on TV and such. I've never heard anyone talk about there being any pain involved."

"Not everyone's gift is the same, and not everyone who has the same gift experiences it the same way."

"You experience pain."

She smiled weakly. "You have to appreciate how supremely unlucky I am to have gotten stuck with the pain while others are making millions."

"That welt on your side…that was more than a bruise."

"What happened tonight wasn't like anything I've ever experienced. This thing…it got inside my room."

"Your room?"

How did she begin to explain something as complicated as her room to a nonbeliever? His expression, however, was earnest and attentive. A long time ago she'd promised to stop lying about who and what she was. He wouldn't understand, but she figured if he wanted the answer, she could give it to him.

"The room is nothing more than a mental exercise. Some of the people at the asylum…"

"Asylum?"

Cass cringed. Of course he hadn't known, and for a second she feared that any credibility she might have gained with him was suddenly lost. It shouldn't matter. She shouldn't care that he didn't believe her, and talking out what happened might be a relief.

"Yes. I was committed. For a time."

Malcolm nodded, then sipped his tea. "Go on."

"Anyway, some of the people there helped. They would try to tell me how to control the voices. Of course, for them, it was crazy voices in their head rather than ghosts, but the principle was the same. Then, a friend at the place where I eventually ended up taught me how to conjure the room to create an atmosphere of control. When I feel a…whatever you want to call it…making contact, I form a mental picture of a room inside my head with a door that leaves them on one side and me on the other. It helps me keep things separate, you know?"

"No. But keep going."

"When the door opens, I see the person on the other side. The dead speak to me, tell me whatever it is they have to say, and when it's done the door closes."

"And no one has ever gotten inside."

"No."

He shook his head. "But you create the room. You think it up. Why did you let it inside?"

"I couldn't stop it. The contact was overwhelming. My brain interpreted that as it being inside the room. Attacking me. Hitting me."

"It hit you in your side. That's why you have that welt?" He set his mug down behind him on the counter and lifted himself off the stool to pace a small area of her living room. "It doesn't make sense. This thing isn't real. Even if it is what you say it is, it's not a corporeal entity. It can't touch you."

"You have to understand that the mind is a truly powerful thing, and it controls our bodies more than we realize. My body simply reacted to the powerful mental image it received."

"Can you fight back?"

Good question. "I don't know. I didn't think about it. It was there and I was afraid. I don't really know how to fight."

Malcolm's eyes fell to the mat and the bands in the corner of the room.

"Yoga and Pilates," she confirmed. "Great for strength, flexibility and relaxation. Not so good against monsters."

"Okay. Let's get back to why you saw it in the first place. How does that work?"

"This has been different, too. Spirits only come to

me when I'm close, physically, to the one they want to make contact with. It's the purpose of a medium."

"I don't understand."

Slightly frustrated at having to explain everything, she paused and tried to clarify her meaning. "*Medium* means 'in the middle.' I'm nothing more than a conduit between someone dead and someone living. But the first time I saw this thing, I was alone in my apartment."

"You think it just came to you?"

"Maybe. At first I thought it could be someone from my past."

"You have a monster in your past? You said you had no family."

Having him say the words triggered a pull in her gut. She thought back to the dream she'd had before it had shown up. She remembered seeing her grandfather. He wanted her to talk to him, but she wouldn't allow it. It wasn't the first time he'd tried to contact her and she guessed it wouldn't be the last, no matter how many times she rejected him. He'd hurt her, yes. Betrayed her. But he wasn't a monster.

"No, no monster," she said, more to assure herself than to answer him. "At least none that I know of. And I don't have a family. My mother left me when I was a baby. I didn't know her in life to know how she would be in death. Same with my father. My grandparents raised me. My grandmother could never hurt me, but my grandfather…"

"He was cruel?"

"He was strict," she amended. "He was old-fashioned. He was straitlaced. But he liked to carry caramels in his sweater pocket and read bedtime stories to me. He wasn't a monster."

"I bet he also wasn't the type to believe in *special* gifts," Malcolm surmised.

The emotional pain came back in a wave that she tried to shrug off. "No, he wasn't. For as long as I can remember I've heard voices. Whisperings in my head. My grandmother called them my imaginary friends. It wasn't until puberty that it started to change. I began to understand that the voices were real. One day my grandmother had a friend over who had just lost her husband. It was like he was shouting at me inside my head. Finally, I stopped and listened to what he was saying. That's when the pain started. I can tell you, I freaked out my grandmother's friend. Told her where to find her missing insurance policy. She didn't know if she wanted to kiss me or run from me. But I couldn't control it back then. It was like if I didn't get the words out, it would hurt even worse."

"You were a kid."

Cass stood, too agitated to sit anymore. She turned her back to him since it was easier to finish the story without looking at him. "It got worse. It seemed like everybody I came into contact with had someone on the other side. I tried to tell my grandparents what I was hearing and seeing. All they saw were the bruises. They thought I was purposely hurting myself. Then Gram got sick and things got worse. When she died, she wanted to tell him goodbye through me. I tried to explain it to him, but he just couldn't believe it. He couldn't believe me."

"It was him, wasn't it? Your grandfather who had you committed."

Cass nodded. "I was sixteen when he sent me away."

"I'm sorry," he said to her back.

Cass smiled sadly. "Of course you are. Because there isn't anything you can do to fix that."

"I know and that sucks."

She turned around and saw sincerity in his eyes. "I don't want your pity," she warned him.

"Okay." In a second, the sympathy she'd seen in his eyes was gone, replaced with something that looked suspiciously like a smirk. "I make it a policy to never feel sorry for someone who drives a scooter."

Cass chuckled softly and felt her insides shift a little in admiration of his attempt to lighten the mood. She really didn't want to like him, but it was getting harder.

"I prefer to call it a minimotorcycle."

"Whatever makes you happy. Back to last night. You said at first you thought it might be someone trying to make direct contact. I take it you changed your mind. And what about tonight?"

"I saw someone. Across the street. A figure in jeans and a bulky hooded sweatshirt. I couldn't make out any features. But the way he just stopped and seemed to be looking right at me… He could have simply recognized me. I couldn't really see him."

"You think that's who the monster was trying to make contact with?"

Cass didn't know. It all sounded so strange, even to her, who had lived with this ability for as long as she could remember. "I know it seems far-fetched."

"Let's not talk about what seems far-fetched, okay.

So you saw this monster through the night," he stated as if trying to lay out the pieces to a puzzle. "When you were alone. That morning you found a dead body."

"A block down the street. I woke up and knew something was wrong."

"Then you see this thing again tonight, but this time there is a figure within view that catches your attention. What about the night before last?"

The night Lauren was killed. Of course he wanted to know. It was a sharp reminder about what he was doing here in the first place. She shook her head. "Sorry. Last night was the first I saw it."

He nodded but didn't comment. His eyes drifted away from her to a spot on the floor. "Are you going to finish your tea? I can warm it up for you."

"No, thanks. I won't sleep tonight. I really need to."

"Yeah." He sighed. "I know what you mean. Are you going to call Brody?"

His question took her off guard. "Why?"

"You saw someone who may or may not be connected to—at the very least—the murder this morning. I would think he'd want to know about it."

"About a faceless figure across the street? Some crazed monster loose inside my head? I doubt it."

"You don't know that." He eyed her suspiciously. "What's the matter? Lover's quarrel?"

"He's not my lover," she countered, probably a bit too emphatically. She felt a rush of heat in her face and was sure that he didn't believe her. She didn't care. The idea of speaking to Dougie again made the nausea from earlier return. No, she wasn't going to call him. Not tonight. Not until she could forget what he'd done. "If you want to, you call him."

"I will."

"Can I ask you something about this morning?" she blurted before she could take it back.

"Okay," he answered cautiously.

"When you touched me…"

"I'm sorry…"

"I'm not looking for another apology," she stopped him. "I want to know if you…if you felt something. Through me. You reacted… There was a change in your expression… I'm making a mess of this."

"You want to know if I felt some kind of presence? Like all of a sudden Lauren was standing behind me? Watching me and telling me to 'get a grip' in the way she used to be able to do with just a soft sigh? If I thought that or felt that then I would have to believe all that stuff I said I didn't believe in, wouldn't I?"

"I suppose."

"Naturally I didn't feel anything. I simply came to my senses."

His eyes remained steady on hers, and it seemed that there were about a hundred different things left unsaid between them in that moment. She understood what he was trying to say, but it didn't make her any happier to know that she'd been right about the change in her gift. Right about Dougie feeling the connection, too.

"I'm going to leave now. Are you going to be okay on your own?"

An idea occurred to her, one that she couldn't

believe she was even considering, but she asked him before she could stop herself.

"Do you want to touch me?"

The question clearly took him off guard.

"I'll let you. You've been nice to me. At least tonight. You're trying so hard to believe me and that means a lot. More than you know. I'll do this. For you. As drained as I am I'll let you touch me so you can feel her. So do you?"

"I do," he said softly. "I do want to touch you. But not so that I can feel her."

Cass let out the breath she was holding. His blue eyes held her completely motionless as the air around them became charged with tension and heat and…wanting.

"Go try to get some sleep, Cass," he finally said. "I'll be back shortly."

"You're not going to look for the person in the sweatshirt? He's long gone by now."

"I don't doubt it, but I might take a look around the area anyway. Makes me feel like I'm doing something constructive. Like I'm not as completely useless as I know I am. I'll need the key to your chain and the key to your apartment so I can ride your scooter back and leave it inside."

"I'll wait up."

"No, you'll be asleep in five minutes. The keys." He held out his hand in a manner that suggested he was used to people doing what he asked. Another sharp reminder, she decided, of the kind of man he was and why she should be wary of him.

"You know it's pink," she told him with a little too much pleasure. "Bright pink."

He grimaced. "Yes, I noticed."

Cass smiled but quickly quashed it. She absolutely did not want to like him. Reaching into her jeans pocket she extracted her key ring. She saw the coffeeshop's key and realized she would have to arrange to have it returned. The idea of job hunting the next day resurfaced and only made her that much more weary.

He took the key ring and listened while she pointed out what opened what. "Go rest, Cass. I'll be back."

She felt Spook and Nosey walk between her legs, rubbing against her. Glancing down, she saw that their faces were pinned on Malcolm, who was walking toward the door. She was sure she was imagining it, but they almost seemed disappointed he was leaving. If she were honest, she was a little disappointed, too.

"Oh, and the bike…" she started to warn him.

"The scooter?"

"Whatever. It shimmies a little if you go too fast."

"I'll keep that in mind."

"Have you ever ridden a bike? Because if you don't know what you're doing and you crash…"

"I won't crash."

It irritated her that she was letting him do this in the first place, but the thought of going back outside into the cold rain was so unappealing.

"I'll be careful." He said it like a solemn promise. She figured she didn't have much choice but to trust him.

"I'll wait up."

He smiled gently and reached out to caress her cheek

with his finger. "I'll be upset if you do. Can I lock this when I leave?"

"Yes. Just turn the lock and close the door hard. I'll leave the dead bolt off."

He nodded. "I'll…call you."

It was the sort of *I'll call you* that sounded more like *I plan on never speaking to you again,* but she let it go. There might have been a moment there between them that had nothing to do with his sister or her monster, but it made no sense to pursue it. They were from opposite ends of the spectrum and it was best that they stay there.

Once he returned the bike, there really was no reason for them to speak again. Not unless she had some answers for him. Currently, she was fresh out.

He opened the door as she stood back. The blinking light on her phone caught his attention and he nudged his chin in that direction. "You've got a message."

"I know." She didn't bother to say that she had no intention of listening to it tonight.

Malcolm opened his mouth as if he wanted to say something else but then seemed to talk himself out of it. "Take care, Cass."

"You, too."

He turned the lock on the door and closed it firmly behind him. As promised, she left the dead bolt off, hoping that the criminal element wouldn't choose this night to test her security system.

"I don't know, girls. I think things were easier when I thought he was a rich asshole."

Her cats raised their heads to her, then quickly

trotted off in the direction of the bedroom, anticipating it was where she was headed next. She thought about camping out on the futon so she would hear him when he returned but figured there wasn't much else to say.

The police would do their job and find the killer. Dougie hadn't been bragging earlier. He knew his job. The ticket would help, Cass was as sure of it as Lauren had been. Which meant she just needed to wait and see if this monster made contact again. Wait and see if her ability was truly changing in a significant way that went beyond being a conduit.

Beyond channeling…to possession.

Chapter 10

Cass woke the next morning and felt a particular satisfaction at seeing her bike in the foyer. He must have known how to handle the scooter. There wasn't a scratch on it.

She made a pot of coffee and some eggs, then picked up the paper from the sidewalk. She was going to have to skip the funnies this morning and move straight to the want ads. Sipping her coffee, Cass circled a few potential opportunities while pointedly ignoring the still blinking light on her phone. What would the repercussions be if she chose not to answer it?

Whatever it was, it couldn't be good news. Frankly, she wasn't sure she had the energy to handle anything else. Three days ago she'd been content with her life, her job and her very good friend.

Today it was as if she didn't know what way was up. Dougie was the enemy. There was a killer on the loose and possibly connected to her, and all of a sudden she was no longer a medium.

She was a something else.

There are those, she knew, who wouldn't understand the distinction between hearing voices and relaying messages and allowing those voices to possess her. *Psychic* was an easy word for believers and nonbelievers to wrap their brain around. Of course there were the con artists who blurred the lines by claiming to be all things: clairsentient, clairvoyant, psychic medium and channeler. Not only did they cause damage through their lies, but they also made it that much more difficult for a truly gifted person to explain to a father why it was she could hear his dead grandmother, but she couldn't find his missing little girl.

Cataloging her skills had helped Cass to get a grasp on her life. Knowing what she was capable of made it so she could define the ways in which she could help people as well as the types of situations and publicity she wished to avoid.

The occasional message passed to the person who most needed to hear it. A human lie detector for the police. These were tangible things that she could do by simply listening to and relating the messages from the beyond. Gifts had to be opened and played with, or what was the point of having them in the first place?

Dr. Farver always used to say that. *Cassandra Allen has a gift.*

But giving up more to the spirits, the ones that up until now had only spoken to her, meant a loss of control of mind and possibly even body that could be dangerous. Hadn't she fallen into the street? And the welt on her side, that was a definite result of the monster getting too close.

She wanted this new ability gone. She'd wanted her old abilities gone once upon a time, too. Never happened. No, there was no going back. Only forward. If only she knew for certain how it would all turn out.

Frustrated and more than annoyed with herself that she'd spent the last half hour dissecting what was happening to her rather than concentrating on her search for a new job, she set the paper down and hit the play button on her answering machine. Moving forward probably meant not being afraid of a phone message.

"You have one new message…beep…Cassandra, it's Dr. Farver again. Listen, I understand why you won't return my calls. I'm…disappointed, but I do understand. I just wanted to say that I hoped if nothing else…well…we could remain friendly if not actual friends. You were here for so long. Mad misses you. I guess I just wanted to be sure that you were all right. I won't bother you again…beep."

The guilt she had felt about erasing his first message returned tenfold. She plopped back down on her single stool and reached for the phone with the intention of returning his call and apologizing. He hadn't done anything wrong. Maybe she had chosen to walk away from that life and his convictions, but that didn't mean he'd ever hurt her in any way. She had to find it within herself to stop blaming him just because he didn't believe her.

Slowly, she lowered the receiver. The answer was there. Cass needed a way to catalog, examine and diagnose the changes she was experiencing, changes that had started over a year ago, she now accepted. Maybe he wasn't a believer, but there was no better scientist for the task than Dr. Farver. Plus, he would have access both to the records of thousands of others who shared her symptoms and to his assessments of those people.

He would also have names. Names of others she might be able to talk to. It was through Dr. Farver that she had met Leandra, another medium who had helped her to refine her mental room to the point where she could open and close herself to contact at will. Dr. Farver hadn't believed Leandra either, but he understood the inherent value of people with special gifts being able to network. It was, after all, a very small community.

Putting extra food out for the girls and leaving her bike behind, Cass decided to forgo the polite ritual of a preemptive phone call and head straight for the source. The Institute of Psychical Studies was located in the northwest section of Washington, D.C. It was only about a two-hour train ride away.

Cass took a cab to 30th Street Station. Inside the spacious building, a beautiful gold angel statue stood bearing the weighty load of humanity while watching over the flood of people who passed under its gaze each day.

A killer had passed under its watch just a few days ago. Cass wondered if it had noticed.

She walked up to the counter, preferring to deal with a human to purchase her ticket than a machine. It was late in the morning. Most of the commuter trains had already left, but she was able to secure a seat on the Boston Coach departing Philadelphia at 11:00 a.m.

Gazing down at the small, white, rectangular ticket, Cass read the name of her train. Like a trolley car, the Boston Coach made the same trip each day up and down the east coast. From Boston to Washington and back, stopping at several cities along the way. Including Baltimore. The Boston Coach had been the name of the train on the ticket found in Lauren's apartment. Quickly, Cass made a mental note to call Dougie and ask him if he'd made any progress with that.

That's when it hit her that she couldn't call him. Not ever again. A paralyzing sadness had her stopping short in the center of the building as if she'd bumped into an invisible brick wall.

Dougie had been one of the few friends she'd made in this world who wasn't gifted or dealing with some kind of mental ailment. He'd been nice and normal and…and he'd used her and lied to her.

If only he could have been honest. She wouldn't be left with this hollow feeling that their friendship had been nothing more than a ruse to maintain contact with his wife.

Cass tried to imagine a scenario where he'd told her everything the next morning.

Yeah, she admitted to herself. *It probably would have been just as bad then.*

Of course the easy answer was simply to forget what he'd done and forgive him, but she couldn't imagine that she would ever feel comfortable with him again. Absolutely, he could never touch her again.

Some friendship.

A clicking noise distracted her from her thoughts, and Cass looked up at the old-fashioned schedule board that still turned over the departure times rather than posting them on monitors around the station. The Boston Coach was now boarding on track eleven.

For two hours she would have nothing to do but sit and think about Dougie, sit and think about what she was going to tell Dr. Farver and sit and think about whether or not she was somehow connected to a killer.

The good news was that with everything on her mind, she didn't have to think about Malcolm and what she suspected could have happened last night had he actually reached out to touch her.

Definitely better to think about murder.

The route to the institute was as familiar to Cass as breathing. The brick-front town house in the northwest section of the city had really been more of a home to her than her grandparents' house had ever been.

After Cass's mother had disappeared and her grandmother discovered she'd be raising Cass, she had tried to turn the statuesque colonial in the Baltimore suburbs into a home suited for a child. But Cass's grandfather's stern presence had lingered everywhere. There was the No Food or Drink Outside the Kitchen rule, the No Playing Roughly on the Grass rule, the No Loud Noise After Six O'clock in the Evening rule. The No Friends Over for Playdates rule.

None of the rules had been overly harsh or difficult to follow. They had just made being a kid less fun. The feeling that she was a chore to her grandparents, rather than a joy, a burden rather than a welcome addition, had never escaped Cass growing up, and it obscured her memories of the lighter moments. Because there had been those, too.

Helping her grandmother in the kitchen. Working with her grandfather on his model train. It hadn't all been grim. Until Gram's health had started to fail. Then her life had ended quietly with the hospice workers, her husband and her grandchild at her side.

She'd connected with Cass briefly just that once. The message had been simple. Goodbye. I love you. Everything is going to be all right.

But she'd lied. Or she hadn't known what would happen. It didn't matter. What mattered was that Cass eventually had gotten away from her grandfather, away from the asylum, away from all of it.

She stopped in front of the building numbered 802. It hadn't changed. The modest gold plaque by the door proclaimed it to be the Institute of Psychical Studies, as legitimate looking as any other scientific center in the country. And why not? Dr. Farver had earned degrees in psychology, philosophy, religion and parapsychology. He was funded by wealthy donors who believed in his work and his research. He regularly published his findings regarding the evolution of telepathy in the human brain. He was respected by his students, his research subjects and his staff.

Unfortunately, he was considered a quack by most of his scientific peers.

It never seemed to bother him. He didn't listen to the sly whispers behind his back at academic conferences although he heard them. He pretended to imagine that when his colleagues asked questions about his research they were sincere, and so he answered as if they were, although he knew they weren't. At least that was what he had always told Cass.

Knowing that it wouldn't be locked during the day, Cass reached for the door and opened it. Dr. Farver liked to create the feeling that everyone was welcome, especially for those who weren't always so easily welcomed by society.

Madeline "Mad" Edelman had not changed in the five years Cass had been gone. She sat in her spot at the reception desk as always. Her bifocals sat as low as they could go on her nose without falling off. She typed away on the keyboard, gazing at the monitor as if she still couldn't get over that it wasn't a typewriter.

She wore a loose-fitting purple dress that floated around her large, round body like a cloud. Her jewelry was always practical as well as pretty. Hematite today, because it was good for the blood.

"Hey, Mad." The words caught in her throat as Cass announced her presence.

She watched the woman raise her head at the unexpected intrusion, then saw in her face, her emotions transform from surprised to happy to nostalgic when her eyes landed on Cass.

"Cassandra." She clasped her hands to her overendowed bosom so hard that her glasses popped off her nose. "I knew it. I knew you would come back some day. Dr. Farver said…well, it doesn't matter. You're here. I was so worried about you."

The guilt that had been plaguing her didn't get any lighter. Cass realized how wrong it had been to cut off everyone from her institute days. Mad hadn't deserved to be ignored. Certainly she deserved more than a lousy Christmas card each year.

It had just seemed that cutting all ties would be easier when she'd left.

And it had been. For her. That didn't make it right. Exactly what she'd done by avoiding her grandfather's funeral. Easy. Not right.

"I'm sorry. I could say that I wanted to call, but the truth is…"

"Stop. Not a word." The woman stood with an easy grace despite her girth and circled the desk with the poise of a dancer. She stood in front of Cass and placed her hands on her cheeks. Cass could see the marks of age that had crept in over the years. The lines around her mouth were deeper, her jowls were heavier. But she still smelled like lavender.

"I mean it. I should have called."

"It's over. You're here. You're good? No, you're not good."

Clearly, Cass hadn't done a very good job of hiding her recent tribulations. Then again she'd never had a very good poker face.

"I'm fine. I need to see him, but I didn't even call to see if he had an appointment open."

"Lucky you, he's free."

"Really?"

The older woman winked at her. "Really. He doesn't know it, but his two-thirty just became his three o'clock. Go on. He'll want to see you."

Cass leaned in and kissed the woman's cheek. "Thanks, Mad." She followed the stairs behind the reception area that led to the second floor and Dr. Farver's office. Students and subjects, those Dr. Farver considered to be especially unique, were housed in the third floor attic. Cass and Leandra had called that attic home for almost six years.

Leandra. Another person she'd lost touch with. Cass's opposite in every way, she'd been tall, blond and built. She laughed hard, played hard and embraced her gift with the same fervor as someone who had just won the lottery. She'd quickly tired of Dr. Farver's testing. She only wanted the credentials of having been "tested" by the institute as a way to get in the door of the higher priced psychic houses on the West Coast. Those that actually employed people with true gifts rather than frauds wanting to separate people from their money.

The blond bombshell had wanted Cass to follow in her footsteps and join her in taking the Hollywood elite for large amounts simply by doing what she did as naturally as breathing.

Cass had passed.

Now Leandra was the famous L. Morningstar, booked years in advance by the stars to do readings. She appeared on *Larry King Live* regularly to thrill the audience and to attract more customers. And why not? Leandra was no fake.

The idea of it made Cass laugh. Her on *Larry King Live?* On the *Late Show with David Letterman?* On the *Oprah Winfrey Show?* No, it didn't work. Not her style.

Still, that didn't mean that they couldn't be friends. That they couldn't do more than exchange Christmas cards once a year. Cass could visit her if she wanted. Vaguely, she wondered if this sudden need to reach out was nothing more than a reaction to losing Dougie. But maybe it went deeper. Maybe she was starting to realize that she'd cut herself off from people. All people. Even the ones who cared.

No time for self-evaluation. Remember, dead monster on the loose.

Shaking her head to clear her thoughts, Cass made her way down the hallway to Dr. Farver's office door and knocked gently. She heard the "come in" and opened the door to find him sitting behind his desk in a gray turtleneck, studying the contents of a folder. Probably the results of a test for his two-thirty.

Tall and whipcord lean, he sported the salt-and-pepper hair typical for a man in his fifties, but his trimmed beard was all white. To say that he looked like the stereotypical fussy professor would be unfair of Cass, as he was the only professor she had ever known. But she wouldn't confuse him with a rock star.

"Hey, Doc."

He flapped the folder shut. Unlike Mad's, his face didn't undergo any transformation. It registered total surprise and it stayed that way.

"I didn't think…"

"I'm sorry about not returning your calls. And for not letting you know my new number."

"Your number was listed but not your address. There was a book I wanted to send you."

"I'll give you my new address before I leave," Cass offered as an olive branch.

He pursed his lips and set the folder down on his desk. "You don't have to feel obligated, Cassandra."

She made a face at the use of her full name said with all the authority of a man who used to get to tell her what to do. It had been his right since he was the one who had rescued her.

Cass remembered the day vividly. He'd shown up at the asylum talking with each of the patients who had been segregated into the nonviolent wing of the hospital. He'd spoken to them, asked them a few questions and moved on. Cass had assumed he was just another doctor coming in to figure out what made them tick.

He'd stopped in front of her bed; she'd been sitting in the chair next to it. He'd asked her why she was there and she had told him because her grandfather had sent her there. Because he didn't believe. He'd asked her what it was that her grandfather didn't believe and she had told him. Then he'd called to an assistant who had been tagging along behind him making notes. Dr. Farver had wanted to know if she sensed anything about the assistant.

It was the first time she'd ever been asked to prove her gift. For a moment she'd been so rattled that the only thought that had emerged was *escape*. Then she opened herself and used some of the skills that she'd recently learned from others who had been labeled "nuts." His aunt had come through. A favorite aunt who had passed away the week before who wanted him to know that she'd always treasured her music box with the dancing Cinderella on top and wanted him to have it.

The assistant had gone white and Dr. Farver had nodded solemnly. He'd appealed to the state to have Cass released into his custody. Since she'd had no history of violence, drug abuse or a criminal record and since she would soon be eighteen and of legal age anyway, the court had allowed it and she had gone to live at the institute.

He'd been her hero. Her imaginary long-lost father. And for a time her very first crush. Until she saw George Clooney.

"I know I'm not obligated. I just…I think I took things a bit too far."

"Yes. So you came all this way to apologize."

"No," she said slowly.

"Excellent. I have a new subject that you absolutely have to meet. She's quite exceptional. Maybe almost as talented as…"

"No. Doctor, I didn't come here to get tested or to test with anyone. I was—this is going to sound really awful, but I was hoping maybe you could help me."

Clearly deflated, he leaned back into his office chair and steepled his fingers together. When Cass said nothing, he indicated the chair in front of his desk where he wanted her to sit, then went back to steepling his fingers, as was his habit.

"What do you need help with?"

Cass sank into the plush seat and tried to formulate a way to say what she needed to say so that he would believe her.

"There have been some changes," she began cautiously.

"With your talent?"

"Yes."

"Do you mind?" He opened a desk drawer and pulled out a mini-tape recorder that she knew he always kept on hand for just this purpose.

"No." Cass wasn't thrilled with the idea of being recorded, but it was how he worked and she was here for his help.

"Explain."

"I don't know that there is any point in explaining." Not when he wouldn't believe her, anyway. "I guess I just hoped you could help me figure out the extent of the change. How do I go about cataloging it? What kind of tests should I do?"

"Cassandra, I can't possibly begin to help you figure out how to test these changes until I know what they are."

"I had an encounter. A physical one. There was a voice in my head and a picture."

"That's typical for you."

"Yes, but this time I couldn't keep it on the other side

of the door. It got inside and I couldn't stop it and…it attacked me."

She watched his face carefully but only saw his lips press together in a pensive line.

"You've used your *room* as a tool for control," he stated.

"Yes." Cass leaned forward, eager to make him understand. "The fact that I couldn't keep it out scares me. What if they start using me? What if I lose control to whomever is making contact? I couldn't bear it."

Dr. Farver shook his head almost sadly. "They?" he questioned. "You mean spirits."

"Yes." She sighed, leaning back in her chair.

"Cassandra, how many times do I have to tell you? You are not hearing or seeing dead people. They're just thoughts. The memories of the person's mind you are reading. And thoughts can't hurt you. You're not a medium. You're a telepath."

Chapter 11

It had been a mistake. She shouldn't have gone. She knew he would probably never believe that what she did was make contact with the other side. A devout scientist, Dr. Farver likely didn't even believe the other side existed. For the six years she'd lived at the institute, he'd tested her regularly, always believing that her gift was the ability to read other people's minds and extract their thoughts and memories.

Cass curled up in her train seat thinking how horrible such a gift would be. It was bad enough that she freaked people out by letting them know what their late aunt Sally had to say to them, but to read their minds? To know their intimate thoughts? People would run from her as fast as they could. Hell, if she were ever confronted with a telepath, she would run, too.

But telepathy, unlike clairaudience, was grounded in scientific theory. A belief that thoughts were nothing more than energy. That the mind was part of a shared network of them. A single consciousness. Dr. Farver believed that some people were born with antennae that allowed them to tap into the network and to access the thoughts of others they came into contact with.

He believed it so adamantly that he summarily dismissed any evidence to the contrary. For example, the things that the living didn't know, that only the person who was dead could reveal.

And the pain. He could never explain the pain.

He had no problem recognizing that severe mental anguish could result in a manifestation of a bruise on her body. That also was grounded in science. It was where the pain originated from and why she experienced it that he could never fathom.

At least she'd gotten to see Mad. The guilt that had been plaguing her for months now was lifted. She'd given Dr. Farver her new address and promised him that she would check in. She'd refused to meet his newest subject, another exceptional telepath, he'd told her, but she had agreed to keep him updated on any more changes in her gift.

Practically, he'd told her to keep a diary and to log what she felt were aberrations the moment they happened. Cass had had to hold back a snort at that point. She seriously doubted logging the fact that she was getting the crap kicked out of her by some crazed beast would help. But it was a step.

The train slowed to a stop and the conductor called out 30th Street Station. Cass grabbed her satchel, left the train and took the stairs up to the main level. It was late, after seven, so most of the daily commuters had cleared through, but there was still a smattering of people milling about the food court area and others on the benches waiting. Glancing up at the center board, Cass could see a train coming in from New York was soon to arrive. No doubt it would be packed with the last of the commuters, and she figured she should get out of the station quickly if she was going to get a cab home.

As she walked toward the doors that led out to the street, she spotted a familiar face. Malcolm McDonough was standing in the center of the station looking up at the board. The *click, click, click* indicated something was changing, and she watched as he read that the inbound train from Baltimore had just arrived at track eight. He walked toward track eight and stood by it, clearly waiting for the doors below to open and the passengers to come filing out.

It was a fool's errand.

Hesitating for a second but ultimately unable to walk away, Cass wandered over to where he stood so stoically. An immovable object, really.

"You think you'll recognize him?"

Startled, he swung his head in her direction. "What are you doing here?"

"I could ask you the same thing."

He sighed and decided not to answer.

Cass nodded. She took in his dark overcoat and the suit underneath it. It was too soon for the funeral—the coroner had only just released the body—which meant he had probably come from work.

"Let me guess. You went back to your office today. Tried to work but probably couldn't focus. Ultimately you gave up. So you checked out the arrival times of trains from Baltimore and figured you would come down here and just see if you could recognize someone getting off this train. A familiar face that maybe you had seen with Lauren at one time or another. What were you going to do then? Tackle the person? Question him or her? Make a citizen's arrest?"

"It didn't sound as foolish five hours ago."

Cass closed her eyes. "How many trains have you been here for?"

"This is the fourth."

"And?"

"And no luck. But you already know that."

Cass held her hands up in defense. "Hey, it didn't take any psychic ability to figure that out."

His impassive expression was replaced by the weariness she'd seen so vividly in him the day before. He walked over to a bench, still within eyeshot of track eight, and sat down. Cass sat next to him.

"You should go home. There's nothing you can do here."

"Her killer came through here. From Baltimore to Philadelphia by train."

"You don't know that," Cass countered. "That ticket could mean anything."

He glared at her. "What the hell is that supposed to mean? You told me she said it was important."

"It was. To her. It doesn't mean she was telling me where to look for her killer."

A line of people made their way up the stairs from the recently arrived train. Cass lost his attention as he scanned the faces of the men and women, most of them in business casual wear, leaving the station. He studied each face individually and a few of the men stared back, obviously not appreciating his intense scrutiny.

"You're trying to find a needle in a haystack," she pointed out.

"But I'm trying," he replied, even as his eyes remained on the passengers.

Knowing she wasn't going to get through to him, Cass turned to leave. Once again the clicking from the schedule board signaled another update. She heard an announcement for a departure to Florida via Washington and one for the arrival of the New York train— although the crush of people exiting from the track next to them was all the announcement Cass needed.

Irritated that she hadn't left when she should have, she was about to snap off a goodbye to Malcolm when a tingle at the base of her neck warned her that something was coming.

Sha-a uh-h-h! Sha-a uh-h-h!

The shout reverberated in her head, instantly knocking her to her knees. In seconds the room took shape in her head, and this time the monster was already in there with her. Shouting at her.

Sha-a uh-h-h! Sha-a uh-h-h!

She cowered at the beast's feet, holding her hands over her ears to shut out the horrible sound of its yell. In the station, she was also on her knees with her hands over her ears, but the action was useless.

"Cass!"

The distant shout reached her, and she managed to look up. She could see that a group of people had formed a circle around her, no doubt wondering what was happening to her.

In her mind the monster reached down, its face coming so close to hers she cringed in both fear and abhorrence. Then it raised a massive arm and brought its hoof crashing down into her face. She fell back at the impact and pain shot through her body. It was as if the blow had started a rippling effect and had broken all of her bones. It kicked her in the stomach and she curled herself into a ball to try and protect herself.

"Cass, look at me. What's happening? Cass!"

Focusing on the actual face above her, rather than the one in her head, Cass opened her mouth and tried to speak over the waves of crippling pain. "Here," she whispered to him, willing him to understand. "Close."

She watched his reaction as the words she had spoken sunk in and she could see he was torn. The fact that the monster was back meant that whoever had brought it must be nearby, but leaving her meant abandoning her with the beast inside her head.

"Can you fight it?"

Sha-a uh-h-h!

Cass couldn't make out what it was shouting, but it didn't matter. Malcolm wanted her to fight it, but she didn't know how. In her mind, she turned over, crawling on her hands and knees to somehow escape it, but it found her and smashed her face down hard onto the floor.

Blood spurted out of Cass's nose, and she could hear the crowd grasp in reaction.

"What's happening? Someone should call 911."

"No," she shouted, but it was nothing more than a breath of air. Again, she turned to Malcolm. "Go. Close. Find him."

Malcolm stared at the woman on the ground, horrified at what he was seeing. He didn't believe in this crap, he told himself, but the proof of her bloody nose and the bruise already forming around her eye was there for everyone to see.

"Step back," he told everyone. "She needs air. She's…epileptic."

A few people nodded, and more than a few who had wanted to help seemed to back off, knowing that the situation wasn't life threatening.

An elderly woman came forward even as Malcolm stood. "Doesn't she need something to bite on?"

"No, she'll be fine in a minute. Just give her space." Matching his words with actions, Malcolm took several steps away from the crowd, his eyes searching for…what? How the hell would he recognize this person when he saw him? *If* there was even a person to recognize.

He glanced at Cass and watched her back arch and her head whip sharply to the side as if she'd been slapped. Something was doing this to her and if it didn't stop, he didn't know what the hell would happen. She was barely bigger than a girl and surely not strong enough to take on this creature she'd described.

Again Malcolm surveyed the area. Some people joined the group of gapers, others just stared at the crowd but kept on their way, and still others ignored the spectacle entirely. And one person stood behind a marble column near the entrance. Watching. His face was covered, but Malcolm could see a pair of jeans and part of his body that was covered in what looked to be an oversize sweatshirt.

Malcolm took a few steps toward the person, trying to make it seem as if his only concern was leaving.

"Hey, dude, you're not just going to leave her, are you?" That from one of the spectators surrounding Cass.

Malcolm ignored him and headed for the figure still by the door.

"That's cold!" someone shouted.

But he kept moving. Suddenly the figure shifted out from behind the column and spotted Malcolm coming directly at him. The hood was pulled down over the face, but Malcolm could make out a thin, pointed chin and slim nose.

The person turned and burst through the doors. Taking off at full speed, Malcolm gave chase. He shoved open the doors but stopped to try to get a sense of which way the person had fled. To his right, he heard a flurry of noise as a woman shouted.

"Rude!"

She'd been pushed to the side by someone moving fast. Malcolm turned in that direction and ran. Weaving through people making their way inside the station, he was finally clear of them and could see the hooded figure running a few yards up. Malcolm gave chase again but paused when he saw the person hail a cab even while running. The cab stopped and the person hopped inside. Malcolm could see the barest profile of a face through the window and then the cab was gone, turning the corner and merging into city traffic.

He let out a heavy breath, then turned and ran back toward the station. When he flung open the door, he saw a significant number of people still hovering over Cass.

Pushing his way through them, he could see that her convulsions had stopped. For a second, with her eyes closed and her body sprawled out on the ground, he feared that whatever had attacked her had killed her. He dropped to his knees beside her and lifted her hand in his. Her pulse was beating way too fast, but it was there.

"Please, give me some room."

"I think something is wrong. She's not moving. Maybe we should call 911." This from the woman who had wanted to help before.

"I've got her," he said.

"Dude, you took off." It was the young man carrying a backpack who had shouted at him earlier.

"I was getting a cab," Malcolm lied. He didn't have time for lengthy explanations. At this point a security guard had come over and joined the group. He reached for his walkie-talkie at his side, but Malcolm shook his head.

"Really, it's okay. She does this all the time. If you call an ambulance it will just be a hassle."

The security guard seemed to waver, but Malcolm didn't hesitate. He bent down and scooped Cass into his arms. She stirred enough to realize who was holding her and for that he was relieved. He was going on his gut that she didn't want the fuss of an ambulance, but that didn't mean he wasn't taking her straight to the emergency room if she couldn't tell him she was okay.

"Did you…?" she asked weakly.

"No. He got away," he whispered back. "Forget about that. Hold on to me."

"Can't. Don't want to touch you."

Malcolm wasn't sure if it was meant to be an insult or not. It didn't matter. "Look, you're as light as a feather, but I still have to get you out of here and down to the garage. It will be easier if you help. Now put your arms around my neck and hold on."

Cass lifted her arms over his shoulders, then linked them behind his neck. Malcolm hoisted her up higher in his arms and her head fell to rest on his shoulder.

"Thank you, everyone, for…" *Watching* didn't seem like the appropriate word, but truly that was all they had done. "Everything," he finished lamely.

The crowd split to let him move, and he made his way to the elevators that would lead to the lower level and his car. Once he reached it, he was able to fish out his keys with one hand while she clung to him. He disengaged the locks and placed her gently in the car.

"I didn't think you would want an ambulance, but I'm taking you to the hospital."

"No," Cass said. "They'll ask too many questions. I won't be able to answer. Please."

"If you're seriously hurt…"

"It's nothing. Bruises and aches."

He looked at her face and saw that while it was smattered with blood, her nose had actually stopped bleeding. "What the hell did that thing do to you?"

"Just take me home."

That wasn't going to happen. Not until he had some answers. But rather than argue, he simply circled the car, got in and left the parking lot.

Cass had dozed off during the trip, so when she felt the car braking to a stop, she had no idea how far they had traveled. She could have been asleep for minutes or hours. It was hard to tell. All she knew was that now that she was awake, she hurt. Her right side hurt so badly, it made breathing difficult and she wondered if maybe she should have let Malcolm take her to an emergency room. But the idea of a bunch of doctors and nurses standing around her and asking her who beat her up was worse than the pain.

They would suspect Malcolm, which she was sure he wouldn't appreciate, and then they would want to call the police. It could get back to Dougie and that would be the last thing she needed.

No, no doctors. There wasn't much they did for bruised ribs anyway. At least she didn't think so. When the car door beside her opened, she roused herself long enough to check out where she was. She was expecting to be parked on her street somewhere close to her apartment building.

She wasn't. She was in a garage by the look of it. "Where did you take me?"

"Home."

Cass had enough energy left to raise an eyebrow at him. "You know I meant my home."

"I figured you did, but I wasn't leaving you alone tonight and that futon you have doesn't look all that comfortable for sleeping."

"You're wrong. It's quite comfortable."

"Yeah, well, we'll both be more comfortable here." That said, he slid his hands underneath her and lifted her from the car seat with the ease of a man who had a great deal of upper body strength. Once again she settled against his broad chest and the impulse to rest her cheek on his shoulder was irresistible.

Cass sighed a little at the cessation of pain. This felt so good, she decided, so good to let someone else carry the load. Then immediately, she struggled to lift her head. When had she ever let someone carry the load for her before?

"I can walk."

"No need." He pulled out his house keys with little effort despite his burden and opened the door that led to what appeared to be a great room. It had two long, brown leather sofas, two more recliners, a large flat-screen TV and a fireplace. Along one side of the wall was a bar and adjacent to that, a pool table.

A perfect man's retreat. Filled with comfort and toys.

Malcolm was certainly the type to have things. Looking around the room at the trophies above the mantel, the baseball that was under glass on one of the end tables and the framed picture of what appeared to be a baseball team with lots of signatures all over it, she wondered if they made him happy. His things.

He set her down on the nearest sofa, and she groaned a bit as the pressure of sitting up was too much.

"Easy. Lie down. That's it." He helped her move into a reclining position and then propped her head up with a few throw pillows. He grabbed some others from the other couch and eased them under her knees.

"I've had my ribs whacked a few times. This is usually the most comfortable position," he said.

"Yes."

"Stay here, I'm going to get some towels to clean up your face."

"Clean it up? That doesn't sound good." Cass reached for her face, but he pulled her hand away before she could touch herself.

"You'll only scare yourself. It's a little blood."

"You hate blood."

He smiled. "I do. I can't believe you remembered that in your condition."

"I can clean it myself."

"Sit tight. I hate it, but I've learned to deal with it."

"It slammed my face against the floor; it felt like my nose was broken."

"Doesn't appear to be broken," he said, studying her face. "I've had a few of those, too, so I know them when I see them."

"Whacked ribs and broken noses. People must not like you."

He laughed softly. "That's probably true, but most of my injuries came from college football."

"And here I thought you were a baseball man." She pointed to the ball on the table.

"That too. I just could never pitch or hit worth a damn. I could, however, tackle. Unlucky for me as there's very little tackling in baseball."

"So I've heard."

There was a weird silence and then finally Malcolm turned away from her. "Stay here. I'll be back."

Cass didn't bother to tell him that wouldn't be a problem. Her eyes fixed on the ceiling above; she noticed the cathedral roof and the thick beams running across it and decided it must be one hell of a gas bill to heat this sucker in the winter. If this was just the game room, the house must surely be a mansion. Still, there was something about the spacing between the beams, the perfection of the angles and the solidity of the wood itself that suggested both an eye for detail as well a sense of intimacy. Then there was the massive fireplace, the centerpiece of the room. It appeared that each brick had been perfectly placed all the way up to the ceiling. So much more than a functional asset. It was a labor of love.

When she heard the rustle of him returning to her, she asked, "Did you build this house?"

"Yeah, I did. My dad started it, but then he passed and it was left to me to finish it."

"Nice work."

He stood over her and smiled down at her. "You've only seen the garage and this room."

"I know quality when I see it." Then again, didn't everyone? Wasn't that the point of quality—to make it known when a person looked upon it?

"Really? This from the woman with no furniture."

"Furniture is only important if you need it. I have everything I need."

"Really," he murmured, but she thought she heard a question in it.

"Really," she repeated firmly. "And you have more than you need, but I guess that's to be expected."

"Why?"

"Because of the money. I'm surprised you don't have someone preparing you a home-cooked meal and waiting for you at the door to take your coat as soon as you come home."

"No housekeeper. I like my privacy. So if that was a ploy for dinner, you're out of luck. There's nothing heating on the stove."

"Not even a casserole?"

"No, why?"

"I figured there would be a bunch of casseroles in the kitchen." Cass pointed to the cutout in the room that led to what appeared to be a massive kitchen on the other side.

"I can state unequivocally that there are no casseroles in the kitchen."

"Huh."

Kneeling beside her, Malcolm dipped a towel into a bowl of water filled with ice. Delicately, he began to run the towel around her face until she felt like a child being wiped down by her mother after an especially messy meal.

"If you get me a mirror, I can do it."

"Stop fussing. I'm almost done."

"I'm not fussing," she retorted. "I feel silly. There's nothing wrong with my arms. Between carrying me in here and wiping my face, you've reduced me to a two-year-old."

"Let it go," he said.

She was about to open her mouth again when he pulled the towel away and dropped it in the bowl. Cass watched as the water immediately turned pink.

"Gross."

"Yep. It's why I hate it. The color. But with the blood gone I've got a better look at your nose. It's definitely not broken. Here. Put this over your eye." He had filled a soft washcloth with some of the ice cubes and laid it carefully over the bridge of her nose and her left eye, which was also throbbing.

It was silly to be vain at a time like this, but her nose was her favorite part of her face. She couldn't help but be grateful the monster hadn't destroyed it.

"What happened?" she wanted to know. "Did you see anybody?"

"A person. Wearing a hooded sweatshirt low over his face. At least I think it was a him. I don't know. I couldn't see any hair. The build was slight, but I saw a chin and nose. Both were sort of thin, almost delicate like yours. And then I saw a profile when…" he trailed off, clearly focusing his attention on the memory.

"What? What did you see?"

Malcolm met her gaze, his brow furrowed with consternation. "You know I'm pretty sure what I saw…was a woman."

Chapter 12

"You think it was a woman," Cass repeated, trying to fit that piece into the puzzle. Hating the idea of having a conversation with him while lying down, she tried to sit up, but as soon as she did, her ribs protested.

With a firm but gentle hand, he motioned for her to stay still and then placed the makeshift ice pack back over her face.

"I know. Hard to believe."

"Why?"

"Well, we're both going to the same place, aren't we? The hooded sweatshirt is linked to the monster. The monster is evil. Someone evil killed my sister. When I think of someone cutting someone else's tongue out…" He stopped and took a moment to gather himself. "I just don't think about that being a woman. It's too gruesome. I don't know."

Cass could have called him a chauvinist, but dropped it. She did, however, have to caution him. "The person at the train station might not be Lauren's murderer."

"I think you're wrong. Put it together. There's a train ticket in Lauren's apartment. You first see this monster the night the psychic is killed, and now again at the train station while a train from Baltimore is arriving. I don't believe in coincidences like that."

"You also don't believe in mediums," she reminded him.

"Yeah, well, I'm starting to be persuaded. Whoever I saw either killed Lauren or knows something about who killed Lauren. I would bet this house on it."

Cass had to agree that the connection between all three events couldn't be ignored. "Did you see the person in the sweatshirt get off the train from Baltimore?"

"No," he admitted somewhat grudgingly. "There was a lot going on at that moment. The train from New York was arriving, another one to Washington was leaving, and the next thing I knew you were on the ground holding your ears. Why were you doing that?"

"It was shouting." It was the only way she knew to describe the terribly loud rumbling in her head.

"What did it shout?"

Cass shook her head, dislodging the ice pack from her nose again. She removed it as the cold on her face became more painful than the comfort of numbness. "I don't know. I couldn't make out the words. It was like noises strung together. It was saying something. I'm just not sure what."

"Is that how it is…you know, when…"

She didn't make him finish the sentence. "No. Not usually. Depending on the connection, the voices can be very clear. Considering this thing manages to get inside my head the way it does, I would have thought that anything it said would have been loud and clear. Then again it's a beast. A monster with a speech impediment and no vocabulary."

Cass glanced up in time to see his disbelief. In a way, she couldn't help but admire him for making the effort. What she spoke of was so much against the grain of reality he based his life on that each word must have hit his ears like a note out of tune. Still, he was trying to understand, and that was more than so many others in her life had done.

Another long silence passed as he sat on the couch, his hip pressed against hers. When the cloth in her hand became too wet to manage without dripping all over herself, she placed it in the bowl on the floor.

"I should go," she said, although not really sure how she was going to make that happen.

He looked down at her, his eyes studying her as if assessing each feature and its place on her face. Cass had a ridiculous impulse to ask for that mirror again just so she could see what he was seeing. Instead, she simply reached up to brush her cropped bangs over her forehead.

Malcolm reached for her hand and rested it on her stomach. Then with a finger he traced the bridge of her nose to its point, then gently circled each eye. Finally he tapped her chin and smiled.

"Definitely not broken. What size are you?"

All thought fled from her mind, making it impossible to answer. She was still thinking about the feeling of his finger trailing down her nose.

"Size?"

"I know small, but how small? Four? Two?"

"Two. Why?"

He didn't answer directly. "Lauren's clothes are still up in her room. The stuff she didn't take with her when she moved out. Mostly it's older stuff, but I should be able to find a pair of sweats and a T-shirt or something for you to sleep in."

"I'm not staying."

"I don't want to argue. Tomorrow I need to go to her funeral. Her funeral is tomorrow." It was as if he forced himself to repeat the words.

"I'm sorry," she whispered. Instinctively, she reached out to circle his wrist. A gesture of comfort she hadn't utilized in so long. Struck by the furred hair on his forearm, its thickness and warmth, she jerked her hand back. Cass tried to make the action more subtle, but failed.

"It's all right. I know you don't like to touch me."

"It's not you. You know that. I just can't stand the idea of being some kind of conduit."

"But you offered to let me touch you before," he said.

"I know."

"You offered to do something you're obviously uncomfortable with. Why? Were you trying to test your-self? Or maybe you were testing me?"

"I thought I owed you. I thought you would accept. People who have lost loved ones want them back. They want to connect and will take any opportunity they've got." Certainly Dougie had.

Malcolm nodded slowly as he came to a conclusion. "You wanted to see if I would take that opportunity. You wanted me to use you so you could prove I was like everybody else. My guess is you've been used before."

"It's happened," Cass said flatly.

"Not by me."

"Not yet."

"Not ever," he countered.

"You sure about that? My best friend couldn't stop himself. You asked about Dougie, if we had a lovers' quarrel? A year ago we were both in really bad places. He'd lost his wife a few months before in a car accident. He stumbled upon me in a coffeeshop. He was a wreck. Claire, his wife, came through loud and clear. I thought I could help him. I thought I could give him some peace. We became friends. Then this one night, both of us were sick with grief and pain. We didn't plan it."

"It happens," Malcolm agreed.

"Anyway, the weird connection thing happened then, too. I didn't understand it, but he did. He felt her and he didn't tell me. He knew she was there. Ever since then he's been trying to talk me back into bed, and now I know why."

"You think it's because he wants to…"

"Be with her. Feel her through me. Yes, I do."

Malcolm nodded slowly. "You never considered he might want you."

"He used me," Cass said bitterly.

"Sounds like you used him, too. To take away the grief and the pain that you were feeling. How was that different?"

Cass looked away from him then, trying to reject what was undeniably the truth. "It was different."

Malcolm chuckled softly and Cass practically groaned at how immature her response sounded.

"Okay. But I'm not going to use you to feel Lauren. First, ew. She was my sister. Trust me when I tell you I never wanted to 'feel' her in life and I certainly wouldn't want to in death. And second…"

Cass looked at him, uncertain about what point he was trying to make.

He ran a hand over the stubble that was starting to become noticeable on his chin. Then, as if coming to a decision, he leaned over her until he was so close she lost herself in the color of his dark blue eyes. His lips touched hers in the barest hint of a touch. Just so that she could register lips upon lips, a hint of breath and heat. Definitely heat.

Sitting up, he gazed down at her, seeing what she knew must be a shocked expression.

"Did you feel Lauren?"

"No!" she burst.

"Me, neither. So now you know."

"Know what?"

"That it's okay to touch. Because sometimes touching simply is what it is." Abruptly, he stood. "I'm going to get you some clothes. You'll sleep in the guest room. That way I'm close if anything happens."

"Nothing is going to happen. You think the person in the sweatshirt is just going to show up?"

"No, but I was more concerned with your ribs. If they start to give you problems or you have trouble breathing, I'll be close and can get you to a hospital faster than an ambulance can get here and back."

Once again, channeling her inner child, Cass huffed petulantly. "I don't have to take orders from you."

"No, you don't. But why don't you do it just this once? You're in pain. You don't want to get back in my car, and I would feel better if you stayed here. If you listen to me, it will make both of our lives a little easier. For tonight, anyway. I think we could use easy for a while. I know I could."

He was hard to argue with when he was right. "Fine," she grumbled, rolling slowly to her side and off the couch until she was standing—hunched over, but still standing—on her own two feet. "But you're not carrying me."

She caught a flash of a wide smile on his face, and then it was gone. "Okay. You win."

Cass walked one step, then two. She shuffled the third. Pressing a hand gently to her right side, she waited, but there was no sharp pain indicating a crack. It seemed that anything that hurt this badly had to be a break, but the reality was she would have been in much worse shape if the ribs were actually cracked. Still, the dull ache of bones and the muscle soreness made movement difficult.

Another shuffle. Then another.

In fact it made movement almost impossible.

"How many stairs in this place?" she asked.

"Let's see. There's three out of this room. About fourteen going upstairs."

Cass stopped. In seconds she felt an arm around her back and then another under her knees as he lifted her easily into his arms. "You're a real hard-ass, you know that?" he told her.

"I would have made it without the steps," she grumbled.

"Like I said, a real hard-ass."

He left Cass in the guest bedroom, which was about the size of her entire apartment. There was a canopy bed, a chair and matching ottoman, a dresser and a vanity with a framed mirror above it. So many things, but his house wasn't any fuller than hers. Not really. In fact, hers had more. She had her animals.

After a gentle tap, he walked into the room with a pair of mismatched pajamas in his hand and held them out to her. "It's the best I could do. They'll be big on you, but they should be comfortable."

She took the clothes and thought about what she would miss tonight. "My cats."

"Will they be okay overnight?"

Would he take her home if she said no? Probably not, she decided. More likely he would go to her place, pick them up and bring them back here. "Yes. They have plenty of water and dry food."

"Good." He extracted a bottle from his jeans pocket and set it on the vanity. "It's aspirin. It will help a little but not much. There's a glass next to the sink in the adjacent bathroom. Take two before you get into bed."

"And call you in the morning," she finished, trying to lighten what seemed to be a room filled with soft talk and tension. It was his fault. He'd made it tense by kissing her.

She felt him looking at her but wouldn't meet his eyes. "You won't have to. I'll check in on you."

He had turned to leave when she suddenly asked, "Why did you do that? Downstairs. Why did you kiss me?"

Slowly, he faced her. "I'm not really sure. To prove a point?"

"You always prove your points by kissing?"

"No, usually I prove them by being right. This time I was. The only thing you felt was me kissing you. Our lips touching. No ghosts between us."

"That's not true," Cass reminded him. "She's there. Whether you admit it or not, you want to hear from her and you know I can help you do that."

He moved farther into the room, no more than a foot away from her, and his expression tightened. "You've got problems, Cass. You can't seem to figure out who wants you for what. I guess I can see why, but we're not all out to use you. Someday you're going to have to learn to take people at face value. Until then, I feel sorry for you."

The words were like a blow to her midsection. "I don't want your pity."

"Tough. You have it."

She smiled at him with little humor even as she felt

the tingle rise up the back of her neck. This wasn't a threatening one. This one was normal. The room took shape in her mind and for a moment she stiffened, uncertain of how contact was going to play out now that she knew her talent was shifting. Still, it was her time to prove a point, so she opened herself to it and the control felt good. Almost healing.

"You were twelve. You climbed up into a tree in the backyard of your house. Lauren wanted to follow, but you told her she was too young, too small. But she was stubborn and she did it anyway. You tried to make your point then, too, and kept climbing higher to show her that she wasn't up for the challenge and should turn back."

"Stop. Don't do this."

"But Lauren kept going until she got so high that she got scared. You had to climb down underneath her to show her the way, to help her down from branch to branch. She says you were so mad at her. So mad that you slipped on the last branch and fell out of the tree. You broke your right arm. She says it was all her fault, for being stubborn, but you took the blame for getting you both into the tree."

The room quickly faded and Cass let out a slow breath.

"That did happen," he admitted.

"I know."

"I didn't ask you to tell me that story."

No, he didn't. But eventually he would have. He wouldn't have been able to stop himself. Just like Dougie. *It's better this way,* she thought. Better to understand the score now than to believe for a second that he was acting in her interest alone.

"You know what's funny about that story," he commented as he made his way out the door. "I was right that time, too. Maybe Lauren was trying to tell *you* something."

The door closed behind him with a soft snick, and Cass was left to think about that all night long.

Chapter 13

The next morning Cass awoke with a deep sense of comfort. The kind of comfort that dared you to move lest you break the fragile boundary between sleep and alertness. The bed underneath her was soft. The blanket that covered her provided both weight and warmth. The air was dry and toasty around her. Unlike the damp coolness she was used to waking up to in her basement apartment.

Don't move, she told herself, although she wasn't sure why it was so important. *Just enjoy it.*

A white fog drifted through her consciousness that she thought was part of the lazy comfort until through the fog she saw her grandfather's face.

Cassie, please talk to me. Cassie. I'm so sorry.

Cass bolted up and quickly regretted the sudden

movement. Pain lanced through her middle and her breath hitched as she tried to pant through the agony without taking the deep breaths that would only exacerbate the problem.

Slowly she lowered herself back into the cushiony deep bed and remembered why moving was a bad thing.

There was a soft knock at the door, but it opened before she could answer.

"Are you okay?" Malcolm asked as he popped his head around the door. "I heard a noise."

"I'm fine. I just moved too suddenly."

"Why?" Pushing the door open fully, he didn't seem at all hesitant about entering her room. Of course, it was his house, but as a man who had shown an abundance of manners over the past few days, the least he could have done was ask if it was all right to come in.

"Why what?" she grumbled, using her hands to lift herself into a sitting position against the pillows. She was in an oversize T-shirt so she wasn't exactly worried about appearances, but she also wasn't wearing a bra. Glancing down to check to see if her nipples were hard would have been a little obvious, but if she had to guess, she would say they were. It seemed to happen frequently when he was around.

And then he'd had to go and kiss her. That certainly hadn't helped.

"Why did you move so fast? Did something startle you?"

Yes, but it wasn't the monster, which was all he wanted to know. "Don't worry about it."

Nothing more than a ghost from her past.

He shifted his head to the side as if considering it but evidently decided to take her lead and drop it. She noted not for the first time how starkly handsome he was. His dark gray suit was cut to fit, and the fine material showcased his physique. A physique she'd gotten an up close feel of when he'd held her against his chest. His face was defined by sharp angles around his cheeks and chin and nose. Had the angles been any sharper he might have looked like a smaller version of Frankenstein; instead, he was closer to Brad Pitt. Only with more intensity.

Again, Cass was pretty sure she wouldn't have even been cataloging his features if it hadn't been for that kiss. It wasn't difficult for her to admit that it had unnerved her. She couldn't get away from it.

It had felt good. Sweet, warm, and she'd wanted more. Everything a kiss was supposed to be. Everything she couldn't have. Certainly not with him.

Shaking herself out of her reverie, Cass stopped admiring him and thought about what he was doing in her bedroom already dressed. "You're leaving for work, and you need to take me home. That's fine. I just need a few minutes to…"

"I'm not going to work," he interrupted. "You forgot. No reason you should remember, but today is Lauren's funeral."

He'd told her last night. It's why he'd asked her to make things easy for him. Cass felt small to have forgotten it. She was so tied up in what was happening to her that she'd neglected to realize that he was still hurting. Still grieving.

"I'll call a cab and I'll go." Pushing the covers back from the bed, she rolled smoothly until her feet touched the floor. Her sides still ached, but it was easier to stand straight today.

She watched his eyes fall to her bare feet, her painted toes barely visible below the overly long pajama bottoms. She wasn't sure if they had captured his attention or if he was merely avoiding looking at her.

"I want you to come."

"I don't understand."

Malcolm moved toward her and stopped. Deliberately, he put his hands on her arms and seemed to pause as if waiting for her to shrug him off. Since Cass felt no strange energy, she didn't see the point.

"I think it might be a good idea," he began, his eyes pinned to hers, hoping, she guessed, that she would see his sincerity. "I saw what that…thing…did to you last night. I know what you suffered. And I wouldn't want you to risk that again. Certainly not for me."

There was a "but" coming. She could practically already hear it. Then Cass was able to figure out what he wanted before he had to say it. "You think the killer might show up at her funeral."

He shrugged. "It happens, doesn't it? They want to see what they've done. Revel in it. He or she, whoever that was in the sweatshirt, might try to lurk in the background and watch, but if you were there…"

"I would know that he was there. Because the monster would come back." Cass pulled herself out of his reach until his hands fell to his sides. He crossed them over his chest and grimaced.

"I did it, didn't I? Crossed that fragile threshold in your brain that signals 'user.' But if you would hear me out—"

"What you're asking makes sense," she cut in, deliberately ignoring the roiling lurch in her stomach. "You don't have to apologize for that. I don't have anything to wear, obviously, but if you take me back to my place I can change quickly."

"Cass…"

"No." She stopped him with a raised hand when he made a motion to move closer. "It's all right. You want to find the person who killed your sister. I get that."

"Did it also occur to you that I might want to find the person who is responsible for that thing that attacked you? Find him so we can stop it from happening again."

"Should it have occurred to me?"

"Yes, it should," he answered tightly.

"You're not making sense." Cass turned away from him to get her clothes that she'd left on the chair.

"There's something there, Cass. Between us. And it sure as hell doesn't have anything to do with your gift. You can ignore it if you want, you can pretend I'm only using you to get after Lauren's killer, but it's not going to change anything."

"Pretend?" she asked, picking the most annoying word out of his speech.

"Yes. Pretend. I'm not going to lie and tell you that your being at the funeral isn't a possible advantage. I'm also not going to tell you that finding Lauren's killer isn't my number one priority. But I meant what I said

before. I saw what happened to you. I know how that
thing hurt you. So the second thing topping my current
agenda is finding out who or what is doing that to you.
Why? I don't know. I like you. You're stubborn and five
foot nothing, but you seem to handle all these burdens.
My dad would say you had grit. But you're so damn
closed I want to shake you sometimes until you admit
that you need people. That you're not as freaking okay
with being alone as you seem to be."

"I'm closed?" Cass laughed, waving her hand
around the room filled with beautiful objects. "I'm
alone? Malcolm, look at this house. If you packed it
full of any more things, you would never have to see
another person again. Some people surround themselves with things because it makes them feel better.
Others do it because they're shallow. Why do you do
it? Why the car, and the watch, and the clothes, and
the memorabilia all tucked into this massive, lonely
house? It's not who you are. Don't try to convince me
that it is."

"I enjoy these things. I have them. It's not to suggest
that they are all I have."

"Really? Then where are the damn casseroles?
Where's the pie and the cookies and all that comes
with it. Your sister died! You're connected to all sorts
of people through your job. Hell, you know the mayor.
Every homemaker within a thousand-mile radius
should be bringing you something to eat, but you said
there's nothing. When my grandmother died, we ate for
months from what people had brought. Here there's
nothing." Cass took a breath because she needed it.

"Don't tell me you're not just as closed as I am," she insisted. "Don't be that hypocritical."

There was a startled silence between them. Malcolm looked over his shoulder toward the door, maybe all the way down to the kitchen, as if to verify that there were in fact no casseroles waiting for him.

"No. No one did bring over any casseroles. A few people sent cards."

Instantly, Cass felt contrite. She rubbed her hands over her face as if she could somehow erase that moment of brutal truth. "I'm sorry. I didn't mean to hurt you."

"I imagine you were just trying to defend yourself. It wasn't my intent to put you on the spot."

He stepped away from her, and that was even worse than the cold timbre of his tone. If only he hadn't pushed her, she wouldn't have had to push back. She wouldn't have been forced to show him that despite what he had, he had nothing.

Of course, then she may not have also realized that for all her pretensions about not needing anything, the result was that she also had nothing. They were so different, yet in this they were remarkably the same.

"I'll go to the funeral," she offered. "It does make sense. And you're right. It's not just about finding Lauren's killer. I have to know who is bringing this monster to me. I have to find a way to stop it. I survived the last time, but I don't know what would happen next time. I have to figure it out before it really hurts me…or worse. You need to take me back to my apartment."

"I was up early this morning. I couldn't sleep. I went to your place. Yes, I took the keys," he said in answer to her shocked expression. "I fed your cats, gave them fresh water and food. They seem fine. I found a dress in your closet. It was black. It was appropriate. Also shoes and some other things I thought you might need."

The audacity of his actions was more than enough to start another argument, but she didn't have the wherewithal to bother. She figured if the monster did show up today, she was going to need all of her strength to survive it.

"Okay," she said.

"I'll get them."

He left but quickly returned with her standard black dress and a pair of old shoes she recognized that matched. Carefully, he laid them out over the ottoman as if they were recently purchased from DKNY. They weren't. He set another bag down beside the ottoman, and she could see it contained her toiletries and a hint of lace, which suggested he hadn't forgotten underwear. The man was nothing if not thorough.

"We need to leave in about an hour."

Cass calculated her preparation time. "That shouldn't be a problem."

"If this person, the sweatshirt, is there, run. Don't think, don't hesitate, just run. The farther you get away from it, the better. I'll take care of the rest."

Run? From something that was inside her head? Cass didn't try to point out the obvious snags in that strategy. Instead, she nudged her chin in the direction of the ottoman. "You should go. I only have an hour. You know us girls," she added as a lame attempt at levity.

He didn't smile or make the obvious jokes. It would have been easier for them both if he had.

"You can't let it continue to attack you," he pressed. "There has to be a way to stop it."

"It's not your problem."

"I think we already established that it is," he declared solemnly. "Get dressed. I'll meet you downstairs. After it's…the funeral…is over, we'll talk more. I want to talk."

The door closed behind him and Cass shook her head. *Great,* she thought. He wants to talk. There was nothing productive that could come of that. At least nothing she could see. Her best bet was to cut her losses. Get dressed, go to the funeral, find the killer then…what?

Cass quickly realized that getting dressed was a much easier option than trying to answer that question.

The day was perfect for a funeral. It was cold, wet, gray and solemn. Cass figured if she was ever going to be buried, she would want it to be on a day like this. The sun shouldn't shine for death. The sky shouldn't be blue. The weather shouldn't be comfortable.

After all, there was nothing comfortable about death.

People should be wet and shivering and sad. They should look miserable because it was a miserable task.

Expectedly, at Lauren's funeral, they did.

There had been a much larger crowd at the church. Malcolm was Catholic, and apparently Lauren had been, too, until her conversion to Wicca. Cass didn't know if Lauren might have wanted a Wiccan service, but, given Malcolm's devotion to her, she had no doubt he would have done that if he knew how to bury someone in that tradition.

As he had mentioned to Cass, the only funeral for witches he could imagine was a stake and a fire, and he said he didn't believe that was appropriate.

The city's elite turned out to pay their respects. The mayor, the chief of police, Dougie's captain and sundry assemblymen. The church was packed with people, and all Cass could wonder was how a man who knew so many people could have so few friends. Some employees had stopped and spoken with him for a time. There was also a slew of Lauren's friends, from high school, college and her coven who offered their condolences. Lauren apparently didn't have Malcolm's issues and seemed to be not only popular but extremely missed.

But there was no one person who was there just because they cared for him. He stood straight and stoic in the church during the service. And now as the priest concluded the rites of burial, he remained the same. Only a smattering of people had followed from the church to the cemetery. Lauren's closest friends, Malcolm and Cass stood in a tight circle around the open grave upon which the coffin sat ready at some near time to be lowered into the ground.

Once the priest backed off, one of Lauren's witch friends offered a prayer as well. When she finished, she was the first to lay a flower on the coffin. Everyone still around the site followed suit and eventually left. There was no announcement to have people back at Malcolm's house, and Cass knew that if there had been, only a few people might have come.

Glancing around the graveyard, she searched for anyone who looked to be lurking. She'd felt nothing during the church service other than the familiar tingling of potential contact that always came when she was in a large group. Anytime she was in a crowd of that many, the odds were someone from the other side would try to make contact. She intentionally shut her mind to it, her belief being that if the monster showed up it would be too strong to be blocked out and, as for the rest, she didn't need the distraction.

With everyone pretty much gone except for Malcolm, who was thanking the elderly priest for his kind words, she felt absolutely nothing. No sensations at all that would lead her to think whoever brought the monster was close.

Still, she wasn't sorry that she had come.

Her eyes fell on two figures who stepped out of a car at the bottom of the hill on which Lauren was to be buried. She spotted Dougie and instantly recognized his partner, Steve.

Steve stayed by the car, but Dougie started walking toward them. No doubt they'd had the same idea about the killer wanting to be at the funeral. They had stood in the back of the church, and the car, she knew, had been driving around the cemetery for a while.

His expression was grim, and Cass had to assume that he hadn't had any more luck than she had had.

"Hey," he began cautiously.

"Hi."

"Can we talk?"

Cass looked over her shoulder. Malcolm was now listening to the priest, who was obviously trying to offer words of comfort to him. She doubted they would help, but it was what priests did, after all.

"Sure." She followed him away from the grave site, as it seemed disrespectful to talk in front of the coffin. He stopped under a tree and faced her.

"What are you doing here?"

"Same thing you are, I guess. Looking for Lauren's killer."

"And how the hell would you know if you spotted him?"

Cass thought about Malcolm's suspicion that the person they were searching for might be a woman but figured there was no point in clouding the issue now. It was time to let Dougie know what had been happening; she just didn't want to do it here. After their fight, for lack of a better word, she'd thought she would have been happy if she never had to see him again, but she could see she was being ridiculous. This case was more important than what he'd done to her.

What he'd done and what she'd done. Yes, he had used her. But, as Malcolm had said, she had used him, too. Was there really any difference?

Regardless of who was to blame, Cass wasn't so immature as to withhold information that might be useful to a murder investigation because she happened to be mad at the lead detective. "We need to talk about this, Dougie. A lot has happened since the other night. The thing that brought me to the psychic's apartment that morning—I didn't want to tell you then because it seemed so far-fetched, but it's happened twice since and I think it may be important. It's why I'm here."

"Detective." Cass turned and saw that Malcolm was a step behind her.

"Mr. McDonough. Pardon our intrusion during this difficult time for you," he said in the manner of someone who has had to give the same speech several times in the past. Cass didn't doubt that, as a homicide detective, Dougie spent a lot of time at funerals. "My partner and I are here because we wanted to see if there were any suspicious people in attendance today. It's not unusual for a killer to want to be a part of his victim's funeral."

"I understand. I appreciate your efforts."

"I was also looking for Cass."

That was news. "Looking for me? Why?"

Dougie turned back to her, his expression even more grim than before. In fact, he looked downright worried. "There's been a development in the case. One you need to know about. It involves you."

"Me?"

He looked away from her as if trying to figure out how to say what he needed to say.

"The murders being so close together puzzled me. Yeah, serial killers tend to kill in a particular area. It's like their hunting ground, whatever. But there was something too coincidental about the two murders. I didn't get the impression that these victims were chosen at random. A witch who worked at a New Age store on Addison. A psychic who gave readings down the block. I knew that they weren't the only eccentrics that lived on Addison."

"Technically, Silvia lived around the corner," Cass pointed out.

"No, her building actually faces Addison. So I went back to your old apartment, the one you lived in only a few months ago."

Cass shook her head, not understanding what he was saying.

"It was a hunch. Just a hunch but…"

"Oh, my God," Malcolm whispered.

"We found another body. A woman with dark hair. Her name was Carol Lyman. She had moved in right after you left. New to the city, she didn't know a lot of people. She'd paid her rent and didn't really know anyone else in the building so no one missed her right away. She's been dead for almost six days. And her tongue was missing."

"Dougie, what are you saying?"

Cass felt a tingle on the back of her neck, but this time it wasn't a precursor of contact. It was that feeling when something horrible was about to happen and there was nothing that could be done to stop it. Her gut clenched and she felt herself break out in a cold sweat. She knew what he was going to say even before he said it.

"We think the killer is after you, Cass. We think he's been looking for you all along."

Chapter 14

The three of them sat around Malcolm's kitchen table. Since his house was the closest and most private place to talk, they had gone there to discuss the issue of the woman found in Cass's old apartment. Dougie had sent Steve back to headquarters and had ridden with Malcolm and Cass to the upscale Gladwyne residence. Dougie's eyes grew big when he spotted the flat-screen TV in the great room, but other than that, he made no comment about the place.

They had just sat down, when—as if to mock her—one of Malcolm's neighbors rang the doorbell. He came back into the kitchen and presented them with a massive casserole dish filled to the brim with macaroni and cheese.

"It's a casserole," he said, his eyes pinned on Cass's.

"I see that."

"Mrs. Norris. Next door. She dropped it off."

"That was very nice of her."

"You want some?"

"I'm not really hungry," Cass replied to his near smirk.

"I am." Unabashedly, Dougie raised his hand.

Malcolm served himself and Dougie, and for a moment Cass considered tossing her pride aside. It smelled delicious, and macaroni and cheese was one of her favorites. Then Dougie reminded them why they were all sitting around Malcolm's kitchen table in the first place, and she quickly lost her appetite.

"I don't get it," she said as the two men went back for seconds. "Why me? It's not like I advertise in the paper. Who would know where to find me?"

"Somebody did," Dougie pointed out grimly.

"You're sure it's not a coincidence?"

The two men exchanged a look, which let Cass know her question was borderline ridiculous. "It's not a coincidence, Cass. But before we get to that, let's talk more about this monster."

"I don't know what else to tell you. The first time I was alone in my apartment, I might have thought it was a dream if the contact hadn't been so strong. When I woke, I sensed trouble. That's why I went outside. I knew there was something wrong. I needed to find out what. The next time was down near Penn's Landing. I left you and started walking, and it just hit me like a ton of bricks. The person in the sweatshirt was there and at the train station when it hit again."

"She's not kidding when she says a ton of bricks, either," Malcolm interjected. "Do you know what happens to her when the dead make contact? It hurts her. This thing messed her up. Almost cracked her ribs and broke her nose. The bruises are faded now but they were there last night."

"Last night?"

"Yes. I kept her here with me. You didn't think I was going to leave her alone."

"No, of course not," Dougie said slowly. "You're a real conscientious fellow, aren't you?"

"Dougie, stop," Cass warned.

"What's the matter, Detective?" Malcolm said. "Am I back on your suspect list? Maybe I killed my sister as part of a more sinister plot to get to Cass. Or are you worried about something else?"

"Should I be worried about something else?"

"Yes, I think you should be."

A silent message passed between them, and Cass figured it was done on a wavelength that only über–macho men and dogs could hear. "Can we please get back on topic? You know…the part about somebody wanting to kill me and cut out my tongue?"

They instantly broke off their staring contest and re-focused on Cass.

"It sort of makes sense," Dougie finally said. "Think about it. There are people who have heard about you. The guy at the coffeehouse heard about you and knew where you worked. Hell, he said he got your name from the postman, who had gotten your name from someone else. Let's say this person wants to make contact with whoever this monster is that died. Maybe he wants a final chance to say 'Fuck you'—who knows. Anyway, he hears about you. He gets your name. Tracks down where you live. Only, you moved a couple of months ago, so he's got the wrong address. He shows up at your apartment, but you're not you. He goes into a rage and kills Carol. Maybe she tells him that she knows you moved only a couple of blocks away. Or maybe he's just got it in his head that you should be on Addison. So he starts to target likely candidates that might be you. A witch, a psychic. When they can't help him, he offs them, too."

Malcolm flinched at Dougie's plain speech but said nothing.

"He's got to be twisted. Whoever the monster is…was…was connected to him in life. That's how it works. Right?" Dougie asked.

Cass nodded. The monster was different than any spirit she'd ever encountered. That was true. The contact was stronger than any she had felt before. So strong she couldn't block it out. In the past, she'd always noted that the stronger the connection in life, the stronger the connection in death. If that theory held in this case, then yes, whoever the person in the hooded sweatshirt was, he or she had been intimately connected to the monster in her head. If the beast had been as evil in life as he was in death then that could make for one very twisted and angry person.

"That's how it works."

"Then what do we do to find him or her?" Malcolm wanted to know.

Dougie shrugged and leaned back in his chair. "*We* don't do anything. Me and my partner will do the things detectives do. We follow the evidence. We found DNA evidence at all three crime sites. I have no doubt that they'll match. Unfortunately, unless this person's been arrested before, that won't help us determine who it is. And those traces take a while. We did have the computer spit out murders where the removal of a tongue had been involved. Aside from our vics, there were three other hits in a five-hundred-mile radius."

"Good Lord," Cass exclaimed. "You're saying that the same person…"

"No," Dougie stopped her. "One was a gang-related thing. One was a domestic dispute. A wife whacked her husband then cut out his tongue, and the other is an unsolved out of New York. We're checking with detectives who worked it to see if we can find any links."

"The wife who killed her husband. What happened to her?" Malcolm asked.

Cass looked at Malcolm and knew he was considering the feminine features he thought he spotted under the hood.

Dougie shook his head. "She did herself in a couple of months later. Couldn't handle the guilt, I guess. Our best shot is the lead in New York."

"But what about the train ticket?" Cass reminded him. "It was from Baltimore."

"Yeah, I thought of that. I don't have any answers yet. Maybe the person had to get out of New York in a hurry. I'll know more as soon as we talk to the detective on the case."

"I was raised in Baltimore. It's been years since I've been there. I can't imagine anyone would go looking for me there but…"

"I'll add it to the list. In the meantime, watch your back."

Watch her back. That seemed like the understatement of the year.

Dougie stood up. "I've got to go. I want to check in at headquarters and see if I can't put a rush on the DNA matching."

"I'll drive you," Malcolm offered.

"Uh. Yeah. Thanks."

Cass stood as well. "Let me just get my clothes from upstairs, and you can drop me off, too."

"That won't be necessary." Malcolm reached out and caught her arm before she could leave the room. "You're staying here until this person is caught."

"No, I'm not."

"Cass," Dougie interjected with somewhat of a pained expression on his face. "He's right. You can't stay in your apartment, not by yourself. You either stay with me, stay with him, let one of us stay with you, or if there's someone else…"

"There's no one else," she snapped. No girlfriend or family or anybody she could call in the middle of the night and ask if she could crash for a while. But she didn't like any of her other options, either.

"It's settled," Malcolm concluded. "Your place is too small and as I told you before, I'm not sleeping on that futon. I have plenty of room."

"I can't leave my cats for another day."

"We'll get them and we'll bring them here. Cats love space."

Cass looked to Dougie for help, but he was watching Malcolm with a stony yet resigned look. Part of her was tempted to tell Malcolm that she'd prefer staying with Dougie, but in the end she wasn't ready to deal with Dougie on a personal level yet. Maybe she could forgive what he'd done, but she couldn't forget it. Not right away. And besides, staying with him would mean regular contact from Claire. The energy it would take to keep her out would be draining. That wasn't the case with Lauren.

"I guess I don't have much of a choice," she relinquished.

"In this, no," Malcolm said. "I think more than enough women have lost their lives and their tongues to this murderer. Let's go."

They dropped Dougie off first and then headed to Cass's place. When she unlocked the door, she did so with a smidgen of trepidation. But she concluded that if the killer was inside, waiting for her, she would have felt the monster by now. No tingles this time. No charged air.

"Let me." Malcolm pushed in front of her and switched on the lights. The place was exactly as she had left it. No disturbances. No intruders. Just Spook and Nosey sitting together on the futon, keeping each other company no doubt until their mom came home.

They pushed themselves up and trotted over to greet her and get patted. First from her, then they wandered over to Malcolm. Obligingly, he bent down and stroked them in long, fluid movements.

Strong hands, Cass noted. Strong, but with the ability to show gentleness. Her pets lapped that gentleness up.

"Do you have a carrier for them?"

"I'll get it."

"Tell me where it is. I'll corral them while you pack."

Packing implied a significant amount of time. And he said it as if it were the most natural thing in the world for her to pack up and move in with him when she'd only known him for days. This morning they had stood across from each other and she'd said horrible things to him and here he was still petting her cats, who were purring so loudly, she thought they might shake apart.

"Why are you doing this? You don't even know me."

"Let's put aside for a moment the fact that I don't think that's true." He stood up and loomed over her. "I think we're a lot alike, you and me, and if we had met under other circumstances…"

A harsh laugh escaped her throat. "You mean if you had just wandered into the coffeehouse someday. You in your thousand-dollar suit and ten-thousand-dollar watch. You would have taken one look at me behind the counter in my green apron and what? Fallen madly in love? Get real."

"I would have noticed your eyes. Bright green and exotic the way they tilt up ever so slightly at the end. And your nose. I would have noticed how delicate and fine it is. How delicate your whole face seems to be. I might have ordered my coffee to stay rather than to go. I might have ordered a second cup."

Her soft gasp was barely audible and she hoped he hadn't heard it, but there was a look of satisfaction in his eyes that told her she hadn't gotten that lucky.

"The point is we'll never know. Instead we met at a police station with me at my worst. I wanted to throttle you, I was so angry. The next morning I came close to actually doing it. There really aren't a whole lot of reasons for you to trust me. My one advantage is that currently you trust the detective less. I'm not going to let you stay here because I'm not going to risk your dying. That is the simple answer. Why I can't risk it…that gets a little more complicated."

That bothered her. "I think you believe if you save me it will erase the guilt of not saving your sister." That was reasonable. That made sense. Nothing else.

"That is definitely a factor. And doesn't that make it easy for you? Help exonerate me, Cassandra, and go pack."

"Only two people I know call me Cassandra."

"A shame. It's really rather lovely."

Cass didn't know what to say to that. She didn't know how to respond to any of it. He was making her nervous and making her think and she wanted to push him out the door and lock it behind him.

She didn't scare easily. In fact, death wasn't really something that frightened her at all. She knew too much about the peace and serenity that was to be found afterward. However, she also wasn't stupid. There was a killer on the loose and it was hunting her. With a knife and a monster. Even if she found a way to avoid having her tongue cut out, she was pretty sure she couldn't beat the monster.

"Their case is in the closet next to the bathroom. And their food. And you'll need their litter. They're not outside cats. Do you have some kind of box?"

Satisfied he was going to get his way, Malcolm was clearly willing to be accommodating. "I'm sure I have something that will work. If not, I'll build them a box."

He seemed so serious, she smiled. "Cardboard and a plastic bag as a liner will work just fine."

Just then the phone rang and Malcolm seemed as startled by the intrusion as she was. Cass considered letting the machine pick up, but since she had only one regular caller these days, she figured she might as well talk to him.

"Hello?"

"Cassandra," came the voice from the other end. One of the two other people to use her full name.

"Hi, Dr. Farver."

"I just wanted to make sure you made it home all right. I was worried about you. You seemed upset, and I don't think I did much to help."

"I made it home fine. Don't worry."

"Okay. Well, it was good to see you. Mad said so, too."

"It was good to see you and Mad."

"Last chance to maybe come down and meet my student…"

Cass smiled into the phone at his near pleading request and this time she felt none of the guilt. "I can't be swayed. But I will check in soon. I promise."

And she meant it. Just because she wasn't part of the institute anymore didn't mean she had to leave behind the people she cared about. Malcolm leaned against the refrigerator in a negligent pose and watched her as she hung up the phone.

"Are you ill?"

Her brow furrowed when she realized she'd addressed Dr. Farver by name. "No, he's not a medical doctor. He's a psychologist who specializes in parapsychology. He founded and runs the Institute of Psychical Studies in Washington, D.C. That's where I was coming from when I saw you at the train station."

"Is he serious? I mean his work…"

"It's legitimate. Funded by a lot of people who are less into science and more into the 'unknown,' but he takes his work and his research very seriously. I owe him a lot. He basically saved me. After my grandfather dumped me in the asylum, Dr. Farver found me and realized that I wasn't crazy."

"A believer."

"Not really," she mused. "He thinks I'm a telepath."

"A tele-what?"

"Telepathic," she repeated, using the more common term. "He thinks I can read minds. He doesn't believe in an afterlife so it stands to reason he doesn't believe that people from there would contact me. Instead, he thinks I can read people's minds, access their memories. When a person dies, the living usually think about them more intensely, about their past together. That's what he thinks I can do."

"But you can't."

"Nope. Don't have a clue what you're thinking right now."

"Good," he stated somewhat enigmatically. "Let's go."

It took longer to corral the animals—they associated the carrier with the vet—than it did for Cass to pack. In the end she pleaded with them to be good girls and finally they allowed themselves to be lifted and placed together inside.

When they got back to the house, Malcolm found a crate that worked well with a plastic kitchen bag for a liner, and the cats seemed to acclimate to the new surroundings almost immediately.

"They'll get lost," Cass worried as she watched them search out each new smell and new crevice in the spacious home. "They like to sleep with me. What if they can't find me?"

"They'll find you. Cats are very resilient creatures."

"You had one?" Cass asked, noting his comfort with them.

"Lauren did. It liked me and I didn't mind it."

"Spoken like a true man."

His lips twitched. "Like I said, pink and cats—two things men never admit to liking." He walked over to the fridge and opened it. He pulled out the casserole dish and got a bowl from a cabinet. "You didn't eat earlier, but I saw you eyeing it up. Come on, admit it— you want some of my casserole."

She did. "Fine, I'll eat it, but my point still stands."

Malcolm heated some up for her and then decided he could have another round. He put two bowls of the heated macaroni and cheese in front of them, along with two glasses of ice-cold milk. They ate at the table and the strange hominess of the act wasn't lost on Cass. It had been so long since she had sat and eaten at a kitchen table that it actually unnerved her. She fiddled with her fork, pushed the food around and squirmed in her chair.

Malcolm raised an eyebrow in question.

"I usually eat in front of the TV on a mat," she explained.

"I usually eat in the other room," Malcolm said. He put down his fork. "You know, you were right about the casseroles. About me, I suppose. I don't make friends very easily."

"Why not? I mean, for me it's a no-brainer. I'm weird. I hear dead people," she whispered dramatically. "I couldn't cope as a teen, and school was filled with people who had lost grandmothers and grandfathers and such. Then after the asylum I didn't want to trust anyone ever again. I got along with the people at the institute. At the time I would have called them my friends. But it was so easy to walk away and not look back. Too easy. I'm trying to fix that now."

"That's why you went to see the doctor."

Cass shook her head. "I was hoping he might help. Part of dealing with this gift is having control over it. Knowing every nuance of it. The channeling is new to me, relatively new, and I wanted a way to categorize it. Dr. Farver was methodical in his testing. I went looking for some ideas, but because he doesn't believe, he couldn't really help me. Anyway, that's my story. Now yours."

"Well, I don't hear dead people. I wasn't committed to an asylum. I'm not considered to be a freak by anyone—that I know of—merely reserved. I was raised by a loving father and an absent mother until I was eleven. Then my dad met Lauren's mom and we became a family. We were happy."

"That's not really an answer."

"I don't know that there is one. Yes, I lost my father and it crushed me. Soon after that, Lauren and I lost Becca. She had also been crushed by my father's sudden death. Neither of those things had been easy. When Dad died, I took over the business and discovered it wasn't in great shape."

"You didn't know?"

"No. He wouldn't have said. He had too much pride for that. It had been hard enough for him to marry a woman he knew had more money than he did, but to tell her that he had turned around and lost it… Anyway, when I saw the condition things were in, I knew where the stress in his life had come from."

"I'm sorry."

Malcolm's mouth turned up. "No point in apologizing for something you can't fix. I should have known he was in over his head. Dad was an ironworker but wanted to build a construction company. He had all the people skills he needed. People loved him. I'll never understand why my mother didn't. But he didn't have much business sense. It was his dream that McDonough Contractors would some day be 'and Son,' but he wanted me to be a college-educated man first. He died right after I graduated. When I saw that the money was gone, I put everything I had into saving the company. I didn't want Becca or Lauren to know. I became consumed with hiding the fact that we were all broke. I'd been broke before but they hadn't. I couldn't let them down, for their sake or my father's."

"All the things I said about you and your money. I thought it all had come so easily." Cass didn't have to say any more to know he understood that she was sorry for that, too.

"Not so easily. It took sacrifice. I didn't take time out for drinks with the boys or poker on Fridays or parties on Saturdays. I had a fiancée when I started. We'd met in college, but she quickly realized that my first priority was the company, and she couldn't accept that so she left me. She got most of my remaining friends in the split."

"Ouch."

Malcolm shrugged. "I've got to tell you, though, I wasn't the chattiest or most popular little boy on the block, either."

Cass smiled at the image of a very serious boy who had been his little sister's hero. "Me, neither," she admitted. "I loved books. Getting lost in them."

"I loved sports. Watching them, playing them. Getting lost in them, too. I took them very seriously."

Cass thought about the sports memorabilia in the great room and frowned slightly. She'd been so judgmental about his things and his need to surround himself with them that she hadn't been able to take them at face value—as pieces of sports history that he enjoyed owning.

Knowing that made the house and everything in it much less intimidating. It made him less intimidating, too. More real. More touchable.

Abruptly, Cass pushed herself away from the table. She scooped up her bowl, rinsed it and dropped it in the dishwasher with a loud thunk as it slipped from her hand. Her back to him, she found a sponge and started absently wiping down the counter in front of her.

"I'm really tired, what with everything that happened today. I'm sure you are, too. I'm going to go to bed now. Probably be out like a light in seconds." Cass heard the rambling quality in her speech but couldn't make herself stop. "You'll want to close your door, though, in case the cats get in. They can be pretty nudgey in the morning when they want to be petted…"

She felt his presence before she felt him. The barest touch of his chest against her back letting her know he was close without overwhelming her.

"Don't be afraid of this."

"I'm not," she insisted. But it was a lie. There were so many things that scared her. Malcolm scared her.

"But you are. You're afraid of what's happening between us and that's okay. Fear is a part of life. It's overcoming it that makes you brave." He turned her so that she faced him and cupped her chin in his hand so that she couldn't avoid his eyes. "Be brave for me tonight, Cass. Be with me tonight."

The sponge dropped from her hand. She opened

her mouth to answer him but before she could, his mouth descended on hers, taking her breath and her response with it.

It would have been yes.

Chapter 15

They were standing in his master bedroom, a massive room done in masculine deep brown and beige colors. Although how they got there Cass couldn't say. She remembered him kissing her. She remembered kissing him back. She remembered feeling like the more she wanted, the more she needed, and the more he gave. She remembered holding on to him and feeling her feet leave the ground and she remembered not being afraid.

Be brave, he'd told her. She wasn't sure that she could be, not in this. Maybe if she just let it be sex, then it would be okay. Yes, they had a connection. He'd mentioned it often enough, and though she'd never bothered to acknowledge it, she'd never made a point of denying it, either.

She was a woman, after all, and he was handsome and strong. But gentle, too, in his way. He held her doors open and he loved his sister. He was a good man, but he was alone. Alone like her. And because he was, and because she was, and because they were attracted to each other, there was a connection.

They could have sex, and it would satisfy the temporary hunger and when all was said and done, they could return to their respective corners. There was no lingering presence in her head to suggest that Lauren was a part of this, and so the morning-after-meaningless-sex hangover would be much less nasty than it had been with Dougie.

Yes, she could do this. She could be brave enough to have this. But she wanted it fast and furious. Done and over and satisfied and back to their corners as quickly as possible.

She reached for the belt at his waist and started to unfasten it.

His lips, which had been grazing her neck just below her ear, lifted and he took a step back. He caught her hands in his and waited until she looked up from his waist, where she could see the faint outline of his erection against the fine fabric of his pants.

"What?" she asked, not understanding why he had stopped. He wanted her. She could see it; if she could just reach out and touch him, she could break his control.

"No, not that way," he answered calmly.

"Not what way?"

"Your way. This isn't going to be fast and over quickly."

She lifted her chin, ignoring the fact that this time he'd been the one to read her mind. "What if that's how I like it?"

He lowered his head until his lips barely brushed hers. "Then that's how we'll do it...next time. Turn around."

Cass hesitated, but the gentle push of his hand on her shoulder had her obeying. Suddenly the sense of being out of control mingled with the excitement of desire. Both overrode the fear of letting him get too close. She felt the slow, gentle tug of the zipper being pulled down her back.

The dress he'd picked out was her standard all-purpose dress. Long-sleeved, knee-length with the barest scoop neck, it could appear elegant at a wedding or appropriate at a funeral. It had been the easy choice.

The other choices he made had been slightly more startling. He'd picked a black lace thong instead of her more prevalent white cotton panties, and he'd picked a pair of thigh-highs that she had purchased months ago on a whim, which she'd never actually worn, rather than the single pair of black nylons she knew were in her underwear drawer inside her closet. The bra was a simple black garment—her only black bra—but it seemed boring in comparison.

"Did you do it on purpose?" she asked as the zipper fell to her lower back, and she knew the lace along the top of her thong was revealed.

He kissed a spot in the center of her back and she felt him smile against her skin. "You mean my choice of undergarments? Hell, yes."

His hands found her shoulders and he pushed the

dress off one, then the other and let it slip down over her arms, her hips, until finally it pooled in a lifeless heap on the floor.

"You're beautiful." Cass felt his hand slide from her bare shoulder to her nape, then a single finger traced her spine until the warm, heavy palm of his hand rested on her bare buttock.

For a moment, she stood trembling. She couldn't recall a time when she'd been studied like this. He'd left on the single lamp by his bed, which gave off more than enough light. He saw everything she had to offer and there was nowhere for her to hide. Dougie hadn't been her first, but there hadn't been many experiences besides that one. Most had been rushed and frenzied. This was anything but, and she wasn't sure she would be able to withstand the tension Malcolm was building.

Another gentle push and he had turned her to face him. Holding her hands, he helped her step out of the remains of the dress and then he led her to sit on the bed. It was huge and soft, and she felt herself sinking into it. She pulled her hands away and used them to brace herself.

Malcolm stepped between her legs, which were still covered in black silk. She thought he might remove the delicate stockings, but instead he traced the length of her leg, down her thigh, under her knee, circling her ankle, until he popped off her very practical shoe. He repeated the process with the other leg, and it was all she could do to sit still while he performed the ritual again.

"You are a contrast," he said as he moved farther between her legs, making her spread them wide enough to accommodate him. "So small and delicate, but then I see your arms and they're so sculpted. Your legs are so toned. And your belly..." He ran his hand over the flat skin that was stretched over firm muscle. His fingers brushed the top of the lace and lingered until she almost begged him to dip them farther below. "Softness over steel."

Since she was unable to form a truly coherent thought, the only thing that emerged from her dry throat was, "Yoga."

"And Pilates. I know."

He met her eyes and smiled. Truly smiled, maybe for the first time since she'd met him. It removed all the sharp edges from his face and made him seem younger. Lighter.

Cass smiled back and he traced it with a finger. Then he was pushing her back onto the bed until she was in the center of it and he was over her. He lowered his head and kissed her like he had all the time in the world. His tongue ran along hers in a slow, leisurely manner, tasting, testing, sucking. Then he delved into her mouth with a steady, heady rhythm that gave her body a hint of what was to come. And the hint was so delicious, so tempting, she found herself arching against him, testing both his endurance and his will-power.

He apparently had plenty of both.

But when her hand searched for and found the outline of his straining erection, he was forced to pull back.

"Not yet."

Cass almost screamed in frustration. She did in fact whimper.

Malcolm merely smiled again. He moved off the bed and removed the tie he still wore that had already been loosened. He quickly unbuttoned his shirt and stepped out of his shoes, throwing the clothes behind him in a careless fashion that suggested while he did possess expensive things, they weren't overly important to him. Finally, he pulled off his undershirt and pushed down his pants and briefs. For a moment he stood in front of her and let her study him as he had studied her.

He was beautiful, too. Built the way a man should be built, with heavy muscles, a defined chest and thick forearms that suggested years of conditioning. His thighs were equally strong. It was no wonder he was able to lift and carry her about as effortlessly as he did. His sex sprang up tall from a nest of dark blond curls, and for the first time, Cass was awed by the powerful sight of an aroused man. Her breath caught in her chest, and instinctively she used one of her hands to reach for him so she could touch him and feel all that pulsing power in her hand.

But Malcolm shifted his hips and his erection out of reach. "No, I'm too close to the edge. It will be over…too soon. My way," he reminded her, although she could see what it cost him.

He leaned toward her and again turned her so this time she was lying on her belly in the center of the bed. She could feel the dip in the mattress as he climbed onto the bed with her and she waited for the next touch.

"Do you know what I discovered about you?"

"Mmm?"

His lips found the base of her neck, a place she

hadn't realized was so sensitive. His tongue traced the line of her vertebrae, and then his teeth ever so gently bit down, making her neck arch much like her cats did when she found a particularly sensitive spot.

"You work so hard not to touch people, but you love the sensation of touch. You love it." He trailed kisses down her back and quickly dispensed with the unfastening of her bra so that he could continue his trail.

"It's there in the way you stroke the cats. The way your fingers run over the steel of a fork or the way they caress the surface of the glass in your hand. When I'm done with you, I'm going to love having your hands on me."

Cass would have told him she wanted to put her hands on him now, but the words got caught in her throat as his mouth pressed against the small of her back. He played there for a while, teasing the shallow dimples that framed her ass. The exquisite torture was like nothing she had ever known. She felt him pull the thong over her hips and down her legs, careful to leave the thigh-highs in place. Then he rolled off her and moved to sit up in the bed with his back propped against the pillows.

"Come here. I want you this way."

She crawled up next to him, the loose bra falling from her shoulders and onto the bed, not that she noticed. Her hands reached out, seeking his leg this time, his hip, his chest, the nipples that were tight, the shallow of his ear. Yes, she thought. She did love to touch. And he was ultimately touchable.

He helped her climb on top of him, with a silk-covered thigh on either side of his legs. He stroked the material and she watched his eyes linger on the sight of his fingers moving from her pale, creamy thigh to black silk to creamy skin again. "That is hot," he muttered gutturally.

Then his eyes moved to her breasts. She looked down with him and saw that while her breasts were small, merely a handful each, her nipples had never been harder or more pronounced. She watched as his hand moved up to cup them and the sensation was almost too intense. When his fingers tightened on one nipple, she felt it all the way down to the pit of her stomach.

She sighed and he turned his attention to the other one. She knew that he was watching her face, and she could only imagine what he saw there, but she had no power to hide it.

Then she felt his hand once more on her bottom, this time guiding her, moving her forward so that her knees were just about on either side of his waist, and when she lowered herself, she felt the brush of his cock against the center of her.

He reached over her to one side of the bed. She heard the slide of the drawer and the crinkle of a packet and realized that the thought of protection hadn't even entered her consciousness. Thankfully, it had entered his. But rather than don the condom, he placed it on the bed beside him.

One hand stayed on her ass, the other cupped her chin so that she was forced to meet his very intense steel-blue gaze. "Just for a minute. I want to feel you without it. Okay?"

Numbly, she nodded. She'd never done this without the barrier before. Even during the frenzied mating with Dougie she'd been aware enough to realize the necessity of a condom. This would be new.

Guiding her, he lowered her until she felt the thick head of his erection probing between her slick folds. He slipped inside, and then pulled her knees farther up so that she naturally sank down on him, skewered, while he was slowly enveloped.

His harsh breathing and her delicate sigh were the only two sounds in the quiet room. Then she slowly lifted herself up his body, barely holding him inside her, only to sink down again, squeezing herself around him as she did.

"Yes," he hissed, then repeated it as it seemed to be the only word left in his vocabulary. He held her in place and kissed her again. His tongue plunged deep and rough inside her mouth in a way he wouldn't let his body duplicate. Instead, he remained still inside her, high and hard, pulsing but not moving. The sensation of connectivity was unlike any she had ever known with the living or with the dead.

"Now," he barked. With his hands wrapped around her waist, he lifted her until he was free from her body and she heard a small gasp escape his lips. With ruthless efficiency, he put the condom on and then quickly dragged her back over him and buried himself inside her as if each second apart from her had been torture.

The barrier was mildly frustrating only because she preferred the intense heat of his skin inside her, but she dismissed it as unimportant to the pleasure she felt.

This time, rather than concentrate on staying still, he thrust upward as she slid down. The rocking was intentionally slow and steady and deep, so deep. She could feel his erection inside her, the round head of it rubbing against a spot that brought a new burst of sensation each time he moved. He pushed harder into her and wrapped his arms like bands of steel around her back. In turn, Cass closed her arms around his neck and clung to him with all her strength, afraid that if she let go she might fall into some endless black hole.

So tightly entwined, they could move only at the point where their bodies met. Malcolm began to snap his hips furiously, and the pressure was suddenly too much. She felt something shatter inside her and the rush of pleasure was so overwhelming, she feared she might faint. She closed her eyes and saw splashes of color and pinpricks of light. Her body stilled then but tightened even more around him so that her knees gripped his thighs, her arms closed around his back. Afraid of her reaction, she needed to cling to him for reassurance. But how was it possible to be afraid of something that felt so good? Her orgasm was like a heated wave crashing out to her limbs only to slowly recede, taking with it all of her strength, all of her reason and all of her resistance.

In the end, her head fell limply against his shoulder. She felt the wetness on her cheek and knew what it was, but she was too spent to be embarrassed.

"Shh, shh, don't cry."

He must have felt the tears on his shoulder.

They sat there for some time, each content not to move. It wasn't until the sweat created by their activity started to cool and Cass's legs began to ache that she felt compelled to move.

"Wait." Malcolm shifted her so that her legs came out from under her knees and circled his waist underneath the pillows at his back. Then he lifted her off him and slipped out. Reaching for a tissue, he removed the condom and tossed it quite competently in the wastebasket situated against the nearest wall.

"Nice shot," she murmured against his neck.

"I told you I liked sports. I'm best at football, but not half-bad at basketball."

She chuckled and the movement caused her body to jiggle against his. The matted hair on his chest, though damp, was still enough to tickle her breasts so much so that she reluctantly pulled away.

"We're a mess," she said, wrinkling her nose.

"Yeah. Come on, we'll shower."

She rolled off him and thought how easy it was to take his hand and let him lead her into the bathroom conveniently situated off the bedroom. It, like the rest of the house, was spacious and filled with all the conveniences. The oversize claw-footed bathtub, the centerpiece of the room, was especially impressive.

"Do you ever actually use that?"

"No," he replied quickly. A little too quickly. She glanced at him now suspiciously. "Cats, pink and baths. I left one out."

He slapped her pert buttocks and pushed her into a shower that felt like it had fifteen showerheads. He washed her thoroughly, but not to arouse. He, however, was not unaffected when she returned the favor. She leaned into him and let her hand trail down to where he was once again hard and nearly scalding hot. He dropped his head back and let her tease for a few minutes, let her feel the size and the width of him, let her test the heaviness of his balls underneath until he once again twisted out of her reach.

Taking her palm in his hand he lifted it to his lips and kissed it. "You had a tough day and I can still see the bruises along your rib cage. If I take you again I might hurt you and I won't do that."

"I don't hurt now."

"Tomorrow you might. Come on, you need some sleep." She felt much like an obedient child being led around by the hand by a parent as he escorted her out of the shower and took the time to dry her off with a fluffy brown towel. Back in his bedroom, he offered her one of his T-shirts, which she quickly accepted and then went about turning down the bed.

Naked, he crawled under the covers and made a space for her to join him. Not that there wasn't plenty. Six people could have slept in that bed together and not known the others were there. Somehow Cass didn't think that would be the case with them.

She hesitated before getting in the bed, a lingering doubt nipping at her heels. What had happened to returning to their corners? If she slept with him, let him hold her, then it wouldn't be meaningless sex.

It wouldn't be meaningless anyway.

The echo of truth in her head was as loud as a spirit making contact. No, it hadn't been meaningless. It had been intense and now that the lethargy and woozy good feelings of it had passed, she could see that it was going to be something real she had to deal with. But maybe she didn't have to deal with it tonight.

His hand was still stretched out to her. "What happened to being brave?"

"I was," she said pertly.

"You were." He sighed. "You are. Brave enough to talk to ghosts and brave enough to survive being committed and brave enough to take on a monster. So be brave enough for this, too, and come to bed."

She hesitated only for another second and then climbed into the bed with him and let him settle the covers around her. He pushed up against her side, clearly not satisfied with just having her within reach, and spooned her from behind.

After a moment she could feel sleep begin to pull at her. She thought about how delicious the macaroni had been, how cold the milk. She thought about how heated the sex had been, fluid, then intense. She thought about Malcolm and the way he seemed to take control so effortlessly and decided she was going to have to find a way to stop that.

Tomorrow though. Tomorrow would be soon enough to find a way to take the control back.

Then she felt the familiar bounce of first one then another cat leaping silently onto the bed near their feet. They did their normal midnight ritual and circled each other until eventually they found spots where they were comfortable and settled down.

Cass moved as if to shoo them off the bed, uncertain about how Malcolm would feel about having more than one visitor in his bed at a time. But his arm merely tightened around her waist and pressed her more firmly against him.

"It's all right," he whispered in her ear.

"But how did they get in?"

"I left the door ajar. You said they liked to sleep with you. I figured they would find you."

The consideration of the act touched a nerve under her heart and for the second time that night, she felt her eyes well with tears. She said nothing, but instead swallowed the lump in her throat and pretended to be unaffected.

The distant purring, the rumble of his breath in her ear, the warmth of his embrace around her body had her tumbling into sleep in minutes.

It was the same dream as before. She was back in the glittering ballroom, only this time Malcolm was holding her hand. He was dressed in a tux. The color contrast of the black on white seemed so stark. Just like him and the way he saw things in black and white… Only he didn't. Not really. He said he didn't believe in the things she told him, but he did believe her.

What was that if not gray?

He reached out his hand for her and she took it. This time, though, she noticed she was in a ball gown. Her shoes sparkled, and when she reached for her hair, she felt a diamond tiara perched on top of her head. She pulled the tiara off and looked at its glittering diamonds.

She frowned slightly at the frivolous accessory. She didn't want him to give her things. She didn't need things to make her happy. *Things* had no meaning. *Things* didn't follow you when you died.

Only love did. And hate.

Suddenly, it was no longer Malcolm reaching out to her, but her grandfather.

"Please, Cassie. Talk to me. Let me talk to you. I need to say I'm sorry. You need to let me."

Cass woke with a start and clapped a hand over her mouth, hoping to smother any noise she had made, but she wasn't quick enough.

"What is it?" Malcolm stirred beside her, his arm still wrapped tightly around her waist as if he was afraid she might bolt in the middle of the night.

"Bad dream."

"Was it…?"

"No. No monster. Just a bad dream," she assured him. The lie rolled easily enough off her tongue, and for a second she felt guilty about it, given that they were currently tucked together in bed. It didn't seem like the place for lies. But she dismissed the guilt she felt. He didn't need to be bothered with the truth. Frankly, she doubted he would care.

No, that was probably a lie, too. He might care. That's why she had to lie.

"Will you sleep?"

No. "Yes. Go back to sleep. If I can't, I promise I won't wake you."

He moved then until he was on top of her, his face above hers so that she could make out the shape in the shadows of the room. Captivated despite herself, she ran a finger over the bridge of his nose. She found a bump there and remembered what he'd told her about having it broken. The small imperfection only added to his appeal in her eyes. It made him that much more touchable. More reachable, too.

"Are you feeling okay? I mean it wasn't too much…"

"No. It was perfect. I feel fine."

"Fine, fine?" His voice rose an octave and she smiled at him, knowing what was coming next. "Then I think I can help you get to sleep," he whispered, lowering his mouth to hers so that his lips just touched hers then pulled away.

"Really?" she said, her smile growing wider as she sensed his playfulness. Suddenly, she had an urge to play along. "Do you have a sleeping pill?"

"Pill? No. It's more of a therapeutic approach."

"Like deep breathing?"

She could see his white teeth against the dark and knew that he was smiling again. For whatever reason, it made her happy. Cass couldn't remember the last time she had felt this way. Tonight she could play with him. Then when she needed to, she could back away from him.

"There will be deep breathing involved," he assured her. "Plus a muscle-relaxing technique that, while I have often found requires a certain amount of exertion at first, eventually results in a lassitude that makes sleep easy."

His hips settled between her open legs and she felt him press against the sweet spot between her thighs. The last thing she thought before he slid inside her was that this would be different than the first time. It wasn't going to be slow and intense or fast and frenzied. It was going to be fun.

And she gave herself over to it.

Chapter 16

Cass felt a firm spank on her naked bottom and she was pretty sure it wasn't one of her cats.

"Get up, sleepyhead. We've got a big day."

Turning over, she saw that Malcolm was already up, dressed as if he was headed for the gym and so chipper she wanted to slap him. In the two days she'd been living with him, she'd come to discover that he was a morning person. And he had discovered that she was not.

"What time is it?"

"Almost ten in the morning," he told her.

Cass's eyes popped open. Ten was late even for her. She couldn't remember the last time she'd slept so late. Although sleeping did come much more readily in a big

warm bed after a night of passionate sex. It was definitely a pattern she could get used to.

"Seriously?"

He smiled mischievously, and once again, she was
reminded of how much younger he seemed when he
did. "Seriously. You went out like a light after another
of my special relaxation therapy treatments last night,
and you haven't stirred since. But it was getting late
and I was starting to worry about you so I figured I
would wake you."

"I'm glad you did." For two days they'd both been
content to just be. They'd read the paper. They'd talked.
They'd eaten. And they had made love. Last night,
however, Cass had decided it was time to get serious
about finding a new job. This fantasy world she was
living in was only temporary, and she needed to be
prepared for what came next when it ended.

"I would hold off on your shower this morning
until after."

"After what?" she asked tentatively. "Are you
planning on seducing me again this morning, Mr.
McDonough? Because I have to say if you are…well,
that would be fine."

Malcolm laughed and the sound made her heart
bump heavily against her chest. "As enticing as that
sounds, I have another idea. I came up with it this
morning. Trust me, okay. I want to take you to this
place I know. I think it might help."

"Help what?"

"I don't want to say. I don't want you to nix the idea
before you've had a chance to see what I'm talking

about. Get dressed in what you would wear to work out, and I'll meet you downstairs."

"Malcolm…"

"Trust me."

He left before she could protest, and she huffed with irritation. Trust him. Like that was the easiest thing in the world to do. She briefly recalled making a mental pact to stop letting him lead her around. To take back control. But the idea of stubbornly refusing an offer of help for no reason was silly.

Figuring the job search could wait, Cass decided that whatever he had in mind couldn't hurt. She found a sports tank top she'd packed and matched it with a pair of her yoga pants and sneakers. A normal workout outfit and one that she would have donned to do her exercises anyway.

Skipping down the staircase, she made her way to the kitchen and found a glass of juice and toast waiting on the counter for her.

"You want eggs?" he offered with his head still inside the oversize refrigerator.

"Toast is fine."

He closed the door and shrugged. "Good, because I don't have any. I'm running out of everything. I really need to do some grocery shopping."

Cass stared at him, her orange juice glass suspended halfway to her mouth. "You grocery shop?"

"How else do you think the food gets in the refrigerator?"

Right. Maybe a man who had money all his life would have a staff of people on hand to do his cleaning and grocery shopping, but that wasn't Malcolm. He would do for himself. It was time that Cass stopped trying to fit his round pegs into the square holes she'd created for him in her mind.

"Do you clean bathrooms, too?"

"Are you insane? I hire somebody to do that."

Cass shook her head with a rueful grin on her lips and sipped her juice. At least some of the pegs fit. "Where are we going?"

"I'll tell you when we get there. Why don't you take the toast to go?"

He was anxious. That much was obvious. And she was certain he wouldn't take her anyplace that would deliberately hurt her. Still, surprises in general weren't a good thing for her. Especially now, when she had no idea how she would react in certain situations.

"Malcolm, I'm not great in large crowds or places where I might pick up on a lot of…activity. You know what I mean?"

"Not exactly, but this place won't be crowded. Especially at this time of the day."

Speaking of which… "You've already blown off work for a few days so you could babysit me."

"Can you not use the term *babysitting?* Considering what we've done these past few days, it makes me sound like a pervert."

"All I'm saying is that taking off to stay with me really isn't necessary. I can handle being on my own."

"I don't doubt it. But it's not an issue. I let them know at the office that I would need a bit of time off. I think I surprised a lot of my employees. They probably thought I would be back to work immediately after the funeral." He sighed. "I don't know. If all this hadn't been going on, maybe I would have been. I would have had nowhere else to go. But right now I'm not in any hurry. Nothing is pressing and the company can live without me for a few days."

Cass bet that was probably the first time he had ever admitted such a thing. "Okay. Lead the way."

The surprise was Hank's Gym. The sign actually read Han 's Gym, but Cass could make out enough of a faded *k* to figure it out. It was a squat cinder block building in a seedy section of northeast Philly that looked like it smelled of sweat and testosterone even from fifty feet away. Malcolm parked the car and found a kid riding by on his bike, who gladly took a ten spot to keep an eye on the car for him. Malcolm led Cass across the street. She stopped short at the door.

"Are you trying to tell me I need to work out more? You know that's the kind of thing that can get a man into trouble with a woman, especially when she knows he's just seen her naked."

He laughed and grabbed her hand to pull her forward. "Certainly not. My stepmother taught me better. This isn't your average workout place."

The grimy sign and soap-covered windows gave that much away. Malcolm opened the door and caught the eye of an older man with thinning white hair dressed in a stained blue sweatshirt sitting behind the desk. He appeared to be counting cash. Lots of it.

"Hey, Johnny," Malcolm called out.

"Hey! Mr. M. Good to see you," he rattled out

through smoke-filled lungs. "I was sorry to hear about your loss."

"Thanks."

That was it. The man turned his attention back to the cash in his hand and went back to counting. "Johnny is a pretty popular bookie around here. He watches over the place for Hank when he's in the hospital."

"Hank of Hank's Gym is in the hospital? That doesn't bode well."

"I guess not. He's getting his hip replaced."

"I see." Cass looked around at the large, cushioned floor mats spread about over an open area of concrete. The back wall sported some spot-riddled mirrors, in front of which two overly large men were lifting free weights. There was a bench with a rack above it loaded with round weights and, next to it on the floor, a bunch of handheld weights in various sizes.

No leg lift machines, no bicep curl machines. Just the weights and the bench. To her left, there was a row of punching bags. Two heavy bags hung on the wall some distance apart, and between them was a smaller punching bag that, given its height over the floor, Cass was certain she would not be able to reach. Behind the punching bags was a tight wire about shoulder height that ran the length of the wall and was secured to either end with hooks.

On Cass's right, a small, wiry, brown-skinned man with long dreadlocks jumped rope so quickly that she couldn't be absolutely sure he was even holding a rope.

"You brought me to a boy gym."

"We like to call it a 'real' gym," Malcolm corrected

her. He moved her toward the punching bags. There was a squat shelf loaded with gloves of a few different sizes and a roll of white tape. Grabbing the tape, he motioned for her to hold out her hands.

"Here's what I was thinking," he started. "This person is looking for you. We know he's dangerous. Lauren wasn't exactly tough, but she was a scrapper. She would have fought to live."

He stopped and Cass waited while he tried to shake off what must have been a rush of grief.

"Not that I'm going to let anything happen to you, but if this person also comes with this…thing…it leaves you vulnerable. You're going to need to find a way to fight them both off or at least avoid them. I can't teach you martial arts or any fancy tricks quickly, but throwing a punch and ducking a punch…that's pretty standard. At least it will serve you better than yoga."

Cass wasn't sure of his logic. "You make it sound like I have control over what happens with the monster in the room. I don't know that I do."

"It's your room, isn't it? You visualize it. It stands to reason you can do anything you want inside it. For example, it's not like it's a real monster. It was a person. Only you're seeing him like you do. I thought if we could teach your body how to fight, maybe your brain will catch on and it will be easier to visualize the next time you have to defend yourself."

"That makes sense, I guess. The first time it came after me, my only reaction was to huddle into a ball."

"Ducking is not a bad place to start, but if you can imagine hitting him back…"

"But he…it…is so strong," Cass muttered.

"Only in your head. And mentally—I think you've got some game yourself. You just need the right tools."

Cass stared at the bag, then at the worn gloves on the shelves. "Okay, but I'm not putting my hands in those things."

"We'll start with tape. If it hurts badly enough you'll beg for gloves."

More pain. Terrific.

Malcolm walked her through the basics of how to shape her fist, how to swing through the punch, how to hit the bag with maximum impact. With her right and then her left hand, she hit the bag repeatedly, first jabbing it, then hooking it, then uppercutting it. She hit it until her fingers were swollen and her knuckles were scraped. Until the tape began to fray around the edges.

"Enough with the bag," Malcolm finally said.

Cass agreed thankfully. She didn't doubt the usefulness of the workout, but her hands were numb and her shoulders and arms protested.

"We're done?"

"Do you have a little left in the tank?"

Unfortunately, Cass was the type who, even if she didn't, wasn't going to admit it.

"What next?"

"Something more important than hitting. Ducking."

The taut wire that ran the length of the wall behind the punching bags was expressly for that purpose. Cass ducked and weaved over and over again, moving from one side of the thin rope to the other. Making her legs move forward. More often than not she misjudged and came up directly under the wire. One time she came up so hard the wire snapped her back and sent her tumbling to the mat. She was pretty sure she heard a few chuckles from the other side of the gym.

But she got up and she kept going and after a while the motion became almost effortless. Until she was ducking and weaving in a fluid motion. When Malcolm swung his arms at her, she moved underneath one, underneath the other and landed a gentle jab to his midsection.

Granted, his arms weren't moving very fast and his intent wasn't actually to hit her so it wasn't a great test, but she did feel more confident.

"Good start," he congratulated her. "I think that's enough for today, but we'll come back tomorrow. For now you can hit the showers."

Cass glanced down at herself. Her sports top was damp with sweat and there was a fine sheen of it all along her skin and she knew her hair was plastered against her neck. Turning her head, she caught a glance of herself in one of the spotted mirrors. With the tape still around her hands, and her muscles more pronounced through both the effort and the gleam of sweat, she looked rather tough. Almost indomitable. For a woman of her size, that was quite a feat.

Malcolm stood behind her and she could see the intensity of his gaze reflected in the mirror. "Like I said before. There's steel underneath. We'll come back again."

Yes, she decided. She would come back again.

"You ready for a shower?"

She looked at him over her shoulder with a dubious

expression. "Oh, I know you don't think I'm taking a shower here."

Malcolm smiled. "No. Mostly because they only have men's facilities. We'll take you home and get you cleaned up."

The word *home* stood out in her mind and she felt the perverse need to correct him by telling him his home wasn't her home. She opted to ignore the phrase and take the offer at face value. After all, she smelled and she really wanted that shower.

The next morning when she came downstairs, there was a pair of boxing gloves waiting for her on the kitchen table next to her toast, orange juice and a plate of scrambled eggs. They had gone grocery shopping together the night before. Technically speaking it had been their first date.

"You're going to spoil me." She smiled, looking down at the small, red, overly cushioned gloves.

"Please don't say anything as corny as 'you couldn't possibly,'" he teased. "It would make me happy if you accepted them."

Cass considered the state of her knuckles. They were red and still slightly swollen from yesterday's activities. Which meant today was only going to get worse. "I'll take them," she said. "So long as you understand that my affections can't be bought."

"Absolutely."

"Especially with boxing gloves."

He chuckled and they headed out again to Hank's Gym. This time, there were a few more men lifting weights, but none spared Cass more than a cursory glance. She had no doubt that a woman's presence in this gym was a strange thing; she just got the impression that very little rattled these men. Malcolm worked on her technique and added a few basic kicks to her repertoire of moves. Within an hour, she was making him miss and making him gasp anytime she connected with his midsection.

The door to the gym opened, sending a bolt of light inside, reminding everyone it was a bright fall morning. An immediate tension filled the place. Two of the men who had been simultaneously curling a fifty-pound weight while staring at their bulging muscles in the mirror suddenly stopped. Cass watched their attention stray to the door.

She turned, curious who the new visitor was and was surprised to see Dougie's tall frame. That explained the tension. She had no doubt that several of Hank's regulars would rather stay clear of the law. Dougie's badge, clipped to his belt, shone like a beacon of light throughout the space. Johnny went so far as to head for the shower room.

Dougie spotted Malcolm and raised his chin. He walked over to where they were standing and saw that Cass was sweating profusely.

He saw the gloves and shook his head. "Going for the super lightweight class?"

"Funny."

"I thought it might help," Malcolm told him.

"It might."

"You have news?" Cass wanted to know. Dougie had called Malcolm's cell earlier looking for them.

"Not great news. The New York connection didn't pan out. The DNA found at that scene didn't match our guy. Or I guess I should say our girl. The lab came back on a hair sample we found. There was a trace of a strawberry extract, probably residue from shampoo. I don't know a lot of guys who use a strawberry-scented shampoo so for now we're going to work that angle. The fact that it is in all likelihood a woman trigger anything with you?"

Cass used her teeth to untie the laces on her gloves, then pulled them off by wrapping her arm around the opposite hand and tugging. "No. Should it?"

"Maybe you heard about someone asking for you. Maybe down at the coffeehouse."

Cass shook her head. "No. Nothing. But then I'm never really sure how my name gets around. It just does. Either way, the coffeehouse would be the last place anyone would look now. I was fired a few days ago."

"Why?" Dougie asked.

"You were fired?" Malcolm asked. "Why didn't you tell me?"

"Not much to tell." Cass shrugged, not understanding why Malcolm was so annoyed at the news. "An upset widower, who turned out to be a murderer, came looking for me. He scared some customers before I could disable him with a stun gun. The manager figured it was bad for business."

"That's not right," Malcolm said. "It wasn't your fault. I can fix that."

"No, you can't, because it wasn't wrong of the manager, either," Cass stated. "He's got a business to run, and I freaked out the help. It's not the first time it happened."

Dougie, however, seemed especially annoyed. "This isn't good."

"I'll find another job. Seriously, it's not that big of a deal."

"That's not what I meant. I was hoping…"

His voice trailed off and Malcolm stared at him, his eyes narrowing with suspicion. "You were hoping what?"

"Look, we have no more leads. We know this girl is probably not from around here if the train ticket is any indication. You've got Cass tucked away in the mansion and that's great. But our killer is going to do one of three things—track down some other psychic somewhere and kill her, give up and leave, in which case we might never find her, or eventually she's going to find a way to get to Cass. Let's not wait for her to act. Let's bring her to us instead. We do it this way and we're the ones in control."

"I can't believe you would even think it," Malcolm said coldly. "You know what she did to Lauren. To that other woman. I've told you myself how the monster affects Cass. How it hurt her."

Cass, who was slightly worn down from the intense workout, shook her head to clear the cobwebs and concentrate on what the two men were saying. Dougie was frustrated. Malcolm was angry. It all added up to a crazy sort of sense.

"You want to use me as bait."

"It all comes back to you, Cass. Each death. If we

can set you up someplace where this person can find you, it might be all we need to draw her out and set the trap. Maybe we can't stop the psychic thing, but if we nail her and put her ass in jail, that means no more monster for you, right?"

"No more monster for me," Cass repeated, thinking that there was something she was missing. She pictured what the beast looked like in her head and thought about the figure in the hooded sweatshirt. How he or she had frozen each time Cass had gotten close.

The answer was there. Just beyond reach. She just needed to think about it a little longer.

But then Malcolm was moving to stand between her and Dougie. "You've got to be crazy if you think I'm going to let you risk her life like that. It was one thing for her to be at the funeral in case this lunatic happened to show up. But you're talking about dangling her out there like some kind of carrot. It's too dangerous."

"You mean it's only convenient to use her when it might serve your needs, McDonough."

Malcolm clenched his teeth together. "What would serve my needs right now, Detective, is for you to…"

"Malcolm…"

"No," he cut her off. "He wants to use you. *Again.* This time it would be your life at stake. I won't allow it."

Dougie's face turned hard, harder than Cass had ever seen it. "Maybe you shouldn't talk about things you don't know," he said coldly.

Cass moved around Malcolm until she was once more between them. "Stop it. I need to think. I don't know what I want to do yet, but I can promise you both it will be my decision either way."

"Tell that to your new lover boy, Cass. Looks to me like he's sort of a control freak. First he moves in on your life. Next thing I know he's moving you into his place. What's next—daily readings from your sister's ghost? Is that what this is about, McDonough?"

Cass felt Malcolm jump, but given her position directly in front of him, it wasn't like he could reach Dougie. Dougie took a step back, his hard gaze still pinned on Malcolm.

"Think about it, Cass. Think about it long and hard. Until we end this, you're not safe."

"Excellent," Malcolm sneered. "You can't do your job and find this person, so let's scare the victim into offering herself up. You're a real hero, Detective."

"I don't owe you any explanations. Call me when you're ready to do this, Cass."

He turned and left, and the atmosphere, which was thick with heat, sweat and tension, returned to just heat and sweat.

"Can you believe what he's asking you to do?"

"Yeah, I can believe it," Cass said, tying the gloves together and flopping them over her shoulder. "And I'm going to do it."

Chapter 17

"I don't suppose I get a say in this."

Cass leaned back and let Malcolm work the shampoo deep into her hair. Ironically, it, too, was strawberry scented. He'd picked it up at the grocery store just for her.

"I let you have a say. And look how right you were. Taking a bath together is much nicer than just taking a shower together," she answered, deliberately misinterpreting him.

"I'm serious," he growled.

"I'm serious, too. I want this done. I would think you would want it done, too."

"I want Lauren's killer caught. Yes. Crazy me for wanting that *and* you safe at the same time." He tilted her head back and filled his palms with water to rinse out the shampoo.

"But I won't be safe until this is over. Eventually, I'll have to go back to my place. It's only a matter of time before she would find a way to track me down there. Dougie is right. Better that we do this on our terms."

"Why do you have to go back?"

Cass stilled as she felt the tension gather in his muscles. "Malcolm."

"You think I'm rushing things."

"Think?"

"Okay." He sighed. "I'm rushing things. It's just… It's been nice."

Cass couldn't argue with that. "Yes. It has been. But a few days aren't real. A week isn't real."

He reached around her body and clasped her hand in his. She felt his thighs brush either side of hers, felt his sex start to nudge a little more insistently against her bottom and felt the swoosh of chest hair along her back. Her heart picked up speed as the now familiar rush of sexual heat churned through her system.

"It feels real," he whispered in her ear before lips claimed the spot right below it. "Maybe you don't want to admit it, and maybe it happened too fast, but there's nothing fake about what's between us."

She tilted her neck to give him better access down the column of her throat. It did feel good. Good to be in his arms, good to feel safe in this house. Good to be touched. No, it was more than the touching. It was the connection. This was what she had wanted so desperately the night of her grandfather's funeral. Not just a cessation of the pain, but also some assurance that she wasn't alone in the world. It's why Claire's intrusion, even when she hadn't understood all the ramifications of it at the time, had been so hurtful.

"I don't know what's real anymore," Cass confessed. And that was the truth. She couldn't tell anymore the difference between the people who cared and the people who merely wanted to use her. Yes, Dougie wanted to use her as bait, but she knew that was only business. Yes, Malcolm wanted to protect her, but to what end?

"I'm real." He pushed his hips against her and she smiled at the physical reminder of just how real he was.

She could lie back in his arms, let him make love to her, stay with him here in this house and what? Live happily ever after? It didn't seem possible. Not because it was Malcolm, but because being happy on a permanent basis wasn't something Cass had ever figured into her future.

How depressing was that?

A tingle ran down her spine and, for a second, she mistook it for a zing of desire produced by Malcolm's creative mouth. But the familiarity of the sensation took over, and Cass felt herself mentally withdrawing from him into her white room.

The door opened and she braced herself for the pain, but this time there was surprisingly little. A mere jolt. Lauren's face shimmered in the mist, and she was smiling.

You can be happy if you want it. You make him happy. That can make you happy, too, if you let it.

Cass had an irrational desire to talk back to the voice

in her head, but quashed it. There was no point in arguing with a spirit, and she had to figure that Lauren was slightly biased when it came to her brother.

I was afraid to leave him alone. I was afraid he would isolate himself completely. It's right that he found you. Right that you found him, too. You'll see. Let me say goodbye.

And that's when it changed. All of a sudden, Lauren was inside the room with her, a place only the monster had come before. This encounter wasn't violent, but it was just as disturbing. In her mind Lauren was holding on to her hands. In the bathtub, Cass was turning, craning her neck so she could see Malcolm.

Her mouth opened and she felt herself saying goodbye before she could stop herself.

Instantly the room in her head was gone, but it was too late. Malcolm jerked back in the tub, causing water to slosh over the side of it.

"What the fuck…"

Cass couldn't speak. She didn't want to speak. She wanted out. Trembling despite the warm temperature of the water, she lifted herself out of the tub, stepping over him in her haste.

"Cass, what just happened?"

Cass reached for the towel and circled it around her body like a shield of armor. She heard another splash behind her, but she kept moving. She needed clothes, she needed her things, she needed her cats.

"Talk to me."

"No," she muttered, stepping into a pair of panties and a bra that she'd left on top of the bed.

"What did I do?" Malcolm raged.

"Nothing. You did nothing, but don't pretend you don't know what happened."

She didn't bother to glance up. His silence was enough of an answer.

"It was weird. It wasn't you," he whispered, his voice shaking. She imagined that was to be expected, considering he had just spoken to his dead sister. Or rather she had spoken to him.

"No. It wasn't."

"She was saying goodbye."

"It doesn't matter," Cass snapped. "It doesn't matter what she said—it's what it means. I can't do this. I can't be with you when I know she's there. Waiting for whenever the hell she wants to make contact. To take control and use me like some kind of puppet. I won't allow it."

"You would have to have known Lauren to know she wouldn't do that. If she did what she did it was just to say goodbye. I think she's gone, Cass. Permanently. I felt it."

"You don't know that." Still on the move, Cass pulled on her jeans and shrugged herself into a sweater. Malcolm was standing in the bathroom door, naked and wet. Perfect. Except he wasn't. Not for her.

"You're not leaving."

"See, that's how well you still don't know me. Of course I'm leaving." She searched for and found the duffel bag she had used to bring her clothes over. Stuffing into the bag everything she had neatly laid out on the chair brought with it a certain satisfaction.

"It's too dangerous. You want to be mad at me, for what, I'm not sure—fine, but I'm not letting you go with that nutcase still on the loose."

"You don't have a choice."

"I absolutely have a choice," he roared. Cass felt him rather than heard him come up behind her and whirl her around to face him. The bag dropped on the floor at her feet and she was once again reminded of his temper.

"What are you going to do?"

The question was clearly a taunt and a not-so-gentle reminder of what he had done to her not that long ago. She watched the anger drain immediately from his face only to be replaced with a measure of shame. For that, she felt somewhat guilty.

"Still don't trust me?"

"It's not that." She sighed, suddenly weary of all of it. "Let go of my arm." He dropped it. "I've got to go. I have to. I'll call Dougie as soon as I get home. I'll have him set up the trap. He won't let anything bad happen to me. I know it."

"So it's back to him."

"It's not back to anything. I can't stay. Being with you opens me up to her and I won't have it. I should have known better, but I didn't."

"Lauren's gone. I know it even if you don't want to believe it. This isn't about her, anyway. This is about you and whatever the hell it is you're afraid of. Your grandfather really messed you up, didn't he? What he did to you—that's why you can't believe that every man isn't out to use you. Isn't it?"

He didn't understand. It wasn't the fear of being

used that drove her; it was the loss of control. Being committed to the asylum had been worse than jail because she hadn't done anything wrong. She'd simply been herself. That feeling that her life wasn't hers to live had never left her.

Turning herself over to some spirit would be the same. The loss of self wasn't something she could give up again, and she was willing to sacrifice anything to protect herself against it. Including giving up the one thing she had missed the most: connection with another living soul.

Cass shook her head. "You're right. Again. But it doesn't change anything. Let me go. Let me go and don't call and don't come over. If you feel anything at all for me…"

"Feel *anything?* What the hell do you think has been happening in that bed for the last few days? Some casual fucking? A little entertainment to pass the time? If you believe that, then you're messed up, Cassandra. Seriously messed up."

Messed up. It was an accurate description of how she felt. "I need my cats."

"Leave them here. I'll collect them and bring them over. You want to make the dramatic exit, go."

"No. I need them now." There could be no strings. It was the only way. If she so much as left a sock here, it would give him the opening he needed and she couldn't allow it because the truth was she wasn't altogether sure how resolute she would be against any attempt he made.

"Fine." He pulled on a pair of sweats and rounded

up the cats so quickly, it almost seemed as if they sensed their mother's urgency to leave. Despite their cozy surroundings, they knew where their loyalty belonged.

During the roundup, Cass had quietly called a cab. When he came down the stairs dressed and ready to take her home, he'd been startled by the presence of the yellow car in his driveway. In a way it was like a dagger in his back that she hadn't allowed him at least this final courtesy of driving her home. It was a slap in the face to the gentleman he was.

Leaving him standing in the foyer, she carried everything out to the car. She pushed the carrier along the backseat, tossed her duffel on the floor, closed the car door and told the driver to go—all without once looking back.

It was better this way, she told herself, reclining into the cab's seat. He knew that she was "messed up," and she knew that she could never risk that kind of closeness with another person again. She'd been weak and stupid and needy and everything else she had ever detested about herself growing up. Everything she'd learned to overcome in the asylum. She had this gift, this curse, and there was no wishing it away. It required sacrifices. How foolish she'd been to forget that. Tears pooled in her eyes, but ruthlessly she forced them away.

She had made her bed. It was time to lie in it.

The apartment was exactly how she had left it. Nothing was disturbed. There had been no attempt to break in. Feeling slightly more secure, Cass stepped inside and tried to shake off what had been a crushing afternoon. Letting the cats free, she noted for the first time that what she once thought looked uncluttered, aside from the dishes in the sink and a frying pan left on the stove, now seemed…barren.

It was easier not to have things. Easier to move around, easier not to form attachments to them. But looking at the near-empty living area with nothing more than the mats, the squat table, the tiny television, the single chair, Cass came to the conclusion that a couch wouldn't hurt.

The phone rang and the glaring noise had her jumping in her skin. She picked up the receiver cautiously, although she wasn't sure why.

"Hello?"

"Is anything disturbed?"

Cass listened to Malcolm's tight voice and decided she was deluding herself if she thought the break was going to be that simple. Not that it mattered. If she had to cut it with a chain saw, she would.

"Everything is fine."

"Call Brody. Now." With that, he hung up and the click in her ear made her perversely annoyed.

"Call Brody," she mocked in a deep voice. "Maybe I don't want to," she retorted to an empty room. "What do you think about that, Mr. Tough Guy?"

The phone rang again and was no less jarring. Cass snatched it up. "I'll call him when I'm ready. Get off my back."

"Cassandra?"

"Dr. Farver. Sorry, I thought you were someone else. What's up?"

There was a decided pause at the other end of the phone, and Cass found herself getting irritated all over again. She had committed herself to staying in touch with this man, but these weekly phone calls were getting a little ridiculous. "Look, Dr. Farver, if this is about your subject again, I already told you I'm not interested. I'm not going to change my mind."

"It is about her but not what you think." His voice was edgy and tense, and Cass was left with the impression that Dr. Farver was about to do something he rarely did. "I think I've made a mistake."

Like admit to a mistake.

"A terrible mistake. I don't…I couldn't…I don't see how but…"

"Easy, Dr. Farver. Just spell it out."

"Someone broke into my office."

"Okay. Was anything stolen?" Cass wasn't sure why he'd felt the need to call her but replied with the obvious questions. "Was anyone hurt? Mad, is she…"

"She's fine," he quickly assured her. "It happened last night. No, nothing was taken. At least nothing of significant value, but I'm afraid of what this might mean."

"You're going to have to spell it out."

"Chris is an exceptional student. Her talent is truly powerful. Almost as powerful as yours. A telepath, naturally. Like you, she had an extremely difficult upbringing. Maybe even more so. Her parents are both dead. It was a murder/suicide. Awful. Like with you, I pulled her out of a home for the mentally committed. I kept doing that. I kept telling her how much like you she was. How similar your talents were. I don't think I should have done that."

Cass stood in her tiny kitchen and tried to assemble the story Dr. Farver was putting together for her. There was a student, a girl, at the institute who shared a similar talent for telepathy.

Only Cass wasn't telepathic.

And something else. Something about the murder/suicide sounded familiar. Why did it sound familiar? How could it?

"I told her you didn't want to take part in the research," Dr. Farver continued, his tone more jittery, more nervous than she would have believed possible of the reserved doctor.

"Okay."

"She seemed upset by that. Even disturbed. She kept insisting that I try to talk you into it. I think she was counting on the fact that you and she were connected in some way. That you might help her develop her gift even further. When I finally told her that you had absolutely refused testing, it was like…I don't know. Something snapped."

"Dr. Farver," Cass said calmly, although the answers were starting to stream in like sand that was suddenly allowed to flow through an hourglass. It was just a matter of time before all the sand was weighted on one side and the full picture revealed. "Why do you think she broke into your office?" The someone no longer being in doubt.

She heard him sigh on the other end of the phone. "I'm not sure. I can't be positive. It's just that she's gone. We've looked everywhere for her. It's not like she's a prisoner here. Of course she's free to come and go as she pleases. But recently she's been gone for days without a word to us. When she came back the last time, she seemed out of sorts. Rattled. High-strung. She kept asking when you were coming. I told her you'd been here and what you'd decided. I came into the office this morning and everything was turned over. Papers everywhere, drawers opened."

"And?" Cass prompted, waiting for the punch line he clearly did not want to deliver.

"And…your folder. It was on top of my desk. I was sure I had put it away. The sheet of paper with your new address was missing. Cass, I think she's coming to look for you."

"I have to go, Dr. Farver."

"I'm sorry. I'm truly sorry. I shouldn't have gotten her hopes up so much. It's just that you two were so much alike. Even the bruises that you would get, she would get, too."

Numbly, Cass hung up the phone. A girl with her talent. But not telepathy. Cass closed her eyes and thought back to the contact with the monster on the street. The person, the girl, in the hooded sweatshirt had stopped, had looked at Cass.

Why?

Anytime before when Cass had done a reading, the living were never aware of the dead's presence. If Cass chose not to say anything, which she often did with the occasional stray contact, the living person would have been oblivious.

But when the monster came, the hooded figure stopped. Stopped and looked and watched. Like she was aware of the monster, too.

Cass shook her head and paced the living room. That didn't make sense. If this Chris was another medium, then that would mean that she was a conduit, too. That she had to be channeling for someone else. Someone else who brought the monster into both of their lives? It seemed too far-fetched that there was another person involved. The only time Cass had ever had direct contact with the dead had been with…her grandfather.

Family.

Cass ran back toward the phone and punched in Dougie's cell phone. It took him a few seconds to answer but eventually he did. "Hi."

"Hey," he replied, recognizing her voice. "Tell me you came to your senses and you're ready to set this trap. I know McDonough is worried, but I promise we can do this safely."

"Dougie…"

"You can't talk. Is that it? Is McDonough in the room with you?"

"No, I'm home."

"What the hell are you doing there? You're not alone are you?"

"Forget about that for a second," she cut him off irritably. "Listen to me. When you were checking into those stories about the other people who had had their tongues cut out, you said there was a domestic dispute case."

"Yeah. The wife offed her husband. Apparently he

was abusive. But I told you, she's dead. She killed herself a few months later."

Murder/suicide.

"Did they have any children? Specifically, did they have a daughter?"

"A daughter?" Dougie repeated. "You're thinking…"

"Can you check?"

"Yeah. Hold on. The file is on my desk somewhere."

She waited while he moved through his office, then she heard the rustle of papers and had to bite her lip to keep herself from shouting to him to hurry.

"Here it is. Wallace and Patricia Rockingford. They had… No, a son. Christopher. No, wait. It's just listed as Chris. I guess it could be…Christine. Holy shit, Cass. You think this is our girl?"

"I'm pretty sure it is. She lives at the institute in D.C. I'm not sure why she would have taken the train from Baltimore unless she had my old address and went looking for me there…. It doesn't matter. It's her."

"Stay put. I'm on my way. Keep the door locked, and whatever you do don't let anyone in."

"Right."

Cass hung up the phone and wrapped her arms around her waist. Dougie was on the way. They had a very solid lead on the person if not responsible for the murders then certainly connected to them.

It couldn't be coincidence. Chris's mother had cut out her father's tongue. Why? Why the tongue? And which one was the monster? Not that it mattered. Either way, the daughter had to be severely messed up.

Messed up.

Malcolm's words came flooding back, and Cass found herself wishing desperately that he was here with her. She'd never let herself get close to anyone. Had avoided it on purpose. In a week he had become this anchor of stability. She'd said it couldn't be real and maybe it wasn't, but it didn't feel like such a short time. It felt like years. If only there were no Lauren. If only there were no opening for her to be used, she could have had…what?

Instead she was standing in her empty apartment. Alone with her cats.

Admittedly, petrified.

"Nothing to be afraid of," she told herself firmly. Dougie was on his way. They knew who they were dealing with now. It was just a matter of time.

It was as if the words themselves conjured the tingle that ran up her spine. She barely had seconds to gather her defenses before the pain of impact overwhelmed her, and suddenly there was a monster in her head. In her room.

Inside the apartment, Cass whirled and saw the doorknob on the apartment door turning. She hadn't locked it. When she'd walked inside, she'd let the cats loose and then the phone had rung and she hadn't locked it.

Cass jumped for the door, pushing against it to keep whoever was on the other side out, but in her room, the monster roared.

Sha-a uh-h-h! Sha-a uh-h-h!

It swung at her, and Cass felt the contact immediately to the side of her face. The momentum of the blow threw her back against the wall inside her white room, and physically she tumbled and fell butt first on the linoleum kitchen floor. Too far away now. All she could do was watch as the door opened and a slim figure in a hooded sweatshirt walked through it.

The girl pulled back the sweatshirt. Her eyes were surrounded by dark bruises and her brown hair was cropped short. She smiled and when she did, Cass noted that a tooth was missing.

"Hi, Cassandra. It's so good to finally meet you. And I see you've met Daddy."

Chapter 18

Sha-a uh-h-h! Sha-a uh-h-h!

"Can you hear him?" Chris asked as she stood over Cass. "Yes, you can. That's what I've wanted. What I've waited for. Ever since Dr. Farver told me about you."

In her room, Cass shuffled back, away from the monster. Its foul face and form didn't seem to move but stood over her, still shouting the same unintelligible words.

In the kitchen, she tried to get to her feet but stumbled backward as the two worlds vied for her attention.

"Chr-Chris," she stuttered, but for the life of her she couldn't think of a thing to say. Not to a multiple murderer.

The younger woman moved inside and bolted the

door behind her, something that Cass would curse herself forever for not doing as soon as she'd walked through it.

If she ever got out of this mess.

Cass figured the girl couldn't have been more than eighteen or nineteen. Like one of the baristas she had worked with at the coffeehouse. This girl should be making frappuccinos, not removing women's tongues.

She was tall and, although she was slim, she still had probably about twenty pounds on Cass. She wasn't weak. That was certain. Not if she'd managed to kill three other women of varying sizes. And, of course, it took a decent amount of hand strength to cut out a tongue.

"We're going to be friends," the girl said, smiling, even as she opened the drawer nearest to her and extracted a medium-size steak knife.

Cass thought about her stun gun, really the only other weapon in the apartment. She kept it in the cabinet above her refrigerator. But when she glanced over her shoulder from her position on the floor, it seemed so far away. She needed time. Time to think about the next move.

"I don't see how that's possible if I'm dead."

"Oh, I'm not going to kill you. I never wanted to hurt you, Cassandra. I only wanted to find you. I needed your help."

Inside her head, the beast suddenly charged and Cass found herself huddling into a tight position as its hooflike foot kicked her back.

Get up. This time the voice inside her head was hers. Rolling to her knees, she scrambled between the beast's legs and, once clear of it, she managed to gain her footing. It turned and howled again, but this time Cass was ready. It swung its arm at her and, instinctively, she put into play what she had practiced and dodged the blow.

Charged with a surge of confidence that her mental form was using what her body had learned, Cass once more focused on Chris, who was now moving about the apartment, the knife gripped in her right hand.

"Those women didn't deserve to die."

"I know," she whispered. "I couldn't help that. The first lady, she was supposed to be you, but she didn't hear Daddy. I asked her over and over again and she said I was crazy. I'm not crazy. The voice is real. You know that."

Chris turned around and faced Cass, who had managed to pull herself off the floor using the refrigerator as leverage even while in her mind she continued to duck the blows of the raging monster.

It wasn't possible. She was never going to be able to defend herself against two enemies.

"No, you're not crazy," she assured her. "The voice is real. I can hear it."

"Yes," Chris burst with excitement. "You can hear it. But that lady couldn't and I got so mad. When she told me to leave I got so mad. Then I saw the knife on the counter in her kitchen. It was just out there. She'd been cooking when I walked in and the words kept coming back. *'If you don't shut your mouth I'm going to cut out your tongue.'* That's what Daddy always said. He said it when I told him about the voices. He would beat me and say it when I cried. He would rape me and say it when I told him I was going to tell Mommy. *'I'm going to cut out your tongue. Shut up. Shut up or I'm going to cut out your tongue.'"*

Cass cringed at the image the girl painted and now the mental image of a monster made sense. He wasn't a man. He was evil. And he had hurt his daughter in every way that he could.

"Is that why your mother killed him? Did she finally see what he was doing to you?"

Chris laughed, but there was no humor in the sound. She wiped her forearm across her brow, brushing the knife perilously close to her face, but it was evident that she wouldn't have felt the sting of any cut, as far lost in her insanity as she was.

"Mommy didn't kill Daddy. Mommy couldn't have. She was weak and pitiful and scared of him. More scared than I was."

Another revelation. "You killed him. You killed him and cut out his tongue."

The look of pure joy that shone in the girl's dark eyes was more frightening than her father's form.

"I did. I killed him and I cut out his tongue. I thought it would be over. I didn't think he could be a voice. But he is. He came back. He came back and now he haunts me and he *won't shut up!"*

The sick joy in her expression was replaced by rage. "Over and over again. He yells and it hurts. It hurts as bad as when he used to hit me, and I have to make it go away. They put me in the hospital, but he didn't go away. They gave me all these drugs, but he still wouldn't go away. Then Dr. Farver came and he

believed me. He believed that I could hear things and
he told me about you and how you used to hear things,
like me. He said we would be able to communicate
without words. He said you would know what was
inside my head. Do you, Cassandra? Do you know
what's inside my head? I think you do."

Her attention distracted, Cass felt the impact of
another blow to her body. She hadn't moved fast
enough and the pain was startling. She should be used
to it, but each time he landed a hit, it was like her body
trembled from the inside out. She slid boneless back
down the refrigerator to the floor.

"Call him off, Chris. Block him out," she urged,
thinking that possibly the girl wielded some control.

But she merely shook her head. "I can't stop Daddy."

"You can. My grandfather. He tries to come through,
too, but I won't let him."

"No. Daddy is too strong. I can't block him out. Not
like I can with the others. But now that you're here he's
not as loud in my head. I don't feel him like I normally
do. He's distracted by you. That's good. That's very,
very good. That's what I'd hoped. That's why I had to
keep looking for you. When I realized you weren't at
the address that was listed in Dr. Farver's folder, I went
to the other place."

"What other place?" Cass gasped as she backed
away from what she saw in her mind as another swing.

"Your home. Where you grew up in Baltimore. But
there was no one there. So I thought maybe I would just
come back to Philadelphia. Maybe the number of the
apartment was wrong. Dr. Farver made mistakes. He

made lots of mistakes. He didn't know about the voices. He thought I could read minds."

Cass shuffled back against the white wall as the monster moved closer to her. One step, then another. The urge to panic was escalating. She didn't know what to do. Which one to focus on. The dead. Or the living.

"So I just started walking up and down, up and down on the street where you were supposed to be. That's when I found the New Age shop. The lady who worked inside was a witch. I thought you could be a witch. Witches have powers, right?"

"Only in books." Cass closed her eyes as she listened to Chris recount Lauren's last minutes on earth.

"I followed her home and when I saw she lived on Addison, I thought it could be you. She was so nice. I said I was like her, and she thought that meant that I was a witch, too. She invited me in for tea, but when I asked her if she could hear Daddy, she...she said she couldn't."

"You didn't have to kill her."

"You don't know what it's like!" Chris shouted back. "You can't understand what it is to hear him every day. *Sha-a uh-h-h, Sha-a uh-h-h.* You know what he's saying, don't you? Shut up. Over and over again. Shut up. I have to take their tongues. It makes him quiet when I do it."

"No," Cass countered. In her mind, she focused on the monster that hovered over her, waiting to serve up his next blow. To inflict pain. That's what it wanted to do. That's what his daughter had learned from him. "I don't think that's true. I think you do it because you liked hurting those women. I think you do it because you want others to suffer like you did. You took that other woman's tongue while she was still alive."

Chris shrugged. "She was nasty. I heard her mother in my head. So I did a reading for her. Me reading for the psychic." She giggled. "But she didn't like what I had to say. She didn't like that I had the power and she didn't. That's how I knew she was a fake. I had to kill her. Just for that."

Cass gasped as the beast's hoof slammed into her stomach. Her body screamed out at the brutal punishment, and for a time she couldn't see anything at all except his arm swinging at her over and over again. She couldn't hear anything except for the muted roars of a tongueless beast.

Sha-a uh-h-h. Sha-a uh-h-h.

It was enough to drive a person insane.

You can fight him, Cassie. You can fight him off. You know how. You just need to be strong. I believe in you. I'm so sorry I didn't before. But I'm here now. I won't leave you again.

The voice in her head echoed over the muted roars of Chris's father. It was coming from outside of her white room, just beyond the open door. She had never let her grandfather get through. She'd never listened to him, never let herself hear his pleas for forgiveness. Partly because she didn't want to forgive him. And partly because she couldn't forgive herself.

He had been dying and still she wouldn't go see him. They had buried him, and she was not there. For what? A grudge. In the end it seemed like such a trivial reason.

Gramp? Cass tried to concentrate. In the room, she shuffled away from the beast toward the open door. It howled, but she closed her mind to it and instead tried to focus on letting her grandfather come through.

You can fight him.

He's too strong.

He's not. Only in your head. Only because you let him be.

He's a monster.

No, he's just a man. See the man. Remember what you were taught.

Cass looked up at the beast, its foul face moving closer to her with each step it took. There was nothing there that resembled a human. Nothing that she could see. A faint whisper of smoke drifted in front of her, forcing her back into reality.

"We need them to think you're dead. Burned up."

Cass watched as Chris dumped a packet of matches into the smoke smoldering on the futon, and suddenly the smoke turned to flames. Flames that were eating up the cushions at an alarming rate.

"This will work," Chris said. "This will work perfectly. There will be a fire. Nobody will find your body, but they'll have to think that you're dead."

"What does that get you?"

"That gets me you. Forever. We'll go someplace. Somewhere where we can hide. And you'll keep Daddy occupied and I'll be free. That's all I wanted. It's all I wanted when I killed him. All I wanted when I went to the institute. And now I have a chance. You've given me that chance."

"People will look for me," Cass breathed even as she mentally pulled herself into a ball inside the room. It was coming for her again. It wanted to hurt her again. She didn't know how much more she could take.

"No, everything will be gone. This building will be gone. Everyone will think you're dead."

The flames continued to feed off the wood frame, and Cass could see Chris watch the fire growing, her attention for the moment occupied. Cass needed to act now. She tried to make a break for the apartment door, but when she rolled onto her knees to get to her feet, the beast struck again. Mentally and physically, she was once again down.

"I have friends. I have friends that are coming." Dougie was coming, wasn't he? Cass thought numbly. And Malcolm would call again soon. She was sure of it. All she needed to do was hold on.

"We'll be gone before they get here," Chris assured her. "I just want to watch the fire. It's so pretty. I didn't used to like it. Daddy one time burned my hand with a match. He wanted to teach me that playing with fire was bad."

"I'm sorry," Cass said. "I'm so sorry he hurt you. That doesn't mean you have to do this. Help me. Help me stop him."

Chris turned away from the fire that had now consumed the futon and was moving onto the old rug. The apartment was quickly full of smoke, and Cass felt the heat in her throat. Chris started to cough, too, but she didn't seem to be in any hurry to escape.

"I told you I can't. He's too strong. You'll just have

to learn how to deal with the pain. Me and Mommy did. We were one big, happy family. One big, happy, hurting family." Chris coughed again as the smoke became that much thicker. She reached into her jeans pocket and pulled out a worn and tattered piece of paper. She held it out for Cass, who was still on the floor.

It was a picture. A picture of three people.

"See, just one big, happy family. Of course you can't tell from this, but Daddy had beaten me up pretty good the night before. I have all sorts of bruises under my dress."

Cass squinted against the smoke and looked hard at the photo. Not at the girl in the dress with the sad expression on her face. Not at the fragile woman standing just behind her. She looked at the man. He was short and pudgy. Balding with a weak chin and beefy hands that he had clenched into fists.

He was just a man.

Instantly, the beast inside her white room transformed. The tusks receded. Hooves turned into hands. The snout was gone, to be replaced by a broad nose and a weak chin, and suddenly Cass found herself confronted with nothing more than a man.

A man she could fight.

She pushed herself back onto her feet and slid out from the corner of her white room.

You're not so tough now.

Sha-a uh-h-h! Sha-a uh-h-h!

Internally, Cass moved closer to him. She felt strong. She felt…invincible.

It's your room, isn't it? You can do anything you

want inside it. Malcolm's words returned to her, as did his instructions. Stay on the balls of your feet, keep your target in sight and swing from your gut.

Cass swung her fist in an arc and felt contact with the man's face. He was taller than she was but not by that much. She landed a right and left to his head and then an uppercut into his soft, fat belly.

Dancing around him, infused with a power that she was only starting to comprehend, she raised her foot and sent it into his backside. He toppled over onto his belly, and she moved on him with a swift kick right to his groin. He squealed and then he was the one curling himself into a ball.

What's the matter? You can dish it out, but you can't take it?

At her feet, he actually whimpered.

Shut up.

He did. The door to the room opened, and the mist beyond it looked sinister and cold. She turned back to the pathetic figure huddled on the floor and as abruptly as he had broken through the barrier and made contact, he was gone.

The room was empty now. Cass closed the door.

"Come on, Cass. It's time to go."

Cass could feel Chris tugging on her arm and lifting her to her feet. With the man/monster gone, she was able to give all her attention to his daughter.

"I'm not going anywhere with you." She hurt, but for the first time since making contact with the beast, she felt as if her body was back under her control.

"Don't make me use the knife," Chris pleaded,

digging the sharp blade against Cass's side. Cass knew that with just a little more pressure it would slide through her sweater into her ribs. "I really don't want to hurt you. But if I have to, I will."

Cass turned her head and saw the fire moving in on them. With the knife at her side and the fire growing more threatening, the smoke practically robbing her of breath, Cass decided to let Chris lead them out of the apartment. She would stand a better chance of confronting her once they were on the street.

Together they made their way to the door, where Cass saw her cats waiting, she knew, for their mother to save them from the fire.

"My cats. I have to take them." Pretending she was worse off than she was, Cass reluctantly let Chris tug her along, allowing her knees to buckle from time to time to show Chris how weak she was.

"No, you can't take them. Daddy doesn't like pets."

"I'm not leaving them to burn."

"They can get out when we open the door."

Chris let go of Cass and made a move to unlock the door when a loud knock came from the other side.

"Cass! Cass, are you in there! There's smoke coming out from under the door and near your window!"

It was Malcolm. Oddly, Cass found herself wondering what he was doing there and then realized she'd just been saved.

Chris pulled away from the door as if stunned that something wasn't going according to plan.

"No. No, we have to leave. We have to escape. Everyone has to think you're dead."

The girl stomped her foot and stood glaring at the door as if it were the enemy. Struggling to hold her breath, Cass used the distraction Malcolm continued to provide by pounding on the door. The knife practically dangled from the girl's hand.

Glancing to her right, Cass saw her single frying pan sitting on the stove where she had left it the last time she made an egg. Praising herself for being the lousy house-keeper she was, she reached for the pan and swung it with all her might at Chris's right arm just at the elbow.

Chris screeched and reached for her arm, but, more importantly, dropped the knife. Diving for it, Cass felt her hand wrap around the wooden handle. But as soon as she did, Chris was falling on top of her, pulling at her short hair with enough force to tear it from its roots in an attempt to get Cass to drop the knife.

"No! Give it to me!"

"Cass!" This time it was Dougie shouting from the other side of the door. "We're here, Cass. Open the door! Now!"

How typical, she decided, for a man to be giving her orders at a time like this. Rolling from side to side, Cass struggled to unseat Chris from her back. But the girl had the talent of a bull rider and held on with all her strength. She let go of Cass's hair but only to reach over her to try to wrench the knife from her grasp. Together their hands grabbled for the sharp blade, vying for control of what really wasn't much of weapon. But to Cass it felt as if all the power rested with the knife and the first person to gain control of it would win the deadly battle.

"If you don't give me that knife, I'm going to cut out your tongue!" Chris growled in her ear.

"It's over, Chris," Cass tried to reason even as she used her elbow to jab at the girl's ribs. She heard a whoosh of breath, but Chris fought back, using her feet to kick any part of Cass she could reach. "Can't you hear them? They're waiting for you on the other side of the door. You can't escape now."

"No! I have to. I have to get away from him. You have to help me."

Cass heard the panic in her voice and in just that second, she tore the knife away from Chris's hand. Cass rolled to her side and brought the knife closer to her chest. At that moment, Chris leaped on her, and without having a second to think, only to react, Cass pushed the knife out in front of her and sank it deeply into Chris's chest.

The first thing that registered was the girl's eyes. They were dark and brown and filled with both pain and sadness that seemed hauntingly familiar.

"No," Cass gasped even as she turned and let Chris roll off her. The base of the knife stuck morbidly out from her chest directly over where her heart beat. It had cut through the thick sweatshirt and had sunk in all the way to the hilt.

Scrambling to her knees, Cass leaned over the girl and contemplated the harm or benefit of pulling the knife from her chest. Instinct told her to get it out. Get it out quickly and maybe it would be like it hadn't happened, but reason took hold.

"Chris. Just stay still. Don't move."

Cass tried to stand. She needed to unlock the door.

Dougie was still hammering away at it. She could hear him shouting. She didn't know where Malcolm had gone, but if she could get the door open and get some air, she could pull Chris free.

The sound of breaking glass registered, as well as the call from another voice, but she was too focused on getting to the lock. Smoke clouded her vision and the air in her lungs felt heavy and hot. What had seemed like such an easy thing at the time, reaching and unlocking the door, now felt almost impossible. The lock was so far away, and standing up, where the air would be so much thicker, didn't seem like a good idea at all.

In front of her, she saw her cats moving around each other, pawing at the door, sneezing in the way that cats do when something smells horrible.

"Cass!"

She didn't know where the shout was coming from this time. From the other side of the door, from inside her head. It was hard to keep it all straight. She looked down again at Chris, whose eyes were open and focused on Cass. Smoke swirled around them, but Cass could still see the desperation in Chris's face. She was going to die and she knew it. Cass felt the weight of what she had done, what she had taken. Chris had come looking for someone to save her, but Cass wasn't sure that she could anymore.

Worse, she wasn't even sure she could save herself.

"I'm sorry," Cass whispered to her. The last bit of oxygen left her lungs and she slumped down to the kitchen floor.

"Don't be sorry," Chris wheezed. "You saved me. I don't hear Daddy anymore."

Don't worry, Cassie. He's coming. It's going to be all right.

Her grandfather's voice might have been reassuring if she weren't so certain that he was wrong. Cass tumbled over Chris's body as consciousness quickly slipped away. Her last thought was that she hoped one of the guys would be able to get through the door before the fire got too bad so that at least Spook and Nosey would make it.

Chapter 19

Cass blinked her eyes open and quickly closed them. Everything before her had been a blur, but it had also been white. All white. For a second, she feared she was back in her room with a monster there waiting to pounce. Then she realized her mind was quiet. Free from voices, human or otherwise. Was this death? It didn't feel like it. She was too conscious of the aches in her body.

She opened her eyes again. Yes, the room was white, but it was real. Solid. She turned her head and saw a machine that beeped steadily to her right. She saw that there were bars on the bed, and she felt the outline of a mask covering her mouth and nose.

She tried to inhale and instantly started to cough.

Her lungs seized until it felt that someone was sitting on her chest. Eventually the spasms stopped and her chest eased a bit.

Okay. Breathe gently.

A hospital. She was in a hospital. Which meant somehow she had survived.

She blinked again, and this time a looming figure moved into her view. She pushed herself back into the bed, but when her eyes finally adjusted to the light, she could see that it was Dougie.

"What happened?" she whispered. But with the mask over her face she had no idea what he might have heard.

"Cass, can you hear me?"

Slowly, she nodded.

"You're in the hospital. McDonough got you out. Do you remember?"

She had heard someone call her name. She had seen Chris's eyes go lifeless. Her grandfather had told her it was going to be okay. But she hadn't really believed him. How could she? She had felt so close to death. After that there had been nothing.

Guess her grandfather was right after all.

"McDonough broke through the window over the futon and managed to get the front door open. He pulled you out."

"Spook. Nosey."

"I had an officer take them to the vet. They're going to be fine."

Malcolm broke through the window over the futon to get to her. Something about that didn't sound right.

She closed her eyes and tried to imagine the apartment and what it had looked like at the end. Fire had consumed the futon and had progressed to the carpet. Smoke had filled the room so that she had barely been able to make out her hand in front of her face.

"No futon," she whispered. "Fire. Too much fire."

"Yeah." Dougie grimaced. "He got pretty burned up."

Frantic, Cass tried to sit up, but her body rebelled and she began to cough. It was as if her whole body were filled with smoke that was leaking out in spurts.

"Hey, easy. Easy. He's okay. It's just his arms. He's down on the third floor getting patched up. I tried, Cass. I tried but I couldn't get the damn door open."

"Good locks," she wheezed after a time, reminding him that he had been the one to suggest the extra dead bolt. The dead bolt that if she had only remembered to engage it when she had first gotten home would have prevented everything. Cass made a mental note not to let Dougie know about that.

She saw him smile at her answer and was pleased that the guilt-stricken look was gone. She knew Dougie enough to know that he would have hated to take the backseat to Malcolm, that he would have rather been burned than be considered less heroic.

He was a good man despite his faults.

"Can I see him?"

"Sure. He'll be up soon, I imagine. Do you feel strong enough to tell me what happened?"

"She was from the institute. Dr. Farver's patient." The mask began to irritate her so she pushed it up and off her head. Gingerly, she took shallow breaths and found that as long as she didn't inhale too deeply, she was okay even though her voice was limited to nothing more than rasps.

"She was Wallace Rockingford's daughter," Dougie told her. "I didn't even consider her. She was only a kid, fourteen, when her father was killed. The cops closed the case on the wife, and she killed herself before sentencing."

"Chris killed her father. She took out his tongue. She was abused. Raped. Beaten. God only knows. But she was also a medium."

His eyes sprang open. "Are you shittin' me?"

As if now would be the time to bullshit him. "No."

He seemed to struggle with that.

"It's how she ended up at the institute. With Dr. Farver. He promised her that there were others like her. He told her I could help her."

"You're saying she heard her father. In her head."

"He was the monster," Cass revealed. "Evil. She heard that there was someone that could help and she tracked me down. Dr. Farver didn't have my new address until recently."

"And the ticket to Baltimore?"

"She went back to my grandparents' house. To look for me there."

Cass waited for all the pieces to fall into place for him. Eventually, he nodded, satisfied. "Would you have been able to help?"

She could see his face scrunch in a way that suggested he probably didn't want to know all the answers. "She said I distracted him. She wanted me to go away with her. It's why she set the fire. But we struggled. She fell on me and the knife… Oh, Dougie. It was horrible."

He reached for her hand, but instinctively she pulled it away. As soon as she had, she felt bad about it. It wasn't her intent to dismiss him but to avoid contact. She didn't have the strength for contact with anyone right now, and she was too skittish to risk what might have been a harmless touch.

"I'm sorry," she apologized. "It's not like you think. I just can't…"

"It's okay."

"No, it's not. Not really. I don't want to be enemies, Dougie."

He looked away, then looked back and smiled softly. "We're not enemies. We're friends. Good friends, but just friends. If you can forgive me?"

She wanted to. She very much wanted to. "Friends. Just friends. Really?"

"Really. In fact I can't stay with you much longer. Steve set me up with his wife's sister. Apparently, Marilyn has decided I'm ready to get out there and date again."

"Good for Marilyn," Cass said.

"Okay. Well, I'm going to go. You sure you'll be okay on your own?"

"Yep."

He stood and walked to the door but looked over his shoulder at her. "I really hate to leave you alone."

"She's not." Malcolm walked in at the same time Dougie was voicing his concern. Dougie took that as his cue to leave. Apparently joining together to rescue her hadn't brought them any closer. No male bonding going on there at all.

"Later, Cass. I'll be in touch if we need anything else from you."

The door swung closed behind him, and Cass watched as Malcolm moved toward her. Her chest tightened and her throat clogged, but she doubted it had anything to do with smoke inhalation.

His forearms were covered in white gauze, and there was a clear gel smeared on his left cheek. There were other bright red marks on his forehead and chin but nothing else bandaged.

"Your face," she whispered.

"It hurts like a son of a bitch," he quickly confessed.

"My hero." She smiled.

"No," he said. "You're mine. You did it, Cass. You held them both off. Just long enough for me to get to you."

"How? I mean how were you there?"

"As soon as I hung up with you, I started pacing. I couldn't stand it. I just knew something bad would happen, and this time I could try to stop it. I got in my car and drove over. Figured I would stand watch in case anyone tried to break in, but it was too late. She was already inside. I didn't know anything was wrong until I saw the smoke."

She saw his jaw clench and reached out to touch his arm to assure him it was okay, but this time he was the one to draw back when she made contact with his covered forearm.

"Sorry."

"It's all right. They'll heal." He wore an enigmatic

expression on his face as if he didn't know what to think of her reaching out to touch him first.

She wasn't really sure what to think of it either. Hadn't she just warned herself against contact? Somehow, though, with him it seemed safe.

"You remembered what I taught you?" he finally asked.

Limply, she nodded. But that wasn't truly how she'd fended off the monster. It had been Gramps. Silently, she apologized to him for all the times she'd shut him out. For everything that had happened before that, too. It had been so easy to dismiss him at the time. She'd been young and hurt. She'd wanted so badly for him to believe her, but instead he had betrayed her. So she'd betrayed him back.

Through hindsight, though, she saw a different picture. He hadn't really betrayed her. He had truly thought he was helping her. He'd never understood that she wasn't sick. Cass felt him there at the edge of her consciousness, and this time she reached out to him.

You loved me.

I did. I didn't know how to show it. I didn't know how to deal with you. I thought you were sick, Cassie. I wanted to help. I'm sorry.

I'm sorry, too. For not being there for you at the end.

There is no end. Goodbye, Cassie. Remember, don't ever fear love. Embrace it. It's a gift, too.

"Cass? Cass, are you okay? Do you need me to leave?"

Her sudden silence must have worried Malcolm as she had given her full attention to her grandfather. She noticed that the contact with him hadn't hurt her at all. She wondered if Malcolm had something to do with that.

"Do you want me to go?"

"No," she said quickly but then started coughing as her lungs seized.

"No? Then I'll stay."

After a few breaths, she was able to answer his original question. "I did remember. Everything you taught me. But it wasn't just that. At first I was losing to the monster. It was too strong for me. I could duck one blow, but then there was another after that. Then Chris showed me a picture of him. I saw his face, and suddenly the monster was gone and it was just a man…. Then I kicked the crap out of him."

Malcolm chuckled. "Good girl."

"It was my room, after all. Nobody messes with me in my room."

He smiled and reached out to let an undamaged finger brush her cheek.

Her eyes drifted shut, but she tried to fight off sleep. She wasn't ready to say goodbye to him yet. There were so many things that they still needed to talk about, but she quickly felt the option slipping out of her control.

"You need sleep."

"My cats," she murmured. "The vet."

"I'll get them."

It was asking a lot. It was asking more than a simple favor. She wondered if he knew that.

"You don't have to."

"You're right. I don't."

With that, she let sleep overtake her without a single worry about her cats. About anything, really.

* * *

The next day, Cass was released from the hospital under the instructions that she was to continue to drink lots of water and get plenty of rest. Her lungs would remind her for a while what she had suffered at the hands of a distraught medium, but eventually they would heal.

Eventually, she would heal, too.

Dougie had offered to pick her up, but she had gently declined. Instead, she had asked him how his date went, to which he had groaned loudly.

"Welcome back to dating," she'd teased.

"This sucks."

"It does. But sometimes things work out."

"You and McDonough?" he had asked her.

But she hadn't really had an answer for that. She'd just wished him luck on his next date and told him she would be in touch when she figured out where she would be staying for the indefinite future.

Her scooter nothing more than twisted metal now, she was forced to hail a cab. She climbed into the backseat and thought for a minute about her options. Her apartment was out of the question, considering it was burned beyond recognition. Her renter's insurance would cover her for the scooter and the futon and her clothes, but other than that, she hadn't lost much.

No, there was only one place she really wanted to go. And her cats were already there waiting for her.

"Gladwyne," she finally told the driver.

The cab pulled into the circular driveway of the address she'd given the driver. Cass hesitated before getting out. Looking at the massive house, she couldn't fathom calling a place like that home. There were so many complications it brought with it. But her cats were inside. And she suspected her future was inside, too.

She paid the driver and got out. She rang the bell on the front door and waited without having any idea what she was going to say.

When Malcolm opened the door, she could almost see the look of relief on his face.

"I wasn't sure if you would come."

"I wasn't sure either," she answered honestly. "But I didn't really have anywhere else to go."

He shook his head at her. "Sorry. That's not a good enough answer. You need a place to go? I'll build a house for you."

He was dead serious.

"You're going to make me ask?"

He folded his arms over his chest, careful not to put any pressure on his burns. "I think I have to. I think I need to hear from you that this is what you want."

Bastard. Of course it didn't help that he was right. She'd been the one to leave. She'd been the one to reject him. She didn't see how it was possible that whatever they had between them could work, but the difference now was that she was willing to take the chance.

Don't ever fear love. Embrace it. It's a gift, too.

It was the best advice her grandfather had ever given her. That and to always buy regular gas.

"I want this. I want…you. I didn't come here

because I didn't have any other place to go. I came here because this is the place I wanted to be."

He smiled. "That hurt, didn't it?"

Cass let out a slow, long breath. "Worse than getting beat up by a monster. But I think it might be worth it."

Malcolm stepped back, opened the door wide, and Cass bravely stepped through it to the other side.

* * * * *

New York Times *bestselling author Linda Lael Miller is back with a new romance featuring the heartwarming McKettrick family from* Silhouette Special Edition.

SIERRA'S HOMECOMING
by Linda Lael Miller

On sale December 2006,
wherever books are sold.

Turn the page for a sneak preview!

Soft, smoky music poured into the room.

The next thing she knew, Sierra was in Travis's arms, close against that chest she'd admired earlier, and they were slow dancing.

Why didn't she pull away?

"Relax," he said. His breath was warm in her hair.

She giggled, more nervous than amused. What was the matter with her? She was attracted to Travis, had been from the first, and he was clearly attracted to her. They were both adults. Why not enjoy a little slow dancing in a ranch-house kitchen?

Because slow dancing led to other things. She took a step back and felt the counter flush against her lower back. Travis naturally came with her, since they were holding hands and he had one arm around her waist.

Simple physics.

Then he kissed her.

Physics again—this time, not so simple.

"Yikes," she said, when their mouths parted.

He grinned. "Nobody's ever said that after I kissed them."

She felt the heat and substance of his body pressed against hers. "It's going to happen, isn't it?" she heard herself whisper.

"Yep," Travis answered.

"But not tonight," Sierra said on a sigh.

"Probably not," Travis agreed.

"When, then?"

He chuckled, gave her a slow, nibbling kiss. "Tomorrow morning," he said. "After you drop Liam off at school."

"Isn't that…a little…soon?"

"Not soon enough," Travis answered, his voice husky. "Not nearly soon enough."

nocturne™

**Explore the dark and sensual
new realm of paranormal romance.**

HAUNTED
BY LISA CHILDS

**The first book in the riveting
new 3-book miniseries, Witch Hunt.**

DEATH CALLS
BY CARIDAD PIÑEIRO

**Darkness calls to humans,
as well as vampires...**

*On sale December 2006,
wherever books are sold.*

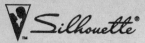

HARLEQUIN® *Romance*®

From the Heart.
For the Heart.

Get swept away into the Outback
with two of Harlequin Romance's
top authors.

Coming in December...

Claiming the
Cattleman's Heart
BY BARBARA HANNAY

And in January don't miss...

Outback Man Seeks Wife
BY MARGARET WAY

TAKE 'EM FREE!

2 FREE ACTION-PACKED NOVELS PLUS 2 FREE GIFTS!

Strong. Sexy. Suspenseful.

YES! Please send me 2 FREE Silhouette Bombshell™ novels and my 2 FREE gifts. After receiving them, if I don't wish to receive any more books, I can return the shipping statement marked "cancel." If I don't cancel, I will receive 4 brand-new novels every month and be billed just $3.99 per book in the U.S., or $4.47 per book in Canada, plus 25¢ shipping and handling per book plus applicable taxes, if any*. That's a savings of at least 20% off the cover price! I understand that accepting the 2 free books and gifts places me under no obligation to buy anything. I can always return a shipment and cancel at any time. Even if I never buy another book from Silhouette, the two free books and gifts are mine to keep forever.

200 SDN EEZJ 300 SDN EEZU

Name	(PLEASE PRINT)

Address	Apt. #

City	State/Prov.	Zip/Postal Code

Signature (if under 18, a parent or guardian must sign)

Mail to Silhouette Reader Service™:

IN U.S.A.
P.O. Box 1867
Buffalo, NY
14240-1867

IN CANADA
P.O. Box 609
Fort Erie, Ontario
L2A 5X3

Not valid to current Silhouette Bombshell subscribers.

Want to try two free books from another line?
Call 1-800-873-8635 or visit www.morefreebooks.com.

* Terms and prices subject to change without notice. NY residents add applicable sales tax. Canadian residents will be charged applicable provincial taxes and GST. This offer is limited to one order per household. All orders subject to approval. Credit or debit balances in a customer's account(s) may be offset by any other outstanding balance owed by or to the customer. Please allow 4 to 6 weeks for delivery.

SBOMB06

USA TODAY bestselling author

BARBARA McCAULEY

continues her award-winning series

SECRETS!

**A NEW BLACKHAWK FAMILY
HAS BEEN DISCOVERED...
AND THE SCANDALS ARE SET TO FLY!**

She touched him once and now
Alaina Blackhawk is certain horse rancher
DJ Bradshaw will be her first lover. But will
the millionaire Texan allow her to leave
once he makes her his own?

Blackhawk's Bond

On sale December 2006 (SD #1766)

Available at your favorite retail outlet.

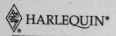

Silhouette®
BOMBSHELL™
COMING NEXT MONTH

#117 DAUGHTER OF THE BLOOD—Nancy Holder
The Gifted

For New Yorker Isabella de Marco, serving as Guardienne of the House of Flames in New Orleans was a birthright she still hadn't come to terms with. The ancestral mansion was in the midst of dangerous transition, and powerful demonic forces were aligning against her. With her partner and lover both wounded, Izzy comes to rely on a mysterious new ally for help...but does he have a hidden agenda to bring about her eternal damnation?

#118 VEILED LEGACY—Jenna Mills
The Madonna Key

Adopted at birth, Nadia Bishop never knew her roots—until she came across what seemed to be her own photo on the obituary page! Was this the lost sister who'd appeared in her dreams? Tracing the murdered woman to Europe, Nadia discovered the key to her own life—her blood ties to an ancient line of powerful priestesses made her a target...and her child's father might be part of the conspiracy to destroy her.

#119 THE PHOENIX LAW—Cate Dermody
The Strongbox Chronicles

The biggest threat in former CIA agent Alisha MacAleer's new life was babysitting her nephews—until an ex-colleague showed up on her doorstep, dodging bullets and needing her help. Suddenly she was thrust back into the world of double agents, rogue organizations and sentient AIs, while also helping men who'd betrayed her before. As avoiding death grew more difficult for Alisha, could the phoenix rise from the ashes once more?

#120 STORM FORCE—Meredith Fletcher

Taken hostage by a gang of escaped prisoners during one of the worst hurricanes in Florida history, Everglades wilderness guide Kate Garrett was trapped in a living nightmare. Her captors were wanted for murder, and though one of them might be the undercover good guy he claimed to be, it was up to Kate to save her own skin. For the sake of her children, she had to come out alive, come hell or high water...or both!

SBCNM1106